A MEMORY OF MANKIND

THIS ALIEN EARTH BOOK TWO

PAUL ANTONY JONES

AETHON
BOOKS

A MEMORY OF MANKIND
©2019 PAUL JONES

Aethon Books
PO Box 121515
Fort Worth TX, 76108
www.aethonbooks.com

Print and eBook formatting, and cover design by Steve Beaulieu.

Published by Aethon Books LLC.

Aethon Books is not responsible for websites (or their content) that are not owned by the publisher.

ALSO BY PAUL ANTONY JONES

Published by Aethon Books
The Paths Between Worlds

Published by 47North
Extinction Point
Extinction Point: Exodus
Extinction Point: Revelations
Extinction Point: Genesis

Toward Yesterday

Published by Good Dog Publishing
Extinction Point: Kings
Ancient Enemies (Dachau Sunset - short story)

For Molly. You got the thing!

And for CoCo Mo

ALEXANDER - INFINTY OF WORLDS

Alexander wept when he heard Anaxarchus' discourse about an infinite number of worlds, and when his friends inquired what ailed him, "Is it not worthy of tears," he said, "that, when the number of worlds is infinite, we have not yet become lords of a single one?'

ONE

I SWUNG my sword in a fast, wide arc, aiming for Weston Chou's neck. Chou dodged my attack easily, stepping inside my guard while thrusting the knife she held in her right hand toward my heart. I twisted sideways, and the blade slid off my chainmail shirt. Then, I brought my sword hand up and tapped Chou on the side of her temple with the sword's pommel, lightly enough that it wouldn't hurt but hard enough to push her off balance. Chou toppled sideways, then rolled away. She forced herself to one knee and stared up at me, barely even breaking a sweat, while I was panting hard from the exertion of the past hour's training.

"Vell done, Meredith, you got her good that time," Freuchen said. He was busy tending to the campfire. A brace of roasting birds that—with the help of Albert—he'd caught earlier that afternoon hung over it. I had a sneaking suspicion they might be dodos. Albert sat next to the big Danish man, and both the man and boy clapped enthusiastically at my victory.

Silas stood in a patch of light, soaking up as much energy as his damaged batteries could hold as the afternoon sun edged toward the western horizon. His eye-bar followed Chou and my movements, but he said nothing.

"You let me have that one, didn't you?" I leaned in and offered Chou my hand, pulling her to her feet.

"Perhaps," Chou said, her face creased into a smile. "Either way, you are improving quickly."

I accepted the compliment, but I wasn't under any illusion that Chou hadn't been holding back. She had attenuated her attack to match the skill of an average human, so it would be a fair fight for me. And "average" wasn't a word anyone who had encountered this woman from the future would use to describe her. Chou could've run rings around me if she'd wanted to. Instead, she'd devoted several hours a day since we'd left Avalon to teach me all that she knew of sword-fighting (of which she was frighteningly proficient).

I'd managed to resist an overwhelming temptation for the first two lessons Chou had put me through. However, on day three, I'd finally cracked. Holding the curved scimitar I'd taken from the body of one of the men who'd tried to kill us that first day we'd arrived on Avalon, I said in my best Spanish accent: "Hello, my name is Inigo Montoya. You killed my father. Prepare to die."

Chou had looked at me oddly, then said. "I can assure you that I did no such thing."

I'd explained that it was just a quote from a movie, *The Princess Bride*, one of my favorites. "You know, the six-fingered man... never mind." Chou had just shaken her head and proceeded with the lesson. I guess she was finally getting used to me.

Six days had passed since we stepped off the *Alexa Rae* and begun our journey into the heart of this strange, unknown continent we referred to simply as the Mainland. I was still trying to wrap my mind around it all. Everyone in this world had been brought here at the point of death. Either by an entity we called the Architect, as my companions and I had, or by another, mysterious enemy we'd named the Adversary. The Architect had left a message in the care of Silas, the last of the robot caretakers assigned to help humanity through the shock of arriving here on this future Earth. I had to find Candidate One; she or he was the only person who could put right the damage that the Adversary had wrought on the Architect's plan. The Adversary wanted me enough that it had sent a group of Nazi stormtroopers to try and catch me. Something that had cost the life of Benito, one of the Garrisonites, along with more Candidates from alternate dimensions than I cared to remember. Oh, and in case I ever thought that the limit on craziness was exhausted, in one of those other infinite copies of the universe, a version of me was the President of the United States. I know, crazy, right?

In the six days we had been traveling together, I'd become a better fighter than I could ever have imagined, thanks to Chou's tutelage. At least, in theory. We hadn't seen another human being during the entire time we'd been walking through the thick forest that seemed to cover every square inch of Mainland. So, there was no way to know just how impressive I actually was.

Albert had named the vast unending woodlands of firs, conifers, oaks, redwoods, and other trees none of us could identify as the Everwood. That's what we called it now.

We'd set our sights on reaching the Collector, the huge mega-structure that dominated the skyline that we believed gathered the energy from the Dyson Swarm surrounding the sun, then distributed it out each night in the form of the aurora that powered the healing nanites—or pixie dust as we liked to call them. That's where we thought we would find Candidate

One and, hopefully, the answers to the mystery of why we were all brought here.

"Come and eat," Freuchen said, lifting the roasted birds off the fire and placing them on a makeshift plate of large leaves he'd pulled from a nearby fern.

We sat around the fire, eating silently, watching the forest vanish into the darkness. We were averaging about ten miles a day, depending on how dense the trees and undergrowth were. Mile after mile after mile of nothing but forest. It was exhausting, tedious, and sapped, not just the energy out us, but our emotion too. Even Albert, who had been so fascinated by the curious world around him, had fallen silent for most of the day.

We chatted half-heartedly for a little while after dinner, sharing memories of our old worlds, our left-behind lives, before, one after the other, we said our goodnights. We turned in with little expectation that the following day would be anything different than this one.

TWO

WE BROKE camp just after dawn, but by late afternoon, the air had grown steadily heavier with moisture. I had a nagging headache over my right eye for the last hour or so from the air pressure as gray clouds filled in the open spaces of the Everwood's canopy, and were gradually replaced by blacker, angrier versions.

Distant thunder rumbled over the trees. Instinctively, I glanced up but saw nothing but bruised clouds through the thick, verdant canopy. A minute later, another crash of thunder rolled in. This time, it sounded closer. Much closer.

"Storm is coming in fast," Freuchen said. "Ve should think about finding cover and making camp early, just to be on the safe side before everything gets too vet."

Chou nodded her agreement.

We quickly found a spot for the night in the twisted roots of an enormous oak, laid down our packs, and set about collecting dry wood for a fire. This part of the Everwood hadn't seen any rain in quite a while judging by how brittle everything was. We quickly gathered a pile of tinder and fuel, and within a couple of minutes, Albert had a fire burning.

The forest darkened as more clouds blotted out what little light remained. Not long after, the first flash of lightning illuminated the canopy, and thunder crashed across the heavens, loud enough to make us all flinch and silencing every other creature. The pitter-patter of the first raindrops hitting the leaves above us quickly turned into a hiss as the storm let loose its deluge.

Freuchen flinched as a trickle of water dropped from above and down his neck with perfect precision. He cursed, smiled at us, and shifted a couple of feet to his right. Chou placed her canteen under the tiny waterfall and filled it. We all did likewise.

"*I think it best if I shut down early tonight and conserve energy,*" Silas said, sitting cross-legged beneath the tree. Each night, the robot lost portions of his memory. Soon after we'd met him, he started jotting down the day's activities in his digital language. He'd just updated the slate on which he'd written today's log, and handed it to me. "*If there's nothing more, I wish you all a safe night.*" His eye-bar dimmed and vanished.

Lightning flashed every few seconds, briefly illuminating the forest around us. The thunder which followed pounded our senses and cowed the three of us into silence as the storm inched slowly over us. I remembered being told as a kid that you should never shelter under a tree during a thunderstorm, but we didn't have much choice seeing as the Everwood was the only shelter for hundreds, if not thousands of miles around us.

It lasted a little more than twenty minutes, finally moving away almost as quickly as it had arrived. By then, evening was fast approaching, and it would have been pointless to break camp.

Slowly, the silence that had descended over the forest was replaced as, one by one, the hidden life within it found its voice again.

We settled into our usual routine. After we'd eaten, we

decided the order which we would stand watch, then chatted quietly amongst ourselves while we waited for the aurora. The day's trek had been particularly hard on us. The ground we traveled over was covered in giant ferns and bracken, which had made walking twice as tricky. If you rubbed up against a leaf at just the right angle, those things could give you the equivalent of a nasty paper cut. Even after the enervating effects of the aurora healed the wounds and carried away the aches and pains of my body, my mind remained exhausted. After wishing everyone a peaceful night, I curled up next to the fire and fell asleep quickly and deeply.

———

I was awakened by Chou, roughly shaking my shoulder.

"Get up, Meredith," she said, panic in her voice. "Everyone, wake up now."

My eyes opened. "What's going on?" I mumbled as Chou moved from Albert to Freuchen, shaking them just as violently as she had me. Dawn illuminated the forest to the east, its orange glow flickering between the trees. But if it was morning, why did I still feel exhausted?

"Why'd didn't you wake me?" I asked, confused as to why Chou had let me sleep through my guard duty.

"There's still an hour or so until dawn," Chou said, stopping to throw first my backpack to me, then Freuchen's and Albert's to them. "It's a forest fire, and its heading our way."

Rubbing my eyes, I looked again to the east. The light I had mistaken for morning's approach flickered and jumped. Chou was right, it *was* fire. And it was getting closer too; I was sure of it.

"Shit!" I hissed.

"It must have been the lightning," Albert said.

"Silas!" I yelled at the robot, still sitting cross-legged beneath the tree.

He woke up. *"Greetings children of Earth—"*

"Silas, stop! Read this." I held the slate in front of his eyes, my other hand tapping impatiently against my thigh as every second seemed to stretch to minutes.

"Thank you, Meredith."

"No time to fully explain," I continued. "Listen, there's a forest fire heading our way. We need to get out of here now."

Silas looked to where I pointed.

"You are correct," he said. *"We should evacuate this area immediately."*

Freuchen swept Albert up into his massive arms, and we took off as quickly as we could, which wasn't anywhere near as fast as we needed to, given the terrain. But the last thing we needed now was for one of us to put our foot in a hole or a burrow hidden beneath the groundcover of ferns and break an ankle.

"Our only hope is to outrun it," Chou said, the same level of concern I had heard in her voice when she woke me still there, which made me even more nervous than I already was.

From behind us, something crashed out of the undergrowth, and I had a second to yell a warning as three giant deer careened past us, narrowly missing Freuchen and Albert. Other animals followed behind them, their natural fear of us overtaken by the fire. In the high branches, I heard the panicked calls of birds and other canopy-dwellers taking flight as the first clouds of smoke moved through their home.

Glowing embers floated, pushed along by a hot breeze that had sprung seemingly from out of nowhere. With it, came the pungent, acrid smell of fire, stinging the back of my throat with every breath I took. I looked back and immediately wished I hadn't. The fire was *much* closer. Close enough that I could see its flames clawing at the trees. Between us and it, smaller fires were sprouting up, the wind-borne embers igniting the dry wood and dead leaves that covered the forest floor.

"If we don't pick up the pace, it's going to catch up with us," I said. "Come on!"

"Follow the animals," Albert yelled. "*Follow* them."

Freuchen said, "I think Albert is right. Look at the direction they are taking."

Rather than running directly away from the fire, the deer and other forest critters were taking an acute route. The kid was right. *Maybe* they knew something we didn't. And perhaps that unknown could save us.

With no other options available, we took off at a sprint, hoping luck would guide our footsteps away from any hazard obscured by the bracken. The sound of our steps and panting breath was blotted out by a growing crackling, hissing roar. I could feel the heat of the fire's approach against the exposed skin of my neck.

Burning leaves and ash floated all around us now in a mocking imitation of the lifesaving pixie dust. I batted at an ember that landed on my neck, scorching my skin.

More deer exploded from the forest; their eyes wild with terror as they careened past us. Another followed behind, this one's fur alight in multiple spots.

A high-pitched squeal filled the air, unlike anything I had ever heard before, and I glanced behind me, expecting to see another burning animal. Instead, I saw a vortex of fire, fifty feet high—a mini-tornado of flame, whirling from side to side, igniting anything it touched. Behind it, the primary fire engulfed trees like the breath from some ancient dragon. It was becoming harder and harder to breathe, the intense heat and smoke choking the oxygen from the air.

"Faster!" Chou urged.

I tried, but my head was swimming; my eyes were filled with tears from the stinging smoke, and my legs felt like they had turned to jelly.

"I'm not going to make it," I said, my voice raspy and barely recognizable.

Then Chou was beside me, her hand on my elbow, urging me forward. "Yes, you are!"

"I... don't... think... I... can," I said.

"You must," Chou replied, her grip on my elbow tightening as she urged me forward. "The future of the world depends on you."

"Over there! I think there's a clearing," Freuchen yelled out, suddenly angling off to his right, unable to point as he still held Albert close to his chest with both hands. Freuchen's bulk hid whatever he had seen from me, but Chou guided me stumbling after him, and ran right into Freuchen's back as he came to an abrupt stop.

Ahead of us, something huge and not natural to the forest rose up from a bed of crushed and broken trees. I could barely see through my watering eyes, but as we drew closer, I began to make out details. A wall of metal painted red and made up of panels held together by the largest rivets I'd ever seen. An enormous propeller, easily twice as tall as Silas, a second next to it, and then a third. It was the keel of a ship, my exhaustion-fogged mind realized, and a huge one at that. My eyes followed the curve of the hull up and up and up. The top disappeared in the smoke billowing around us like fog.

A sudden gust of hot air blew past us, momentarily parting the smoke like curtains, and I caught a brief glimpse of two words painted one above the other in golden yellow across the curve of ship's stern: *Liverpool*, the lower word read, and above that in four-foot-high letters *Titanic*.

THREE

"YOU HAVE GOT to be kidding me," I managed to splutter before Chou pulled me away. She pushed me to the right side of the ship, placing the legendary liner between us and the oncoming fire. Now I had a clear view of precisely what we had stumbled into.

The ground around the enormous ship's keel had been kicked up in an earthen wave. For fifteen feet in all directions, the trees had been reduced into nothing more than matchsticks. Those just outside the perimeter had been snapped in two and now lay at odd angles, slowing us as we clambered over their splintered trunks.

The liner must have arrived at the same time as we all had. Only a small amount of new vegetation grew around the edges of its keel. Additionally, there was no sign of rust or damage to indicate it arrived any earlier. In fact, it looked like it had just rolled out of the dock. Brand new.

"Ve must find a vay in," Freuchen said. "If ve can get inside, ve can shelter until the fire moves past us. It's our only hope."

Behind us, several of the dead trees we'd just climbed over

ignited into flame. Like some unstoppable monster, the main fire would not be far behind.

"It broke in two," I gasped.

"Vat?" said Freuchen.

"The Titanic, in my universe, when it sank, it broke in two. We need to find where the break is."

"Silas," Chou said, "run ahead and see if you can find us a way in."

"*Of course,*" said Silas, then took off, vanishing into the wall of smoke surrounding us while we stumbled blindly onward. He reappeared thirty-seconds later, bounding over the fallen logs that blocked our way as though they weren't even there. "*Meredith was correct,*" he said. "*There is a fissure large enough for us to enter the ship just ahead. Quickly, follow me.*"

With renewed energy, we followed behind the robot as best we could.

"*Here,*" Silas yelled, the roar of the fire deafening again as it closed in on us. Silas stopped and pointed toward a gash running from the ship's keel all the way up through each floor to the top deck. The opening was about ten feet wide, and as I looked into it, I saw buckled metal supports and broken floors. Pieces of furniture and equipment hung from the lip of each shattered level like internal organs. Some of the debris had fallen out and lay scattered around the opening.

"*Quickly,*" Silas yelled, "*there is no time left.*" He leaped up and grabbed ahold of a piece of metal that had been the floor of a corridor, pulled himself up, then turned and reached down for us. One after the other, he drew us to him until we were all safely inside.

Coughing and spitting gobbets of black soot, we moved up the corridor before collapsing to the carpeted floor. We lay there, panting, breathing in the deliciously cool air of the ship's interior.

"*We must keep moving,*" Silas said. "*Upward, We must move upward. The dead and broken trees around the perimeter of the ship will keep the fire from reaching the upper portions of the vessel.*" A dense black and gray cloud of smoke was already flowing into the corridor, rising slowly toward us. The *Titanic* was sinking again, but this time she was being swallowed up by smoke.

We dragged ourselves to our feet and followed Silas as he progressed along the corridor. Beyond the metal bulkheads, I heard the fire roaring, heat already beginning to radiate into the corridor.

"Ve vill be cooked like beef in an oven if ve stay here," Freuchen said.

"*Up,*" Silas repeated. "*We must try to get above the fire.*"

"There's a maintenance stairvell," Freuchen yelled, pointing to an opening in the left wall. We staggered toward it and began climbing the metal steps toward the upper decks.

"Keep going," Chou insisted.

Finally, three decks later, weary and footsore beyond words, we stepped out into a door-lined hallway. Each door had a set of gold numbers on them, which I assumed meant they were cabins. First-class, too, judging by the luxurious carpet, exquisite sconces on the wall, and miniature chandeliers hanging from the ceiling. Freuchen lowered Albert to the floor, then fell onto his back, chest heaving while wiping black soot from around his nostrils.

"Are you okay?" I asked him, leaning against a wainscoted wall while I tried to catch my breath.

He nodded. "I believe I vill live."

Even Chou seemed spent. She sat next to me, her usually pristine white clothing and cloak smudged with black and stained gray here and there from the smoke.

"Do you think we're high enough?" I asked, sliding down the wall until my butt hit the floor next to hers.

"*I believe so. For now, at least,*" Silas said. "*My thermal sensors indicate the heat is being dissipated sufficiently through the ship's hull to no longer be a threat to us* at this time." His eye-bar tilted upward. "*I do not see any sign of fire above us either.*"

Exhaling slowly, I wiped soot from my lips with the back of my hand. I took a mouthful of water from my canteen and swilled it around then spat it out. It came out black.

We rested for a while, none of us saying a word, my mind finally able to take in where I was. I was on the *Titanic*. I let that thought sink in for a moment if you'll pardon the pun. So many weird things had happened to me since arriving on this far-flung future version of Earth. So many in fact that I really *shouldn't* be surprised to have *literally* run into the wreck of the most famous liner ever in the middle of a forest.

Freuchen sat up, placing both hands on the floor behind him. "Vy do you..." He coughed, spat a ball of black crud onto the carpet. "My apologies. She is such a vundrous beast, no? In my timeline, it vas just a few months ago that she sank. But vy on earth do you think the Architect vould bring the *Titanic* here?"

"Perhaps you should ask Silas," I said.

"*While I do not know the precise reason this vessel was brought here, I do know that the Architect targeted specific caches of equipment, artifacts, supplies, and resources that candidates would find useful. It would be expected that some of those caches would be recovered from the site of unfortunate disasters such as this.*"

"So, the Architect is into recycling?" I said, turning to the robot.

"*Yes, after all, it would be a terrible waste of resources to simply leave them to decay.*"

I was beginning to feel better, so I got to my feet, then helped Chou up too. "Let's see what's behind..." I paused to check the embossed number on the nearest cabin, "...door number C-79, shall we?" I said, reaching for the ornate door-knob. It turned easily in my hand, and I pushed it open.

"Wow!" I said, stepping inside. The room was a complete shamble; broken glass lay next to a mirror frame. The king-sized mattress hung half-off the bed, a high-backed easy chair lay on its side, and pieces of broken crockery were scattered all over. But the workmanship of everything was exquisite, and it wasn't hard to see that the room had indeed been first-class accommodation. An ensuite bathroom adjoined the main cabin. On the opposite wall was a porthole. Beyond it, I saw nothing but smoke and the orange glow from outside.

Freuchen approached the porthole and looked out. He shook his head slowly. "The leading edge of the fire has moved past us, but it looks like hell out there. But you are correct, Silas, the flattened trees beneath us have kept the fire from reaching the ship."

The rest of us crowded around the porthole. Clouds of smoke billowed past the window. From this elevated position, I could see the brighter line of the fire's leading edge moving away, just as Freuchen had said. It stretched for miles on a rough path. Everything behind it was aflame, burning brightly but with less intensity.

"There was no way we would have outrun that," I said.

Chou nodded her assent. "Once again, chance has smiled on us," she said.

"Chance or perhaps by design?" I said, not even trying to calculate what the probability was of a safe refuge of this magnitude having been randomly set down here.

"You think the ship vas placed here on purpose? By the Architect?" Freuchen said, both caterpillar-like eyebrows raised.

"Perhaps," said Chou. "The odds would seem too great for us to have simply stumbled upon it accidentally."

"Vell, vether by good luck or design, ve are not getting out of here tonight. Ve are going to be stuck here until the fire dies down."

"Maybe we should rest for a while, then explore?" I said. "There doesn't seem to be much water damage that I've seen, which is weird. And if that goes for the rest of the ship, there have to still be supplies onboard. Maybe something we can use?"

"That is a good idea," Chou said.

I wondered how many historians would have given their first-born to be in my shoes right now. *This was the* Titanic! To have the chance to see firsthand the actual ship behind the legend was an amazing opportunity.

"Vat I vould not give for a Turkish Bath right now," Freuchen mumbled.

I nodded at the adjoining bathroom. "Maybe the faucets still work," I said, jokingly.

Freuchen walked into the bathroom and turned on one of the taps. There was a *pop-clunk* and then the unmistakable sound of water gushing into the porcelain sink.

"No way!" I said, rushing to his side.

"Yes vay," Freuchen deadpanned. He placed a metal plug into the sink and watched it fill with water. "There must be some kind of gravity-fed vater reservoir connected to the plumbing system. The fact that it is still vurking is another stroke of good luck." He picked up two large white towels from the floor, shook them out, then hung them over the bathtub.

"Ladies first," Freuchen said, retreating into the main room and closing the door behind him.

I stripped out of my clothes and dumped them on the commode. They stank of smoke and sweat. I turned and looked at myself in the ornate mirror above the sink. Every inch of me was covered in dirt and soot; even my hair looked more brown than red, but at least I looked like *me*, something I hadn't been able to say for what felt like a very long time. In a wooden cabinet next to the sink, I found several bars of paper-wrapped soap and began working on scrubbing away the grime. The water was cold but felt wonderful against my skin. I was halfway to being clean when there was a knock on the bathroom door.

"Meredith, I have something for you," Freuchen's muffled voice said.

I hid behind the door and cracked it open an inch. Freuchen stood several feet away, his head turned in the opposite direction for modesty's sake, his arm outstretched to me.

"I think these should fit you," he said and handed me a set of men's pants and a thick polo-necked sweater. "Ve found them in the next cabin. The water is vurking in most of the cabins in this corridor. Chou and the boy are cleaning up in them, so take your time. Now, if you vill hand me your clothes, I vill wash them for you."

I laughed and thanked him. "You are a man of many talents, Mr. Peter Freuchen," I said, as I placed my soiled clothing into his outstretched palm.

"It is my pleasure," he said, then turned and left me to my business.

I finished my ablutions and slipped into the clothing Freuchen had found for me. The material was itchy against my skin but comfortable enough and so much better than the alternative.

When I stepped into the main cabin, Freuchen and Albert were already back. Our clothes, still dripping, hung from hangers against the ship's bulkhead to dry. Chou had even abandoned her seemingly indestructible clothes.

Albert wore only a man's sweater, so large it came down to

just below his knees. Freuchen wore a pair of pants far too short for him and a long leather coat that was also too short for his arms. Chou showed up a minute after me, rocking a man's frock coat and wool pants.

"Well, don't we all just look fabulous," I said, laughing.

"Needs must ven the devil drives," Freuchen said, good-humoredly.

Albert giggled and flushed red. Chou raised her eyebrows and shook her head slowly.

Silas said, "*I must remind you that I am running on limited power. I should position myself near the porthole to gather as much of the available light as possible and place myself in standby mode. Is that acceptable?*"

"Oh, my God," I said.

Despite only getting maybe four hours of sleep after the aurora last night, running for your life has a way of blowing the cobwebs from your mind. I had utterly forgotten that Chou had roused us before dawn. "Absolutely, Silas. Go ahead."

The robot positioned himself so the light that came through the porthole would hit the maximum area of his energy-collecting coating, then shut down.

Despite the invigorating energy of the aurora, we humans also needed rest, if we were to stay on our toes until the fire burned itself out. "Maybe we should get a little rest while our clothes dry?" I suggested.

Freuchen nodded. "Ve should stick together for safety. You and Chou and Albert take the bed. I'll be fine in this." He righted the easy chair from where it lay on the floor and settled himself into it. Chou repositioned the mattress back onto the bedframe, then we climbed onto the bed, Albert sandwiched between Chou and me.

I stared up at the ceiling awhile, my mind wrangling with

the reality that I was now a first-class passenger aboard the *Titanic*.

If I remembered correctly, the *Titanic* had been on her maiden voyage from Southampton to New York when she'd sunk, at least in my version of the universe. But her wreck hadn't been discovered until sometime in the '80s, which meant that this *Titanic* couldn't be the one from my universe. It *had* to be from a parallel world where the wreck was never discovered. And I hadn't seen any water damage which meant she'd either never sunk, or the Architect had transported her here before the sea reached this deck, but who knew what the rest of the boat was like?

An hour passed, then another, and I drifted along the fine line between sleep and wakefulness, listening to Albert's puppy-snore and the occasional *creak* from Freuchen's chair as he shifted position.

Though she tried to be quiet, I heard Chou rise from the bed. I sat up too. Light streamed in through the portal, enveloping Silas in orange and casting a shadow across the breadth of the room. Chou silently passed me her canteen, and after a couple of gulps, I handed it back to her.

Freuchen's eyes fluttered open. He stretched, stood up, and checked our clothing. "Dry as a bone," he announced, tossing them to us.

Chou immediately began to undress. She wore nothing beneath her borrowed clothes.

A mortified Freuchen turned and stared at the opposite wall, the back of his neck flushing as bright red as his face surely was. Chou didn't seem to notice or care.

"I'm a little bit more modest," I said and walked into the bathroom to change. When I came back, Albert was awake and dressed, sitting cross-legged on the bed.

Freuchen was re-entering from the corridor, buttoning up

his shirt. "Vell then," he announced, "now that ve are all decent again, who is up for an adventure?"

"I have a sneaking suspicion," I said to Chou, as we followed Freuchen back into the corridor, "that one of these days, those are going to be the last words of our species."

————

Wisps of smoke floated near the ceiling, caught in the beams of the flashlights we'd liberated from the Nazis back on Avalon. We followed the corridor toward the bow, past cabin after cabin. I don't know about anyone else, because they didn't say anything, but I found it eerie, wandering through this empty ship, despite its almost pristine condition. And I still couldn't stop wondering what had happened to the passengers. I would have expected to have seen some kind of a sign that *someone* had managed to make it here alive, but like I said, apart from the obvious external damage that had allowed us to get inside and the disheveled state of the rooms, there was no indication that this *Titanic* had even spent a minute beneath the waves.

"Can you imagine the people who must have been traveling on this ship?" I asked, peeking into an open cabin. The room was just as much of a mess as the one we had left Silas in. Women's clothing was scattered across the floor, and, miraculously, next to an empty champagne bottle, lay two intact champagne flutes.

"Some vould say the very best of our time," Freuchen said.

"You would not?" Chou said, one eyebrow raised.

"I prefer the company of the common man... or voman," Freuchen answered. "Although, I vould very much like to have made the acquaintance of Captain Edwards, as I believe he vas given a rum deal after the disaster."

We reached the end of the corridor and stepped out into a large open section of the ship.

"Oh, wow!" I whispered.

Ahead of us was the magnificent wooden structure known as the Grand Staircase.

"I had heard the Grand Staircase vas a masterful piece of vurk," said Freuchen, running his hands over the smooth lacquered banister. "But I never imagined just *how* exquisite."

I craned my neck over one banister. The staircase swept up to the deck above, then down below us, and down again for several more decks.

"Which way do you think?" I asked.

"I have no knowledge of this vessel," said Chou, "but you and Freuchen seem very familiar with it, so I will leave it to your judgment."

"Vell, if ve could locate one of the dining halls or perhaps the crew kitchen ve might be able to find preserved food or rations?"

I nodded. "Sounds good."

Freuchen said, "I believe the first-class dining hall is on B-Deck."

"Up it is then," I said, smiling.

"Vait a minute. The purser's office is open," Freuchen said before we could take a step. He was pointing back in the direction we'd come from to a recessed alcove I'd somehow missed. A set of wooden roll-up shutters was half-pulled down to an ornate teak counter. Behind the bar, a pigeonhole cabinet took up the back wall, letters and documents still in some of the slots. Adjacent to the counter, a door stood ajar, the word PURSER written in large black letters across the frosted glass.

"It might be vorth taking a look," Freuchen said. "The first-class passengers kept a lot of valuables in there."

"Really?" I said, surprised that Freuchen would take an interest in anything of value.

He must have caught the surprise in my voice because he clarified by saying, "Ve may find something ve can use to barter vith ven ve find other people."

I felt my face bloom red, embarrassed that I'd doubted my friend. Instead of offering an apology, I smiled, shook my head, and walked toward the open door.

The room held three desks with accompanying office chairs and a large filing cabinet. But what was of interest to us were the three large metal safes set against the far bulkhead. There were no combination locks on any of them, just a keyhole and a brass handle. All were closed.

Freuchen tried the handle of the first, but it was locked. I tried the second with the same result. Albert tried the third handle, and, to all our surprise, the heavy steel door swung open.

The safe had four shelves and multiple compartments. Most were filled with rolls of US cash, legal documents, and other now worthless documents.

"Here, take a look at vat is in here," Freuchen said, handing me an embellished gold-plated jewelry box. I flipped the lid. The box contained five rings and a beautiful diamond necklace, all obviously worth more than most people probably made in a lifetime back then. I handed the box to Albert.

"There you go," I said to the boy. "You're now an official millionaire."

Albert smiled broadly and began to go through the box.

Meanwhile, Freuchen had handed Chou a hand-sized satin pouch. She undid the drawstring fastening and pulled out a beautiful diamond-and amethyst-encrusted gold necklace.

"Put's the *Heart of the Ocean* to shame," I whispered.

Chou looked at me oddly and said, "As Freuchen

mentioned, this will make a fine bartering item. Several if we break it apart."

I winced at the idea of destroying such a beautiful piece of art, but she was right.

Several more pouches followed, each containing more stunningly excessive jewelry than the previous. When we were finished, we had a pile of precious stones and metals that was probably worth a half-a-billion dollars in my time.

"Hey," I said, "what about that?" I pointed to the bottom shelf of the safe. Leaning against the back wall was a leather bag, the size of a laptop computer. Freuchen reached in and handed it to me. I unzipped it and pulled out a wooden case.

"What is it?" Albert asked.

"I think," I said, as I turned the case over, "it's a... yes, it *is* a book." The wooden outer casing was just to protect the tome held within. I tilted it so I could see the spine and read the embossed title aloud, "The Rubaiyat of Omar Khayyam." I'd never heard of it, but apparently, Freuchen had judging by his gasp.

"Please, may I see it?" he asked.

"Sure," I said and dropped the encased book into his outstretched hands.

Ever so carefully, Freuchen removed it from its slipcase.

The cover was stunningly beautiful: three peacocks stood atop a heart, tail-feathers spread wide. Flowers were intricately embroidered in gold-leaf and ink across the soft leather. On the back cover, a lute, inlaid using actual wood, was surrounded by more intricate embroidery.

"It is a book of ancient quatrains by the Persian astronomer-poet of the title, translated by Edward Fitzgerald. I had read about it in a newspaper before the *Titanic* left on its maiden voyage, but never had I thought I vould actually place my hands on it. Look."

Freuchen reverently flipped the book open to a random page, and now it was my turn to gasp in astonishment. The pages of the book were even more intricately inlaid with gold and...

"Are those rubies?" I asked, pointing at the small stones embedded within the illustration in their own gold settings upon the page.

Freuchen nodded, flipped the page. "And diamonds."

"Wow!" I said, then added, "I know someone who would like that."

Freuchen smiled. "I vas thinking the very same thing."

"Edward," said Albert.

"Yes," I said.

"Vell, I think it vould be a vunderful gift for the man ven ve make it back to Avalon. Here, you hold on to it for him, Meredith." Freuchen handed me the book, and I placed it back into its slipcover and leather bag then put it in my backpack.

Meanwhile, Chou had divided the other jewelry into three separate piles and placed each into one of the velvet bags.

"Better not keep everything with one person," she said and handed us each a bag of loot. After another quick check of the room that turned up nothing, we left and headed back to the Grand Staircase.

———

We took the Grand Staircase up to C-Deck then followed a sign that indicated the restaurant was back in the aft section of the boat.

"If I remember correctly,' Freuchen was saying, "there is a pantry attached to the first-class restaurant's kitchen. Vith some luck ve vill—"

A man appeared from nowhere, materializing from thin air, his eyes wild with fear as he rushed down the corridor toward us. Chou was the first to react, leaping like a cat to her right, then dropping to a knee, her eyes locked on the stranger. I stood frozen, directly in his path, jaw almost to my knees as the man, dressed in a navy blue double-breasted jacket, with a white and black peeked cap stumbled toward me. In the second or so he remained visible, I saw terror written across his face but no recognition of our presence. It was almost as though we were invisible to him. I turned just in time to see him vanish again as though he had never been there.

Now the corridor held only me and my companions.

"What the ever-loving shit just happened?" I stuttered, looking to Freuchen. He stood unmoving, eyes as wide as proverbial saucers, his back pressed firmly against the wall, staring at the space where the sailor had just dematerialized.

"A ghost," Albert whispered as if his voice might bring the man back. "I think the ship is haunted."

"No," Chou said, moving to the boy's side, "not a ghost. Something... else."

"Vat else could that have been other than a spirit?" Freuchen spluttered, his voice cracking.

"A hallucination. A projection. But no, most definitely not a ghost." Chou knelt down to examine the carpet as though it might hold the secret to what had just happened, then stood again, slowly. "Did you notice anything about the corridor when the man appeared?"

Nothing sprung to my mind, but then my heart was still pounding so loudly in my chest I was surprised the others couldn't hear it too.

"The lights," Albert said. "The lights were all on."

"The boy is right," Freuchen said, regaining his composure. "The lamps in the ceiling were all aglow as if the power had been returned, but they went off again as soon as the apparition vanished."

I had no recollection of *any* of the overhead lights being on. All I could conjure up of the encounter was the fearful look on the man's face.

Chou continued to examine the air the man had walked through as if searching for something. Finally, she said, "Turn off your flashlights, please."

"What? Why?" I said. I don't believe in the supernatural. Still, despite Chou's protestations, I was not sure that what I had just witnessed wasn't *actually* a ghost. After all, it had done a pretty damn good impression of one, that was for sure. I thought it was reasonable that the idea of plunging us into complete darkness didn't appeal to me one little bit.

"Please," Chou insisted, turning off her own light.

Reluctantly, we all did the same.

"I really don't see what we have to gain by standing in the darkness," I said, my thumb nervously caressing my flashlight's switch. Except, we weren't in darkness. Not completely, at least. Suspended in the air between the ceiling and the floor were four irregularly shaped slits—fissures in the blackness. A faint, yellow light leaked from them. There was one at chest height just a few inches from me.

"Is it pixie dust?" I said, reaching out a tentative finger to touch the dimly glowing hole.

"Stop!" Chou said, grabbing my hand, while gently moving it away from the fissure.

"Not pixie dust then," I said, gulping.

"No, not pixie dust." Chou inhaled slowly and deeply. "I believe," she said, her voice just above a whisper, "that some kind of temporal anomaly has taken place here in this corridor. Perhaps a residual effect of the process the Architect used to translocate us here. Look, lean in closer, and tell me what you see. But don't, under any circumstance, touch it."

"Why shouldn't we touch them?" Albert asked, looking sideways at her.

"The results of our reality combining with the other universes would be... unpredictable."

"By 'unpredictable,' do you mean the end of the universe? Everything goes boom, don't cross the plasma streams kind of 'unpredictable?'" I said.

"No, no," Chou answered, slowly circling the nearest anomaly, its light painting one side of her face, then the other. "But the probability is that the stress exerted on the membrane between the two realities is fragile. If it breaks, a large part of *that* other corridor would be pulled into *this* reality."

"That doesn't sound so bad. I mean, isn't that what the Architect wanted to happen?" I said.

"Yes, but the temporal aperture the Architect would have used to bring us or this ship into this reality would have been scaled accordingly. In this instance, I believe the result would be the equivalent of forcing a large volume of water under immense pressure through a hose. Matter from the other universe would be compressed to the size of the aperture and would explode into our reality. It would cut through everything and *anyone* in its way."

"Oh-kay," I said. I leaned in until my eye was six inches away from the bright line. I gasped. Through the hole in the darkness, I saw the corridor. But the ceiling lights, dark in our world, glowed then dimmed like the power was being turned slowly up and down. Men and women rushed along the corridor, dressed in suits and dresses. Every one of them looked terrified.

By the time I had stepped away from the aperture to make way for Freuchen, Chou had moved on to the next, this one about four feet away and close to the floor. She dropped down onto her chest and edged slowly toward its glow.

"Here, come and look at this," she said, rolling aside so I could lie down beside her.

I edged closer. I was looking at the same deserted corridor. The lights glowed strongly now, with no sign of fading in or out. One of the cabin doors opened, and a waiter who looked like he could have worked in some high-end Manhattan restaurant stepped out of the room with a silver tray in one hand. He said something I couldn't hear to whoever was still in the cabin, smiled courteously and nodded, then reached and closed the door behind him. He took a couple of steps down the corridor, checked he was alone, then popped what looked like half of a bread bun into his mouth before walking on.

While all this was happening, Chou had moved to the next aperture, this one also at chest height. She moved aside as I stepped close to her. The version of the corridor I saw through it was awash with water and tilted at a disorienting angle. Only one lamp still worked. Though, it stuttered—off more than it was on, which gave the corridor a terrifying and unnerving haunted house effect.

"This doesn't make sense," Freuchen said after he had looked through each of the tears and allowed Albert to carefully do the same. "It appears to be this very corridor, but each seems to be experiencing a very different reality."

Chou said, "I believe that this is not *the Titanic*...this is *multiple Titanics*. Or at least many *potential Titanics*. The Architect must have established connections between this world and numerous alternate universes. In some, the ship may have sunk. In others, it may never have at all. The Architect would have to have established a temporal connection with these alternate universes to identify whether the disaster had taken place or whether the ship sailed on, its passengers blissfully unaware of the fate they had avoided. For some reason, some of those connections have never disengaged."

"But where did the sailor come from?" Albert asked.

"Perhaps our presence caused his appearance," Chou answered.

"But why on Earth would the Architect be so interested in the *Titanic*?" Freuchen pondered aloud.

Chou thought about it. "Perhaps there was something significant about this ship."

"Or, *someone*," Freuchen added.

"Oh, God. You don't think Candidate One was aboard, do you?" I said.

Chou shook her head. "That does not seem likely to me, Meredith. But I would imagine there would have been numerous well-educated people, along with experts in many fields who would have perished when the ship sank."

"Of course," I said. "It would have been a fantastic resource for the Architect to have brought here."

"And that vould make it a prime target for the Adversary, too," Freuchen added.

"So, I guess the Architect and the Adversary must have gotten into some kind of a struggle that resulted in what we're seeing here in this corridor. But that still doesn't explain what happened to the passengers and crew."

"Perhaps those who made it through vandered off into the Evervood?" Freuchen said.

"Seems like the most likely answer," I said, but that still didn't feel right. And I couldn't shake the feeling that there was something we weren't seeing.

"Ve should continue," said Freuchen.

Chou nodded. "Yes, just be careful. And I'd suggest that we keep only my flashlight activated. That way we will see any other anomalies, should they exist."

She weaved her way between the apertures, and we carefully followed behind. Soon, we passed a narrow corridor connecting the port side of the ship to the starboard. Chou stopped and shined her light into it. A door was labeled 'crew access.' She pushed it open and leaned in, moving her light up and down, illuminating a metal stairwell similar to the ones found in modern apartment buildings.

"It vould probably be used by the crew to move through the ship vithout being seen by the gentry," Freuchen commented.

Chou allowed the door to swing shut again

"The restaurant is this vay," Freuchen said, pointing to a sign with an arrow on the wall. "The pantry vill be somevere vithin it."

Chou elbowed through a pair of red baize-covered swinging doors, holding the left one open while the rest of us stepped through. She shone her light into the larger room beyond, illuminating several overturned wing-backed chairs that lay around a still upright mahogany table. We followed a short teak-paneled corridor through another set of double doors and found ourselves standing in what had been, according to Freuchen, one of several dining halls or restaurants. The room was littered with overturned tables and chairs, broken cutlery, and discarded utensils.

"That vay," said Freuchen, pointing past what had obviously been a buffet station on our right to another set of doors. Once through the doors, we found ourselves in a room with three huge cupboards, two oversized sinks, and an extensive cooking range. Freuchen threw open the doors to the nearest cupboard and flicked on his own flashlight. Instantly, his face lit up with a huge smile. He reached in and pulled out a brown paper bag about the size of a sack of flour. *Darjeeling* was written in extraordinarily neat cursive across it.

"Tea!" Freuchen said. "Finally, civilization has returned to this land." He laughed heartily, unslung his backpack, and dropped the tea inside. "And sugar, too." He pulled another bag from within the cupboard and lowered it into his bag alongside the tea.

"Is there anything more substantial in there?" I asked, unable to keep from smiling at his boyish excitement.

Freuchen shook his head. "Not in this vun. Try the other two."

The second cabinet held masses of flour and other baking accessories. I took a single bag, weighed it in my hand.—it was easily ten pounds—and put it back on the shelf. There was no way to justify carrying that kind of weight when we had no way to make the bread I suddenly missed more than anything else from my old life.

"Oh, imagine a sandwich?" I said. "Or even just toast and jam?"

"Over here," Albert said, stealing me from my reverie. He and Chou stood in front of the largest of the cupboards.

Freuchen ran his light beam over the shelves. They were packed full of canned goods: beef, pork, sardines, condensed milk. The list went on.

"We should take as much as ve can comfortably carry," Freuchen said. "Ven Silas vakes up, ve can have him carry most of it for us."

We packed our backpacks with our newfound bounty, to the point that Freuchen had to help me get mine over my shoulders. Feeling more positive than I think any of us had since leaving Avalon all those weeks ago, we turned and headed back through the doors leading into the main restaurant area... and froze.

In the corner opposite of where we stood, the room was no longer a disheveled mess. Three of the overturned tables now stood upright. Men and women dressed in beautifully tailored suits and long, elegant dresses and wide-brimmed hats sat at each of them, talking amongst themselves while eating off unbroken crockery. Servers bounced between the tables, disappearing in and out of view as they crossed some unseen boundary between our world and theirs.

They seemed totally oblivious to our presence.

"Look at that," Freuchen said, pointing to a table that, in our reality, had been tipped on its side. But in this *other* version of the restaurant, the table was slowly being replaced by one in its upright position, its lacy white linen tablecloth and bone china all neatly placed and waiting for new diners.

"Their reality is expanding, replacing this version with its own," Chou said. "Fascinating."

Near the center of the room, another reality was emerging from the chaos. This time, the restaurant appeared to be empty, the chairs all neatly tucked into the tables, the lights dimmed.

"Vat the hell is going on?" Freuchen rumbled, his gaze shifting from one surreal scene to the other.

"I think our presence here is causing these other universes to attempt to exert *their* version of reality into this one."

"What'll happen when one of them succeeds?" I asked.

Chou said, "I would suggest that we leave this ship immediately."

"What about the fire?" Albert asked.

"Don't vurry, little man," Freuchen said. "The fire has passed beyond us by now. Ve vill just have to be very careful."

I turned to head toward the exit... and again, stopped dead.

Near the entrance to the restaurant, ten feet of water reached from the floor to the ceiling. We'd been so caught up in watching the passengers dining that we hadn't noticed this third alternate version of reality silently slip into existence. It was like looking at a huge, slowly expanding fish tank minus the glass. The restaurant wall beyond that appeared absolutely normal.

The water was expanding outward quickly, twice as fast, I guessed as the other realities, and as it expanded, everything that was pristine and new here, aged and crumbled. *It's as though it's been sitting at the bottom of the ocean for decades*, I thought.

"It's going to cut off our exit," said Freuchen.

He was right. In a few more seconds, the wall of water would grow enough to completely block the one and only way out of the restaurant. And if that happened, we'd be trapped in here with these three competing realities.

"Run!" Chou said and sprinted to the exit, ducking past the amorphous bubble of water.

Freuchen snapped up Albert and dashed for the shrinking gap between the water and the exit. I ran too, managing to slide past just as the expanding water connected with the smaller reality containing nothing but the empty version of the restaurant. The empty restaurant vanished, replaced by the same murky gray water. A large hole appeared in the far wall, ragged and rusted around the edges. Through it, I saw the *Titanic's* decayed prow, everything in between it was corroded and broken. After subsuming that reality, the vast bubble of water began growing again.

"Come on!" Chou yelled, grabbing me by the hand and dragging me toward the staircase. As I turned, I saw the bubble of ocean water touch the oblivious diners' reality and consume it entirely. Instantly, a wave of water exploded through the restaurant, filling the remaining space in seconds.

"Oh, crap!" I squeaked as the water rushed towards us. Everything it touched instantly turned to rot.

Chou, already at the fancy stairs, stopped briefly to check that the rest of us were following, then, two steps at a time, took the stairs down to C-Deck where we had first entered the ship, and where we had left Silas on standby in the cabin.

Freuchen, Albert, and I raced after her.

The water had already reached C-Deck, too, spreading through the rooms and corridor with frightening speed. Chou threw open our cabin door and yelled, "Silas, wake up."

I stumbled into the cabin, pushed past Chou, fumbled for the slate, and thrust it in front of his eye-bar just as Silas said, "*Greetings children of—*" It took him a couple of seconds to read the code from the slate.

"I don't have time to explain, but we need to get out of here, right now. Come with us," I yelled and dove into the corridor. The sound of Silas' heavy footfalls behind me was the only acknowledgment I needed that he'd understood.

The water was less than ten feet from the door and closing in fast. The irony of being chased into this ship by fire only to be chased back out again by water was not lost on me.

Chou, Freuchen, and Alfred were already charging down the metal stairs, heading toward the split in the *Titanic's* side.

Ahead, the opening we'd come through was now just one deck away. I saw Chou leap from the stairs, throwing herself through the fissure. She hit the ground and was instantly lost in a puff of gray smoke. I felt my heart seize... then start again as she reappeared, covered in gray ash—all that was left of the fallen trees around the mighty ship's hull. She stood facing us with her arms outstretched. Freuchen realized what she was asking for and without a word to the boy, tossed a screaming Albert through the remaining space and into Chou's waiting hands. She spun around, ran, and vanished from my sight just as Freuchen hit the ground next to them. He turned and looked back at me, fear in his eyes.

Out of the corner of my own eye, I saw the wall of water was an arm span to my right side now, so close I could see my reflection in its surface. I forced my eyes forward again and locked onto Freuchen's face. I could tell from his horrified expression that he knew I wasn't going to make it. It simply wasn't possible to cover the twenty or so remaining feet before the water caught up with me. *When it did, would I end up like the ship?* I wondered. *Or would I simply cease to exist like the other realities that had already fallen?* It was all too—

I felt a metal arm wrap around my waist as Silas swept me up. Then we were flying through the air, and I caught a final glimpse of the pristine *Titanic's* bow before it turned to rust and crumbled. The four enormous smokestacks bent and warped, decayed, and flaked away, turning the smoky air orange with rust particles. Rigging snapped, and the glass in the portholes cracked. Water gushed out of every space within the ship, spilling through before vanishing as the two competing realities finally synchronized, leaving nothing of the once-mighty liner but rot and rust and steel bones.

I hit the ground and heard a loud crack, like a thick length of wood snapping in two. Silas landed beside me, stumbled, and vanished into the gray fog of smoke that surrounded us. It stung my eyes and clogged my throat. I tried to breathe, but the hot air was just too thick with dust and ash. I felt consciousness fade in, then out... then I was surrounded by blackness.

—————

"Meredith, vake up." Freuchen's voice pulled me back to consciousness. I opened my eyes to my three companions' faces staring down at me. "Are you alright?" he said, his face twisted with concern.

Hot tears began to run down my cheeks as I tried to sit up, then fell back into the gray-white ash, grimacing in agony. "I... I think I broke my arm," I moaned.

"Remain still," Chou said, kneeling next to me. She gently

rolled back the left sleeve of my top. I heard Albert gasp, and I craned my head to look, but Chou said, "Don't look."

"Too late," I whispered as I caught sight of the three inches of white bone sticking out of the skin just below my elbow. I managed to bleat a surprised "Oh!" then I fell back into the darkness.

———

When consciousness returned, I was sitting upright, my back against the rusted hulk of the *Titanic*. My left arm was splinted with two thin pieces of metal and resting in a sling made out of somebody's spare shirt. It still hurt like a son-of-a-bitch but not as bad as it had. After a tentative attempt to get to my feet, I found that moving didn't add much to the pain.

"Sit back down," Freuchen ordered. The rest of my friends were gathered around me, concerned smiles on every face.

"I showed them how to tie the sling," Albert said, his smile broadening.

"I should've guessed," I said, smiling back at him.

"How do you feel?" Chou asked.

"Like I just got hit by the *Titanic*," I said, somewhat mirthlessly.

"*I have performed a full scan of you,*" Silas added, "*and apart from some bruising, I do not detect anything more serious than your broken arm.*"

I hadn't had time to really take in my surroundings, but now that I did, all I saw was a wasteland of ash and burned wood. It was close to noon, judging by the sun, which was for the first time since setting foot on the mainland, fully visible in the smoke-swept sky.

"Do you think you can walk?" Chou asked. "We should try to make it back to the forest if we can."

I nodded. "I think so. Could I get some water first, please?"

Freuchen knelt close to me and lifted his canteen to my dry lips. I drank deeply, swilling my final gulp around my mouth to try to get rid of the taste of smoke.

"Ready?" Freuchen asked when he put his canteen away.

"As I'll ever be, I guess."

He supported my good arm and helped me slowly to my feet. My teeth gritted against the knifing pain that ran up my left, and I took a couple of seconds to steady myself then said, "Okay, I'm good to go."

Silas had both mine and Freuchen's backpacks slung over his arm and carried them as though they were nothing. He led us through the gray wasteland that had been, until earlier this morning, verdant and lush forest. As we moved away, I took one last look back over my shoulder at the remains of the famous ship, unable to shake the sense of sadness that overcame me at such a thing of beauty being reduced to a decomposed pile of metal. Then another bolt of pain pulled my attention back to reality, and I trudged on with my companions.

———

In spite of Chou's excellent first-aid, walking was a lot more painful than I thought it was going to be, especially when, after several hours, we crossed the edge of where the fire had finally burned itself out. Some trees still smoldered, but most were just singed, and past the first couple of rows, the Everwood lay undisturbed.

"Still feeling okay?" Chou asked me after we had covered a few more miles.

"Not really, but I'll be okay," I replied, not wanting to slow our progress any more than I already was. I comforted myself with the thought that, in a few more hours, the aurora would arrive and heal me.

Late afternoon, we made an early camp, and Freuchen and Albert settled me into a comfortable position before turning their attention back to the nightly routine of gathering wood and starting the fire.

"Vell, let's see vat ve have in here, shall ve?" Freuchen said, good-heartedly as he rummaged through his backpack. He pulled out several cans of food we'd taken from the *Titanic*, opened them with his knife, and set them to warm on the edge of the fire.

"Here you are," Freuchen said once they were heated.

I used my fingers to pull the oily meat from it, all while trying to banish the idea that I was eating half-billion-year-old chicken out of my mind.

Later, when the aurora illuminated the forest, I felt an immediate sense of relief as the pain of my broken arm evaporated. I had Albert slip the sling over my head, and we all watched in fascination as the pixie dust went to work on knitting my bone back into place. Then, they rebuilt and stretched the skin over the wound. When it was done, I flexed my newly-mended hand in front of my face.

"As good as new," Freuchen whispered. Then, as a measure of how normal these incredible events had become for us, he threw a couple more branches on the fire and wished us all a good night's rest.

FOUR

TWO DAYS LATER, the forest that had surrounded us since we'd stepped off the deck of the *Alexa Rae* finally faded behind us.

"You have *got* to be kidding me?" I said, stepping out into a wide clearing that ran like a band between the Everwood and the new challenge ahead. Honestly, I'd have been happy with another hundred miles of trees instead of what lay beyond the clearing—a mountain range that reached into the sky for several thousand feet. It stretched from north to south, horizon to horizon, like a granite backbone running across the land. The lower approach of the mountain swept upward in a gradual rise, gently enough, but then it rapidly grew steeper. Not an impossible climb but a dangerous one for sure.

"Maybe there's a cave?" Albert said, his eyes screwed almost closed against the sunlight bouncing off the snow that covered the mountain from three-quarters of the way up the slope to the ragged saw-toothed ridge that was its peak.

"Perhaps," Chou said, laying a gentle hand against the boy's shoulder, "but I don't think we have time to check." She turned to me and said, "Can I have the binoculars?"

I unslung the binoculars from around my neck and handed them to Chou. Even without them, I could see the occasional stunted tree, bedraggled bush, or lonely weed jutting out of the otherwise barren rock, the only things to break up the dull gray monotony of the mountainside. Chou lowered the binoculars and pointed toward a spot about half-a-mile to the north.

"That seems to be the lowest part," Chou said. "We should head for it."

"Do you think we can make it to the other side before sunset?" I asked Freuchen. The idea of being stuck on the mountain overnight didn't appeal to me, and he was the best judge of this situation given the numerous adventures he'd entertained us with each night at camp.

"I don't see vy not," he said. "It's late morning; ve have plenty of daylight left."

I sighed. "Well, it's not going to climb itself, I guess."

Freuchen smiled broadly. "Vunderful!"

―――

We took a diagonal route up the mountain, rather than trying to climb straight up. The approach took a lot of the strain off our legs, but after a couple of hours of negotiating the boulder-strewn terrain, my thighs were throbbing, and my ankles ached. Freuchen, Chou, and of course, Silas seemed completely fine. Albert started to complain not long after we'd set off, his young legs simply not strong enough to take the exertion of climbing at such a steep angle for a prolonged length of time. So, Silas had offered to carry him, and now, the boy was cradled like a baby in the robot's arms.

"I'm sorry, guys, but I need to take a break," I said finally.

Freuchen nodded. "Good idea. Let's get some food in us,

too," he said. "Ve should drink water. It's easy to dehydrate at these higher altitudes."

I sat on a flattish outcropping, stretched each leg to ease some of the tightness in the muscles, then took Freuchen's advice and drank deeply from my canteen, then polished off some jerky. We'd reached the three-quarter mark, and from here on up to the summit, there was nothing but snow, ice crystals glittering on its surface. The air had been growing gradually colder, but now, as I looked at what we had left to climb, I gave an involuntary shiver.

"The snow's going to make the rest of the trek very treacherous," Freuchen said, eyeing the layer of white that covered the mountain like frosting on a cake. "Ve vill need to take our time."

I opened my backpack and pulled out a thick woolen sweater Edward had given to me. I slipped it over my head and instantly felt more comfortable. Everyone but Silas and Chou did likewise. Chou just tugged the white cloak she wore more tightly around her, the two edges connecting by some unseen fastener, so the cloak became more like a poncho.

"That cloak's not going to keep you very warm," I said.

"It will suffice," Chou assured me. I'd long ago learned that my friend's clothing was far more sophisticated than it appeared, thanks to whatever futuristic super-material it was made of. That, plus Chou's genetic enhancements, made her all but impervious to anything but extreme conditions. While I chewed on the last mouthful of my jerky, I took it all in. The forest stretched out behind us, green and lustrous, more like a single entity than a collection of the millions of trees I knew it to be. I watched the birds wheel and dive. Heard the calls of distant animals. Above, the sky was gray-blue and spattered with large white clouds that occasionally drifted in front of the sun, casting huge shadows across the scenery.

"Incredible, isn't it?" Freuchen said.

I nodded. "The Architect should have sent an artist." But I don't think even the most talented painter could have captured the magnificence of *this* view.

We set off again and didn't stop until we reached the beginning of the snowpack. My leg muscles were still complaining, but the short rest had taken some of the dull edge off the pain.

"Be extra diligent from this point forvard," Freuchen said from the head of the line we'd formed. "One wrong step and..." He whistled like a falling bomb while drawing the trajectory we'd take down the mountain with an index finger. "Don't vant to end up a pancake, do ve?" He laughed uproariously as though he had just told the funniest joke ever, his coarse beard bobbing with each mighty guffaw. Then he turned and began to climb the six-hundred or so feet that remained between us and the summit.

I placed one tentative foot on the snow. It crunched beneath my boots, more like ice than the soft powder I'd skied on the one time I'd visited Mammoth for a long weekend back when I turned twenty-three. "Winter is coming," I mumbled under my breath, in my best English accent, then crunched through the snow after my friends.

———

The mountain's summit lay above us just a few more minutes' climb. The gusting wind blew flurries of loose snow off the ridge, sending it swirling over our heads, forcing us to dip our heads against its stinging bite.

Freuchen stopped suddenly. He turned back to face us, smiling, then beckoned to Albert. Silas lowered the boy to the snow and walked protectively behind Albert as he high stepped to where Freuchen waited.

"What is it?" I asked.

Freuchen put a finger to his lips, then when Albert was close enough, he knelt and pointed at a large boulder half-covered in snow on our right and whispered, "Look, over there. Do you see them."

I looked again and saw what Freuchen had spotted. Just below the boulder, almost invisible thanks to its pure-white fur, sat a fox, eyeing us cautiously. Then two cubs, no more than a few months old, I guessed, tumbled into view from behind the rock. They seemed oblivious to our presence as they playfully chased each other up and down the slope and round and round in circles. Their tiny yips of excitement were almost as enchanting as Albert's gasp of wonder at their antics.

"They're beautiful," Chou said, a smile breaking the stone of her face.

"*Vulpes Lagopus*," Silas said. "*And they are, indeed, most beautiful.*"

I could have stayed and watched them play all day, but the wind sliding off the ridge brought with it an uncomfortable drop in temperature that cut through even the thick sweater I wore.

"Best ve keep moving, I think," Freuchen said, seeing Albert scrunch up as the icy wind passed over us.

———

With a final concerted effort, we made it to the top.

The rocks that formed the mountain's ridge might as well have been an undulating wave of slabs jutting out at random angles. The slippery ice made it all but impossible to find a secure footing. Even Freuchen was having problems.

"I vish ve had brought some rope and tackle," he grumbled.

"*Allow me,*" Silas said. The robot reached for one of the slabs, pulled himself effortlessly onto it, and sat there like he was riding a horse. His eye-bar scanned the opposite side of the mountain. *"There is easier ground on this other side,"* he said. He shimmied ten feet or so farther along the ridge, then swung his legs over to the opposite side, so only his upper torso was visible to us. Then he beckoned to us to come to him.

"Peter first, please," Silas said, reaching two metallic hands down to him. Freuchen took them and allowed the robot to pull him up. He scrambled over the ridge and turned back to us. The Dane was shorter than Silas by a couple of feet but still more than tall enough that he could easily reach down and help Chou up and over the ridge.

I checked with Albert. "Ready?" I asked. The boy nodded. I picked him up with both hands beneath his armpits and offered him up to Silas, who pulled him over the ridge, then I took Freuchen's hands and allowed him to help me.

A blast of wind stung my face with icy pinpricks, and I closed my eyes, waiting for it to die away. When I opened them again, I gave a gasp of amazement. Stretching out for as far as I could see, from horizon to horizon, was almost nothing but forest. It must have gone on for several hundred miles in every direction. Looming over all of it like the sword of Damocles, the collector was visible for the first time in all its amazing, terrifying, and unbelievable hugeness. It cast an enormous shadow that slowly moved like a sundial over the tops of the trees.

That first day, when I washed up on Avalon's beach and I'd got my first brief look at this incredible edifice, I'd thought it was made up of facets...and I'd been right. The trunk was constructed from huge, irregular slabs of some translucent milky material, like pieces of a shattered mirror put randomly back together again. They glinted blindingly when the sun caught them. Miles above us, the collector's cone-like bell spread out across the atmosphere like a lily pad on a pond. The trunk— miles across at its thickest point—swept down toward the earth, growing rapidly narrower before broadening again. As it neared the ground, it vanished into tightly-clustered rocks that rose above the trees at its base, oddly out of place in the sea of green surrounding it. Lines of energy moved and shifted within the collector's trunk.

"It does not seem possible. How could something like that even exist?" Freuchen asked, his voice resonating with awe.

"I have *no* idea," I replied, turning to look at Chou, who stood silently next to me, her eyes fixed on the distant structure.

"Look, over there," said Albert. "Smoke!"

We'd been so distracted by the collector that we had failed to notice the five or six trails of smoke rising just a few miles to the northeast. I raised my binoculars and glassed the area.

"It looks like a settlement," I said. "I can make out the roofs of a couple of buildings." I passed the binoculars to Freuchen.

"I think you are correct," he said.

"There are more, too," Albert said. He pointed off into the distance at more streams of gray smoke, several miles from the first. "And over there," he added, pointing further to the north where a single large plume of smoke twirled lazily upward.

"At least three separate camps," Chou said.

"People," I said, turning to look at my companions. "There are people." I felt a thrill of excitement pass through me. We hadn't seen anyone else since leaving Avalon, and I had secretly begun to wonder whether there was actually anyone else on this planet other than the few hundred souls who'd had the good fortune to end up on the island.

"How far away do you think the nearest settlement is?" I asked.

"*Approximately four-and-a-quarter miles from the base of the mountain,*" Silas said.

"Ve can make it by late afternoon if ve get a move on," Freuchen said, and without another word began to climb down toward the forest.

"Silas, will you lead the way?" I asked. Despite the robot's memory problems, his ability to navigate was second-to-none, and we were going to need it now we were back in the Everwood.

"*Of course*," he said, and took his position at the front of the line.

———

The smell of wood smoke wafting between the trees told us we were close to the encampment we had spotted earlier from the mountain. Hunkering down behind the trunk of an oak tree, we plotted our strategy, keeping our voices low so they wouldn't carry to the settlement.

"We need to be cautious," Chou said. "We have no way of knowing who these people are or what their reaction to strangers might be."

"Agreed," Freuchen added. "I think ve should pursue the same strategy as ven ve returned vith Silas to the garrison."

I nodded my agreement. "All of us wandering into that camp is going to set off alarm bells for them. We need to play it cool, and that means Silas needs to stay out of sight until we have a better idea of the kind of people we're dealing with. No offense, Silas."

"*None taken*," the robot said.

"I will enter the settlement," Chou said, as though she would not hear any argument.

I shook my head. "Nope. I'm the one who needs to go in. If these people are no threat, then great, but if there are any agents of the Adversary who recognize me, then it'll be better they don't know about you. In other words, I might need you to come save my ass."

Freuchen said, "I think it vill look very suspicious; a lone woman traveling on her own. I vill go vith you."

Chou nodded.

"*I would certainly feel more comfortable knowing Peter was accompanying you,*" Silas added.

I thought it over for a few seconds, then nodded my agreement. Freuchen was imposing enough to deter any straight-up attack but charming enough that if the people of the encampment were friendly, he would not be seen as an immediate threat.

"Okay," I said, standing and looking to Freuchen. "I'm ready when you are."

Chou shook her head. "I suggest we make camp here until morning so Silas is fully charged and will be able to assist if the need should arise." She was right. It made no sense to enter the settlement tonight only to have Silas shut down until the aurora arrived. We would need him to help us escape if it came to that. Despite the robot's aversion to violence of any kind, the mere presence of the enormous golden robot carried an awful lot of shock value and would, hopefully, scare the crap out of any attacker. They didn't need to know he was a pacifist.

FIVE

IT BEGAN to rain a few minutes after I woke. The first drops pitter-pattering against the forest's canopy before proliferating into a cacophony of white noise. From my backpack, I pulled an oiled poncho that had belonged to one of the dead Nazi's and slipped it over my head. Everyone else did the same, except for Chou, who just raised her hood.

"Okay, are we all clear on what the plan is?" I asked, loud enough to be heard over the deluge.

Silas stood in what had moments before been a pool of early morning sunlight, but which now was just a pool. "*We will wait at this location. If you have not returned by this evening, we will continue to wait until after tonight's aurora, then we will move closer so that we can ascertain whether you need our help. If you do not return by tomorrow evening, we will enter the camp under cover of darkness and locate you.*"

"Exactly," I said.

Chou still wasn't happy. "I do not like the idea of waiting that long," she said. "It leaves too much to chance."

I shook my head slowly. "You need to give us time to feel these people out. The Architect only chose to bring those he thought were worthy, and somehow, I don't think there's much likelihood of that being a camp full of the Adversary's people. We have to gain their trust and make sure that they're trustworthy in return. And it's going to take more than a morning to do that."

Freuchen laid one of his big paws on my shoulder. "Don't vurry. I vill take good care of her."

Chou inhaled deeply, exhaled slowly, and nodded.

"Be careful," Albert said, his brow furrowed with concern.

I smiled. "No need to worry about us, little man. We'll be just fine." I kissed him on the crown of his head and gave him a hug.

"Okay, let's do this," I said to Freuchen, who handed me my backpack. I slung it over my shoulders, and the two of us headed off through the trees in the direction of the encampment.

———

Freuchen and I pushed through the trees. The downpour had turned out to be little more than a squall and had already evaporated, leaving the air fresh and clean. It made following the smell of woodsmoke through the trees as easy as following a path. We walked in silence, communicating only with pointed fingers and nods when we thought we should change direction. I placed a hand on Freuchen's shoulder and brought him to a halt, then pointed ahead of us to a spot just past a thicket of bushes. I leaned in close and whispered, "See him?"

It took Freuchen a second to spot the man sitting on the ground ahead of us, his back against a tree trunk, chin resting against his chest, obviously dozing. He was dressed in jeans and a wool sweater. Occasional puffs of mist escaped his nostrils. Cradled in the crook of his arm was an improvised spear like the ones Albert had made for us.

Freuchen whispered. "Perhaps now might be a good time to announce our presence. Ve don't vant to startle him into doing something stupid." I nodded my agreement but still jumped when Freuchen said, very loudly, "I once stalked a vale for six days along the coast of Greenland. I vas half-frozen to death and starving but there vas no vay I—"

The guard leaped to his feet, a look of shock and sleep-confusion on his face. He spun around a few times, then finally spotted us.

"Hey! You there, stop where you are." His accent sounded Australian. He swallowed hard as he ran his eyes up Freuchen's huge frame. The Dane had two feet of height on the guard and was twice as broad. "Who are you? Where did you come from?" the guard demanded.

"Hey there, stranger," Freuchen said, raising his arms in a gesture of surrender (which I also did) and smiling amicably. "Ve are no threat. Ve are just two explorers washed up on the same shores as you."

The guard was in his twenties, skinny, but savvy enough that he understood that Freuchen could snap him in two and use him as a toothpick if he wanted to. He projected a cocky bravado to hide his obvious fear while he eyed us both suspiciously. He said nothing for a moment, then advanced, his spear held out in front of him. When he was close enough, he reached for my sword, but I stepped backward.

Freuchen stared down at the guard. "Tsk, tsk, that does not belong to you, *little* man. Now vy don't you take us to whoever is in charge and ve promise not to tell him you ver asleep at your post."

The guard hesitated, then motioned with his spear back past the tree where he'd been asleep. "That way," he said.

He waited for us to step past him, then followed.

———

The side of a log cabin, bigger than any of the garrison's huts we had built on Avalon, materialized through the trees. I nudged Freuchen to draw his attention to it. He nodded to the left of the first where I saw a second cabin. Beyond that was a third and fourth. A man stepped out of the nearest cabin and disappeared into the trees, whistling to himself. Next, a woman appeared carrying a child clutched to her breast. She was dressed in a toga, her hair pulled up into a coil on her head. She glanced at us wide-eyed then continued on her way.

"Where are you taking us?" I asked the guard.

"To the Mayor," he said.

"You have a mayor?" I said, but the Australian had gone quiet.

Stepping from between the first two huts, I had expected to see a camp similar to the layout of the garrison spread out through the surrounding forest. Instead, the ground sloped away then vanished altogether, revealing an opening to a vast pit two or three hundred feet across. The ground around the mouth of the pit had been cleared of trees and bushes, but a carpet of deep green moss still hung over the edge, undulating in the gentle breeze.

"That way," the guard said, nudging us toward a set of roughly hewn steps that had been cut out of the earthen side of the pit.

We followed his command, but as my foot touched the first step, I came to an abrupt halt, gave a little gasp of surprise. From there, I could see that the pit was a hundred-plus feet deep. The stumps of trees that had grown along its sides showed where they'd been removed, then used to build numerous cabins and buildings in their place. I quickly counted thirty or so of these large buildings, twice the size of the garrison's. Each was held in place by log stilts similar to homes I'd seen when I'd gone sight-seeing through Hollywood Hills. At the bottom of the pit was a huge beautiful blue-green lake, fed by a waterfall that gushed from a fissure about three-quarters of the way up the northern wall. There were a *lot* of people milling around—at least several hundred that I could see. Some were weaving baskets from the reeds growing in clumps along the shore of the lake. Others were working on new buildings, or cooking meat over open fires and what smelled like bread in a row of six earthen ovens, or just standing and chatting amongst themselves. There was even a woman using a simple potter's wheel to make clay urns or vases. A few faces turned our way as we followed the guard down the winding dirt path into the pit before returning their attention back to whatever they'd been doing. Every face smiled at us.

Freuchen and I smiled back. We exchanged a glance that said *this is a good start.*

About halfway down, the guard said, "That way," nodding toward a path that ended at the door of a cabin. We did as he ordered and stopped outside the door. The guard edged past Freuchen and knocked hard on the door with his stick.

"Come on in," a woman's voice said from within—an *American* woman's voice. The guard pushed the door open then ushered us inside.

The cabin was surprisingly clean. The logs that made up the walls gave it a countryfied feeling. The smell of sap and oak added to what was a relaxing atmosphere. Dust motes floated through the air of the main room with a wall on either side, partitioning off two more rooms. There were no doors in either doorway, so I could easily see into them. One was a bedroom, with two utilitarian wooden beds covered in what looked like brown fur. The other had a sectioned-off area with a row of shelves that held a collection of cans, tools, buckets, and other miscellaneous stuff that I guessed must have arrived with the town's people.

A young woman sat at a table in the main room, eating a meal of leafy greens from a clay bowl. She looked like she was a few years older than me, her long blonde hair tied back in a bun. She had a calmness to her that made me instantly like her. Putting down her fork, she swallowed, smiled widely, and said, "Oh, guests! Welcome."

"I found them in the forest, Mayor," our guard said.

"Well done, Robert," the woman answered, stepping around the table and walking toward us. Her blue eyes turned first to Freuchen then to me. "Do you speak English," she asked, smiling.

"Ve do," Freuchen said.

I nodded. "Yes."

She tilted her head quizzically. "You're American?" she said, with some evident surprise.

"Yes. California."

Her smile grew wider. "What year?"

"2018."

"Close enough to me," said the woman with a wry smile, then after a slight pause added, "New York, by way of Denison, Iowa."

I hadn't noticed the large dog that had been asleep at her feet until it stretched, letting out a loud almost-howl of satisfaction and got to its feet, padding over to where the woman stood.

I offered my hand to the woman, "My name's Meredith, and this is Peter."

"I prefer just Freuchen," Freuchen said.

The woman shook our hands in turn. "My name's Emily," she said, reaching down to stroke the large dog's head, "and this is Thor. Welcome to New Manhattan."

SIX

"PLEASE, HAVE A SEAT," Emily said, fetching two wooden stools from the bedroom and placing them in front of the table. "Are you hungry?" she asked once we were sitting.

"No, but I could use some water, please," I said. Freuchen echoed my request.

"Of course." She filled two mugs from a pitcher and handed them to us.

"Thank you," I said, sipping from my mug. "This place is... amazing."

Emily laughed. "It is, isn't it? We were lucky to find it."

"There are a lot of..." I almost said candidates, but caught myself in time, "people here. Did you all arrive together?"

Emily continued to smile but diverted. "Why don't you two tell me your story first?" She sat back in her chair, her smile broadening.

Chou had anticipated we would be asked about where we were from and had advised us that we withhold all mention of Avalon and what had taken place there. So, before Peter and I left, we'd all agreed on a simplified story of our arrival.

"We arrived off the coast to the south," I said, gambling that everyone else had also arrived similarly to us. "Freuchen pulled me from the water, and we've been looking for others since then."

"You haven't seen anyone else since that first day?"

"Some," Freuchen lied, "but they mostly stayed avay from us, although I can't think vy." He gave a big friendly grin and stretched his huge frame.

Emily nodded silently. I couldn't tell whether she believed us or not.

"The aurora and the pixie dust that first night were our first real signs that we weren't on Earth anymore," I said.

"Aurora? Pixie dust?" Emily looked confused, then gave a little laugh. "Oh, you mean the bliss." She paused for a second, then added, "I think I prefer your names for it. Go on."

I saw no need to tell her that, according to Silas, we *were* on Earth, or, at least, some far-flung future version of it, in some alternative dimension. That I would save for a time when we knew she could be trusted. Until then, we would let this play out, get a feel for what kind of a person Emily, and the rest of her people were, then decide on how much real information we would share.

I continued, "It kind of sealed the deal that whoever or whatever's behind the *Voice* that asked whether we wanted to live or not... well... the probability is that they aren't human. They must be incredibly advanced to have brought all of us here."

Emily smiled.

"And that's really it," I said. "We've been traveling along the coast since we arrived. It was only when we were finally able to make it over the mountain range that we realized there were other... survivors."

Emily stood and walked around to the front of the table.

Then, sitting, she said, "And the sword and armor you're wearing. Where did that come from?"

"Ve liberated it from a dead man," Freuchen said, bluntly. "He no longer had any need for it."

"Can't argue with that," Emily said. She silently looked us both over for several seconds. "Most of the people here arrived at the same location on the coast. We survived the first couple of days together then made our way over the mountain. We lost twenty-three people." She seemed genuinely sad at that. "Then, we stumbled on this place." Emily got to her feet, raised her arms to encompass the whole encampment. "There's a mixture of people from the last five-hundred-or-so years here, enough that the language barriers have been overcome and we've been able to get things done. We opened a school in the first week and started to teach English-as-a-second-language to our residents who didn't speak it. Now, about ninety-five percent of us can hold a basic conversation."

I smiled broadly, genuinely impressed by how organized the camp seemed to be and thankful that I wouldn't have to worry as much about my translative powers giving us away. "So, why New Manhattan? Is that where you were when the *Voice* contacted you?"

Emily took a moment, as though she were wondering whether to answer or share her information with me. Eventually, she said, "I was a reporter in Manhattan and New York. There was an... event, and I was the only survivor."

"Wow!" I said, intrigued. I took a sip of water from my mug. "Nobody else in Manhattan survived?"

Again, a long pause. "As far as I know, there were only a few survivors left... in the world."

"Vat?" said Freuchen.

"You're joking, surely?" I said. "Was it a pandemic? A nuclear attack?"

Emily shook her head. "Neither, really. It all happened so fast, I'm still not really sure *what* it was exactly and, trust me, you probably wouldn't believe me if I told you. Anyway, I made contact with a man who was part of a group of survivors in the Stockton Islands—they're in the far north of Alaska. I was making my way to them when I was attacked in a forest by... some *things*. I think Thor came to my rescue, but by the time he reached me the... creatures had me."

"And that's when the *Voice* asked you to make the choice," I said.

Emily nodded. "This thing had me on my back. It was about to take my head off and then... poof!" She imitated a slow explosion with her fingers. "Time just... stopped. The *Voice* asked me if I wanted to be saved, and the next thing I know, I was dumped in the ocean, along with the back half of one of the things that attacked me... and this guy." She leaned over and scratched Thor behind his ear.

I had no idea what she was referring to when she talked about the '*things*' that had attacked her. Still, I could tell I wasn't going to get any more information out of her on that subject. Not yet, at least.

"Well," I said, "look at it this way: in another universe, there's probably a version of you that survived. And who knows what she might have achieved?"

Emily laughed loudly. "You know, I never thought about it like that. Well, let's hope she has an easier time of it." She leaned back against the table. "Okay, so, tell me, are you passing through, or are you looking for something more permanent? We can always use more hands."

"Stay," I lied, "We'd like to stay and help out in any way we can. Just tell us what you want us to do."

Emily eyeballed us both. "You both look like you can carry your own weight. I'm going to leave you in the hands of our foreman." She turned to the young guard who had escorted us in. "Robert, would you go fetch Bartholomew, please? Let him know we have a couple of new guests."

———

Bartholomew Mwangi was almost as tall as Freuchen and just as wide in the shoulders. His hair was cut so short, it was little more than a burr, his skin the color of umber, a thin sheen of sweat glistening over every exposed inch. He was an imposing-looking man, lean but strongly muscled, his mouth set in an intimidating frown. But that menacing demeanor dissolved the second he smiled, lighting up his face as brightly as the aurora lit up the night sky.

"Bartholomew, I'd like you to meet Meredith and Peter," Emily said.

"Freuchen," Peter said, extending his hand. "Just call me Freuchen."

"I am delighted to meet you," Bartholomew said. His heavily accented voice was deep and melodic, his words forming a sing-song rhythm so fast they almost melted together. He wiped his hands on his dirty jeans, then first shook Freuchen's hand, then mine. His grip was firm but not crushing. I was surprised by the softness of his skin—especially for a man who was so obviously used to hard work—until I realized that any calluses he might have earned would've surely vanished each night when the aurora worked its magic.

"Do you think you can find our new guests a place to stay, maybe put them to work?" said Emily, leaning back on the table, smiling.

"Of course. Of course," Bartholomew said enthusiastically. "Follow me, and I will give you the grand tour," he said, "then I'll show you to your cabin." With a hand between my shoulders, he ushered us out of the cabin and back onto the main path, leading us toward the bottom of the pit.

"Everyone seems very friendly," I said after the tenth person had waved or called out a greeting to him.

"Yes, it's hard not to know everyone when you live as closely as we do here. It reminds me very much of where I grew up."

"Where was that?" I asked.

"Kenya. A town called Voi. My daddy worked the docks in Mombassa until he died when I was nine. My mother died a year later, so I had no choice but to leave. I traveled to Mombassa, found the first crew that would take me, and I rode the sea until the day I was brought here."

"I'm sorry," I said.

He waved his hand as if shooing away a fly. "Pfft! It was a long time ago, and if it had not happened, then I would not be here now. The universe moves with its own will."

I had to smile. Bartholomew was the first person I had met since I'd arrived who seemed genuinely happy to be here on this other Earth.

Freuchen asked, "And vat ill fates caused you to land on these shores?"

"I was the Bosun of the *Kirinyaga*, an oil tanker. We sank on our way to Libya, 16th of June, 1985."

"That's horrible," I said.

"No, no. Thank God we had not picked up any cargo when we went down. It would have been a hell of a mess. A hell of a mess."

I began to suspect that Bartholomew was just one of those permanently optimistic guys who, no matter what life threw at them, would always see the positive side of it. We reached the bottom of the pit and walked to the edge of the lake.

"There is a cave system down there," Bartholomew said, pointing below the water to the right. It was difficult to hear him over the roar of the waterfall as it crashed into the lake, creating a constant foam of bubbles and waves that kept the surface of the lake in motion. "One of our people has managed to go in the lake a hundred feet and says that he believes the caves go about much deeper."

"That seems very deep for someone to dive unassisted," Freuchen said.

"Janus is a free-diver. He is capable of holding his breath for almost ten minutes... the problem is he needed to hold it for twelve, which is how he ended up here with us." Both Bartholomew and Freuchen laughed uproariously at this joke, and I realized that these two men were cut from almost identical cloth.

"Amazing," I said. "The lake is so beautiful."

"Yes, the lake is, as you say, amazing. It is as though we have stepped back into the Garden of Eden. And perhaps that is what is happening, eh? Perhaps, the universe is giving us a chance to start it all over. A second chance to get it right this time. Who knows? Not me." He gave one of those huge grins then said, "Come, follow me."

He led us to a spot on the lakeshore where seven logs had been dropped into the water ten feet apart from each other. The tops of the logs were shaved flat, so it was easy to walk out a good thirty feet or so into the lake. "We wash our clothes here," Bartholomew said. "It's simple but works. And we have several people skilled with the needle who will be happy to patch up yours for you." He pointed at a couple of rips and tears in my jeans. "They are also working at spinning yarn from our sheep."

"Sheep?" Freuchen said, astonished.

"Yes, we have a flock of sixty sheep... well, mountain goats and sheep that we have captured. In the farm."

"Farm?" Freuchen said, looking at me, eyes wide in disbelief.

Bartholomew laughed. "Yes, farm. It is about a mile away. We also have other livestock; bison, wild pigs, deer, rabbits, turkeys, ducks, and some things that we don't ha_ a name for but taste very, very good."

"This land is abundant," Freuchen said, then add_ almost as if someone vanted us to prosper, don't you think? is

Bartholomew made no reaction to Freuchen's subt_ attempt to find out whether he knew about the Architect or, perhaps, even the Adversary. But if he was masking his thoughts, he was giving an Oscar-worthy performance because I saw no sign he was hiding anything from us. Quite the opposite, in fact.

"Yes, yes, you are quite right," Bartholomew said, enthusiastically. "We have had many, many discussions about why we might have been brought here and by who. We have reached no consensus. But the one thing that we do all agree on is that whoever the *Voice* is, he wants us to survive. To prosper, as you say."

I glanced at Freuchen, who surreptitiously raised an eyebrow at me, then said, "Yes, it is almost as if by some design. As if some great *architect* designed and placed us all here for a reason."

There was still no reaction from Bartholomew, and I quickly drew the conclusion that these people knew nothing of the titanic struggle that had, and for all I knew, still was taking place behind the curtain of this world.

"Come, it is time I introduced you to some of the others in the camp. We have some fascinating people. At least, we think they are. There are some here whose grasp of English is not very good, but we are working on that. Even so, they are talented individuals."

"Actually," I interjected, "I'm kind of tired. All of this is just so... overwhelming. Do you think you could show us to our cabin? I know I'd like to rest awhile. If that's not too much of a problem?" The idea of my ability to translate any language being discovered would raise far too much suspicion this early on. These people all seemed friendly enough, but I needed to talk with Freuchen and try and suss the place out a little more before we showed our hand.

Bartholomew shook his head. "Forgive me. Of course. Of course. Come, follow me." He led us back up the path, nodding to people as we passed them. We reached a cabin on the opposite side of the pit, directly across from Emily's.

Bartholomew opened the door and ushered us both inside. It was identical in layout to the one we'd met Emily in. On the wooden table were bowls of fruit and some dried meat. A pitcher of water and two wooden mugs with two wooden cots in the room adjacent.

"I am in the next cabin over," Bartholomew nodded to his right. "If there is anything you want, please just come and find me. If not, I will return for you a little later. Until then, please rest." He stepped to the open door, smiled that ridiculously broad grin again, then closed the door behind him.

———

Freuchen moved to the door, opened it a crack, and looked out. "He's gone," he said, walking back to where I had taken a seat at the table and sat down next to me. I poured us both a mug of water, pulled a strip of dried meat from the bowl, and smelled it.

"Smells good." I nibbled an edge then took a big bite. "Taste's great. I think it might be bacon."

Freuchen grabbed a large piece and devoured it in two huge bites. "Vat do you think of our hosts? Can they be trusted?"

I nodded. "I think so. They seem just as genuine as Edward and the rest of the Garrisonites." I was pretty much convinced by now of my theory that the Architect either selected people who were inclined to getting along with others or that each of the candidates had been altered somehow to be more amicable. If I had to guess, I would choose door number two. A few genetic tweaks here and there and everyone just gets along. It made the most sense to me.

Freuchen nodded as he swallowed another chunk of meat. "I agree, but I think ve should stick vith the original plan. Let's give it tonight, and then ve can assess our situation again tomorrow."

"Sounds good," I said, taking an apple from the bowl and crunching into it. It was deliciously sweet and crisp. "So, how do we keep my... ability to ourselves?"

"You either stay in the cabin, or you take a chance that no one vill notice."

"Or I could just come clean and tell them about it. They're going to find out sooner or later."

"Perhaps. Or maybe ve should just vait. Even if someone notices, there's no reason for them to suspect us. Not if ve stay quiet. But if ve have to, ve can explain your ability and say ve don't know how you got it."

We ate until we were full, then I suggested we should get some rest. It would be nice to sleep with a roof over our heads again.

Freuchen said that he wasn't tired, so I left him at the table and headed into the bedroom. The beds were basic wooden cots with plank supports to lie on. I climbed beneath the fur blanket. It wasn't exactly what you'd call comfortable, but compared to sleeping on the ground, as I'd done since we got here, it was sheer luxury. Within minutes, I was asleep.

SEVEN

WALKING OUT OF THE BEDROOM, stretching the stiffness from my shoulders. Freuchen was asleep where I'd left him, his arms folded on the tabletop, his head resting on them, snoring like a bear.

"Hey! Wake up," I said, shaking him by one meaty bicep.

"Eh? Vat?" he exclaimed, bringing himself to a sitting position, eyes wide.

I gave a little laugh. "Sorry, didn't mean to startle you."

He waved my apology away, shook his head, and got to his feet. "I vas dreaming I vas vith my vife at our home in Greenland, hunting seals."

"You never told me you were married," I said, surprised at this sudden moment of openness from Peter.

Freuchen's eyes became sad, his face flushed red. "Navarana. A fine, fine woman. She bore me two beautiful children before the Spanish Lady stole her from me in '21."

"Spanish Lady?" I said, confused.

Freuchen's lip quivered as he spoke. "The great influenza outbreak. It took so very many around the vurld... millions, they said. And my beautiful Navarana vas the least deserving of death among them all." He sucked in a slow, deep breath, then said, "Come on. Time vaits for no one. Our hosts vill be vundering ver ve are"

Shadows had crept up to the cabin's front door. Stepping outside, we saw a line of large campfires, twelve in all, burning along the winding path back up to the surface. The smoke from them twisted and curled up toward a sky, purple and bruised with night's approach. The smell of roasting meat wafted to us from spits hung over the fires. New Manhattanites were slowly making their way down from the surface and heading to the fires, sitting or standing around them in groups, laughing and talking.

"Everyone seems so relaxed," I said, reminded of weekends barhopping through Santa Barbara before everything went to shit.

Freuchen nodded. "They have an idyllic life here. All the food they need. Freedom from a tyrannical government, illness, and other hardships. Yes, I think I understand vy they are so happy."

"If they only knew the true reality of it all," I whispered.

"My friends, over here," a voice boomed. Bartholomew stood tending a fire between the two cabins next to ours. "Please, come join us."

From somewhere further along the trail, a guitar began to play an upbeat tune, and a woman's voice sang along with it.

Two men and four women sat around the campfire. They were all dressed in modern, store-bought clothing; shirts, pants, jeans, sweaters, leather shoes, and sneakers. All were in their late-twenties-to-mid-thirties and seemed to be conversing quite freely in English. Four seemed to be couples judging by the way they lay against each other holding hands.

I put on a big smile and joined them.

"Here," Bartholomew said. He handed us cups of brown

liquid. Freuchen sniffed his, then sipped the contents. His face cracked open in a huge smile. "Mead! The drink of the gods."

"You have alcohol?" I said, sniffing at the cup. It smelled wonderful—sweet and fruity. "Oh, my God. It's delicious."

Freuchen downed the rest of his drink and smacked his lips loudly. "Vunderful! Ver did you find it?"

Bartholomew filled his cup again. "Not found, my friend. We make it ourselves. A young woman, actually. Originally from Pompeii, a master mead maker who is unafraid to raid some of the local wild beehives and knows her craft so well she has refined the brewing technique to under a month. We are very happy to have her here, as I am sure you can tell, and we are keeping her very busy."

Freuchen raised his drink in a toast. "As am I."

Bartholomew chugged his drink, wiped his mouth, and said, "My manners! Please, let me introduce you." He ushered us into the glow of the fire.

"Hi," I said, smiling, "I'm Meredith, and this is Peter."

There was a flurry of returned smiles and "hellos." Everyone seemed very at ease with each other, and I said so.

"Well, it helps that we knew each other before we all arrived here," said a man who introduced himself as Evan.

"Really?" I said, honestly amazed. "All of you?"

Alysia, a tall statuesque woman with coffee-brown skin, nodded. "Maybe 'knew' is a bit of a stretch, but we all came from the same time and place.

"Uh-uh," a long-haired blonde woman by the name of Denise, who rested her head in the lap of a man. "James, Kelly, Bev, and I all worked together. So, technically speaking, we did know each other. Kind of." She smiled broadly.

"Hi, I'm James," said the man cradling Denise's head in his lap. He'd obviously had a few mugs of Bartholomew's mead already, his eyes wide, words slightly slurred.

I laughed gently. "So, how is it you know each other?"

"We worked at the World Trade Center in New York," Denise said, as if that explained everything.

I knew what the Twin Towers of the Trade Center were but didn't get the reference.

"September 11th, 2001?" Evan said, his head tilted slightly as if anticipating a sudden realization from me at the date.

I shook my head slowly. "Sorry."

"The two planes that were flown into the Twin Towers. No?" said James

The memory of an old news story rose to the front of my mind. I thought I remembered something from around that date. Something about a terrorist attack that had been thwarted by the FBI. Yes, now that I thought about it, I did remember.

"There was an attempted terror attack on New York back in oh-one," I said slowly, as the memories bubbled back to the surface. "A group of terrorists planned to hijack some planes and fly them into buildings in New York, but the FBI got to them before they could follow through. A whole bunch of the terrorists and two FBI agents were killed. The rest ended up in prison."

Denise sat up and met the gaze of her friends. "Oh, wow. We were right. It *was* terrorists. We just assumed you were... you know..."

Freuchen chimed in, "From the same universe as you?"

Everyone's head nodded. "Yeah, kind of."

I took a deep breath, "So you're telling me that in the *when* you're from those assholes were successful? And you would all have died in the attack?"

Denise nodded. "I mean, we suspected it was a terrorist attack. A single jet could have been an accident. But two?"

Freuchen shook his head. "Even though ve are from the same planet, it is amazing how very, very different those vurlds are. It doesn't matter if ve're separated by time or by universe; everything is all so... alien."

"But we're still all human. That is the one thing that binds us all together, no matter where or when we are from," Bartholomew said.

James laughed, "Right. I mean, at least we haven't met any *actual* aliens."

"Mmmm hmmm," I said between sips of my mead. "Not yet, anyway."

From farther up the path, two silhouettes emerged from the growing shadows.

"Hello, everyone," Emily said, her dog Thor padding along at her side, tongue lolling, tail curled into a question mark. There was a chorus of returned greetings, and she took a proffered mug of mead from Bartholomew, thanked him, then leaned against the wall of the cabin while she sipped it. "How are you two settling in?"

"Good, thank you," I said. "We didn't expect this kind of hospitality."

Emily took another sip of mead and paused for a second. "This is a new world. A chance to do things a different way. I think we're all tired of the same dog-eat-dog routine, and I believe that whoever or whatever brought us here did so with a purpose, and it wasn't to keep on doing the same shit we did back on Earth. So, why not try something new?"

I raised my cup to her. "I'll drink to that."

I liked Emily. There was something intangible about her... something powerful—a natural-born leader. I think we would have been good friends if we'd met back on my version of Earth, and I felt a flash of guilt at having to lie to her.

"And you, Meredith? How did you get here?" Bartholomew asked.

All eyes turned to me, and I felt my face flush red.

"Don't be shy, honey," Denise said, smiling her encouragement.

"Suicide," I said. "I tried to kill myself." It felt good being honest about something.

"But the *Voice* thought you were worth saving," Evan said. "That definitely counts for something."

I smiled politely back at him. "I suppose."

"No supposing about it," James said, jumping to his feet. He took me by the elbow and guided me closer to the fire. "Sit yourself down and have another drink." He nodded at Bartholomew, who dutifully topped off my mug.

"No one can deny we're all here for a reason," Alysa said. "All we have to do is figure out what it is."

I glanced up at Freuchen, but he was talking animatedly with Bartholomew. I felt terrible about keeping the information I had from these people, but there was no way to predict their attitude, and the truth was, the less they knew, the safer they probably would be. If the Adversary discovered I was here, there was no telling how many of its robo-bug assassins might turn up.

More people began to approach from the darkness until thirty or so sat around the fire, talking, or just relaxing. Freuchen seemed to be making the most of the almost party-like atmosphere, drinking and entertaining anyone who would listen with stories of his adventures.

The woman with the guitar who everyone seemed to know and called Connie walked from the shadows and sat down next to Emily. Thor got to his feet and headbutted her until she gave him the attention he was looking for, then curled up between the two women.

Emily caught my attention and tapped the ground next to her. "Meredith, come meet Connie Converse."

"Hello," I said, "nice to meet you."

Connie looked to be in her early forties. She had delicate

features, dirty-blonde hair, with only a hint of laugh-lines around her eyes and lips. Every once in a while, she slipped a pair of horn-rimmed glasses off her nose and cleaned them in the folds of her blue dress.

"It's a pleasure to meet you," Connie said. Her voice was deep, American, but I couldn't place from where exactly.

"Connie arrived here from the seventies," Meredith explained. "She's a songwriter and a singer. If you ask her nicely, she might just sing us one of them."

Connie flushed a little red and dipped her eyes to her feet.

"Would you?" I asked. "Please."

From the other side of the fire, someone called out, "Yeah, come on, Connie. Let's hear something." More voices added their encouragement.

"Okay. Okay," Connie said, slipping the guitar onto her lap. She began to strum. The people around the fire quieted and turned their eyes in her direction. She began to sing a melancholy tune about a place between two tall mountains called Lonesome.

Over the next couple of hours, while Connie slowly worked through her repertoire, more people joined us, drawn by Connie's guitar. Freuchen put away enough mead to kill an elephant. He, however, seemed only mildly affected by it, his words slurring only enough to show the alcohol was having an effect. No one seemed to mind, they were all equally relaxed and happy. Occasionally, a couple would pair off and walk hand in hand into the night, but the majority remained, falling asleep around the fire, chatting, or just listening to Connie's haunting voice.

I sat back and watched the people interact—laughing, loving, singing, and for a moment, I got a brief glimpse of what the Architect had planned for all of us.

"Here comes the bliss," someone said excitedly, out of

nowhere. Connie stopped playing and turned her head skyward as, all around us, pixie dust flared, while overhead, the aurora streaked across the sky. It was the first time I'd really seen it since we'd left the island and entered the Everwood.

"I'd forgotten how beautiful it was," I said quietly.

"It really is quite something, isn't it?" Emily said, her voice filled with awe. "The sheer power behind all of this... it's... overwhelming."

I knew exactly what she meant. This nightly display of super-advanced technology that repaired our broken and damaged bodies was God-like. And the aurora was just one small piece in an even bigger jigsaw puzzle of hidden pieces.

"I try not to dwell on it too much. It can drive you crazy," I said.

I closed my eyes and allowed the sense of wellbeing to wash over me.

When I opened them again, Freuchen was seated next to me, a scowl creasing his face. "Vell, this is very disappointing."

I looked sideways at him, puzzled. "What?"

"Not only does the aurora heal us, but it also removes all the effects of intoxication from our bloodstream. I am as sober as a priest."

"Oh, that's too bad," I said, rubbing his back. "But at least it'll save you a hangover in the morning."

"I guess I vill have to start drinking earlier tomorrow!"

I laughed, and before we turned in for the night, Freuchen and I quietly discussed what our next move should be. The people of New Manhattan were genuinely friendly, we both agreed on that. They'd welcomed us into their community with open arms and seemed more than happy for us to stay—an opportunity I would have jumped at under other circumstances. The question now was, could we rely on their help? And how much could we tell them of what we knew of my quest to get to the collector, the Architect, Adversary, and what little information we had as to why we had all been brought here? Emily had no reason to trust us, but she would have a reason not to once she learned that we'd lied to her.

"I feel like they have the right to know that there *is* danger out there," I said.

Freuchen agreed. "But I vurry how they vill react to our mighty metal friend."

"Silas is going to be a bit of a shock for them," I whispered. "But at least they'll know we are telling the truth when they see him. And he can answer their questions directly." I paused for a moment. "I think we should approach Emily directly in the morning. Tell her what we know and offer to take her to meet the rest of the group."

"It vould be better than having them stroll into New Manhattan," Freuchen said. "Can you imagine the commotion *that* vould cause?" He laughed good-naturedly, his beard shaking. "Emily seems like a good leader. I think she vill understand vy ve had to deceive her. And I am sure that the boy and Chou could use some rest and the company of others for a day or so."

"Sounds good..." I stifled a yawn. "...to me."

It was well past one in the morning, and the effects of the aurora had worn off long ago. Now my body just wanted me to sleep.

We thanked everyone for their hospitality, wished them all a good night, and headed along the torch-lit path back to our cabin.

Freuchen insisted I take the bedroom for myself while he slept at the table.

I'd become so used to the constant rustle of the leaves overhead and the howls of the unseen night-things, I found it difficult for my mind to ease into sleep. The cabin's log walls made me feel mildly claustrophobic, and I couldn't get comfortable in my cot. A small tallow candle spluttered on a shelf next to my bed, sending shadows dancing across the floor. I blew it out, and the room vanished into darkness, leaving me with only my thoughts. It was strange being so alone, and my mind naturally drifted to my friends, waiting in the forest for me. I wasn't worried about Chou or Albert or Silas; they were more than capable of looking out for themselves, but I did find myself missing them horribly. Although we hadn't really known each other that long, the bond we'd formed was unlike anything I'd ever experienced before. I missed the sounds of their nighttime breathing. Albert's gentle mumbling as he dreamed. The way Chou always seemed to be awake whenever my sleep was restless—watchful, ever vigilant. Silas' shadowy figure standing silently over us...

―――――

I woke with a start, confused for a moment as to where I was until my sleep-slowed mind reminded me I was in New Manhattan. I slipped from beneath the fur blanket and pulled on my clothes. I wrinkled my nose—they smelled ripe. I was really going to have to take advantage of the washing facilities here.

"Good morning," said Freuchen as I walked into the main room. He sat at the table, eating from a large bowl of mixed fruit. A second bowl sat across from him. "Bartholomew dropped these off for us a few minutes ago. I hold him ve needed to speak vith Emily as soon as possible, and he said he vould come back soon." He nodded at the second bowl of fruit. "Tuck in."

The fruit was delicious, oranges, pears, and a handful of grapes. I held up a fleshy purple fruit, unsure of what it might be.

Freuchen shrugged. "I have no idea vat it is, but it is delicious."

I took a bite. He was right, it *was* delicious, and I eagerly began working my way through the rest of my breakfast. I was almost finished when the door cracked open, and Bartholomew's head appeared.

"Emily is free to see you now if you want to come with me," he said.

I popped the last piece of purple fruit into my mouth, wiped my lips with the back of my hand, and followed Freuchen out the door after Bartholomew.

The morning was hazy and a little on the cool side. The sun was going to have to climb higher than Freuchen and I were used to if it was going to reach us down here.

"You slept well?" Bartholomew asked as we headed toward Emily's cabin.

"Yes," I lied.

New Manhattan was already busy with people going about their business: men and women fetching water from the pool; carpenters working on the half-finished cabins we'd seen yesterday; kids being shepherded toward a large lean-to that must act as a schoolroom; women hanging the hides of deer up to dry on bamboo frameworks; a man baking bread in one of the kilns.

"All these people, from so many different times and dimensions."

Freuchen threw a brotherly arm around the other man's broad shoulders, and said, "Tell me, my friend, what are *your* thoughts on vy ve are all here in this land of plenty?"

Bartholomew said nothing for the next couple of steps. "Some people think we were brought here by whichever god watched over them in their time. Me, I have no time for such superstitions. But to my mind, it seems indisputable that whoever is responsible has brought us here for their own reasons. Whether those reasons are good or evil, that is the real question."

"And what reason do you think that might be?" Freuchen said.

Bartholomew shrugged. "I am just a man. I do not pretend to know the how or why of any of this. I just trust that at the right time, whatever plan there is for us will be revealed."

"And the rest of your people?" Freuchen said. "How do they feel?"

Bartholomew gave it some thought. "The majority seem to feel the same, I believe. Everyone who I have spoken with was facing certain death. They know that they were singled out, saved, and delivered to this land. But they have no more of an idea as to why than I do."

Freuchen clapped Bartholomew hard enough on his back that it would've sent any other man flying. Bartholomew did not budge. "I knew I liked you for a good reason," Freuchen said, grinning.

A deeply-tanned young man approached us, carrying a large bundle of branches stripped of their bark. "Hello, Bartholomew," he said in broken English, "Please tell me where I am to take?"

Bartholomew planted a hand on the young man's shoulder and gently turned him around until he was facing a row of three half-finished cabins.

"That way, Kyril. Just give them to—"

Bartholomew's sentence went unfinished as a dazzling flash of orange-and-white light seared my retinas, momentarily blinding me, but not before I saw half of the cabin Bartholomew was pointing at explode in a ball of fire and splinters. In the instant it took for that image to register in my brain, a crash like thunder engulfed me, and I was knocked off my feet, flying backward through the air, daggers of wood zipping past me. I landed with a grunt on the path, skidded on my back, rolled two or three times, then came to a stop, staring at a bush with a flaming chunk of wood protruding from it. My ears rang while white and orange ghosts of the explosion paraded in front of my eyes.

A pair of booted feet shuffled into my line of sight. I heard a voice, muffled like the words were being spoken into a pillow. The bush was on fire now. I began to get annoyed at whoever the owner of the boots was for blocking my view, and if I had been able to speak, I would have told them so. But my mouth didn't seem capable of forming words just then, and my mind swirled in confusion.

A line of warmth trickled over my forehead then dripped down onto my cheek. I raised my hand and wiped at it, then brought my fingers to my eyes. Blood. My blood. I was bleeding.

The boots' owner kept talking to me, but I just couldn't bring myself to take my eyes off the burning bush. There was something prophetic about it that my brain just wouldn't let go of. The boots were replaced by a man's heavily bearded face. It looked familiar to me. The man's mouth was moving as he yelled something at me... Freuchen! It was Peter Freuchen. As if the realization that the face belonged to my friend and traveling companion had acted in some way to free the stuck gears of my brain, my senses returned with a sound like rolling down a car window when you're doing a hundred on the freeway.

I moved onto my back. Freuchen stood, his hand extended down to me. There was no sign of Bartholomew.

"Come on, Meredith. Ve need to get out of here."

But I didn't move. Instead, I stared past him, my eyes moving over the burning wreckage of the five or six cabins, following the twisting lines of black smoke up the walls of the pit to the pure blue sky far above... and the huge, cigar-shaped airship that hung suspended above New Manhattan. A single word was painted in giant red swooping letters on its silver fuselage, and I strained my eyes to make it out.

I mumbled the word aloud.

"Vat? I can't understand you," Freuchen said, still staring down at me, oblivious to the airship floating high above us.

I raised a hand in slow-motion. Freuchen reached for it. I avoided his grasp and jabbed my finger skyward. "*Brimstone!*" I repeated.

Freuchen turned and looked up, muttered what must have been an expletive, turned back to me, and without another word, grabbed my hand and pulled me to my feet.

"That vas dynamite or grenades," he yelled. "Ve're going to be trapped like fish in a barrel down here. Ve need to get to the surface right now."

I nodded, and together we started to make our way up the path.

"Where's Bartholomew?" I asked.

"Last I saw him, he vas running toward Emily's cabin."

Smoke and fiery embers swirled and danced around us, caught in the updraught created by the burning cabins and numerous fires that ignited bush and brush along the path. A woman screamed above me, and I looked up in time to see a man falling backward off the edge of the pit, clutching his side. He hit an outcropping of rock, spun like a rag doll, then disappeared through the roof of a burning cabin with nothing but an explosion of sparks to mark his passing. More voices screamed incoherently, but above all of that commotion, I heard the unmistakable sound of gunfire. Short rapid bursts of gunfire.

The screaming stopped.

Freuchen pulled me sharply toward a cabin and then around to the back of it, and we paused momentarily in the narrow space between the cabin and the pit's wall. The smoke wafted and twirled like fog obscuring our view to the surface.

There was the sound of more shooting, followed by more screams.

"Ve cannot let you be seen," Freuchen said.

"What? Why? You're not making any sense."

"Meredith," he continued, "vat if they have been sent here by the Adversary. Vat if they are here for *you*?"

His words hit me like a sledgehammer between my eyes. In my literally shell-shocked state-of-mind, I had forgotten about the Adversary. Then an even worse thought crashed into my brain. "Oh shit, what if they tracked us here? What if they somehow followed me? What if I'm responsible for all this?"

Freuchen brushed off my questions. "It does not matter. They are here, and ve must get back to Chou and the others." He pulled me along the back wall to the corner of the cabin. He leaned out far enough to assess whether it was safe, then grabbed my hand again and pulled me at a half-run, half-stumble across to the next cabin.

I coughed loudly as I inhaled thick woody-tasting smoke that stung the back of my throat and made my lungs constrict and my stomach heave.

"Stay here, I vill be right back," Freuchen whispered. Before I could protest, he edged carefully around the side of the cabin, then, after a quick glance left and right, disappeared. I heard movement within the cabin and realized that it was *our* cabin.

A minute passed before Freuchen reappeared. He had his backpack slung over his shoulders and my pack in his left hand, my sword strapped tightly to it. In the other, he held the pistol that he'd taken from the Nazi officer and insisted on bringing with him. I'm not a fan of guns, but I have to admit, I breathed a sigh of relief when I saw it. He handed me my backpack, and I slung it over my shoulder. I began to untie the bindings that held my sword.

"No time for that," Freuchen warned. "Okay, ve are going to make a run for it."

I nodded.

"Follow me."

We sprinted to the next cabin, the sound of chaos only growing louder around us. There were two more almost-intact cabins ahead of us, which took us practically back to ground level, give or take a hundred feet or so. But the cabin between them and us was on fire, burning so intensely I could feel the heat from where we hid. Thick black smoke billowed skyward, but an ever-increasing pall of it was expanding outward onto the path. I coughed again as a hot gust of wind blew a cloud of smoke directly over Freuchen and me. I spat black spittle onto the ground.

"Ve are going to have to use the smoke as cover," Freuchen said. "You vill have to hold your breath, okay?"

I nodded again.

"I vill count to three, then ve run and ve do not stop until ve reach the trees. Chou and Silas vill have heard the gunfire and explosions. They vill be coming for us. Ve do not stop for anything or anyone, you understand?"

I nodded once more.

"Okay! Vun... two... three."

I sucked in a huge breath, held it, then took off after Freuchen, who had already vanished into the wall of smoke covering the path. A few steps in, half-blinded, I ran into Freuchen's broad back. He'd slowed to a walk so I could catch up with him. He reached behind him and found my hand, pulling me after him. My eyes stung. The heat from the burning buildings singed my skin, and the roar and crackle of the fire kept out any other noise. I stumbled over some hidden obstacle lying in the path, and my hand slipped from Freuchen's grasp. I went down hard, skinning the palms of my hands. I let out a gasp of pain and instantly regretted it as I sucked in a lungful of smoke. Coughing and retching, I reached frantically around me, hoping to find Freuchen. Instead, I found the body that I had tripped over. For a second, I thought it might *be* Freuchen but then felt my hand brush against the person's hairless face. Pushing myself to my feet, my eyes watering so badly I couldn't see a damn thing, I staggered blindly in the direction I thought Freuchen had been taking us. Snot and blood filled my nostrils. My ears still rang from the explosion. I felt a gust of cool air blow over me, and darkness changed to light as I stumbled out of the bank of smoke and onto the path. Freuchen was nowhere to be seen, but I was less than ten feet from ground level, and I thought that perhaps he'd made it up already. I blundered along the path, the smell of the forest barely registering through my clogged nostrils.

There were several bodies sprawled on the ground around the top of the pit. My eyes were streaming, making everything appear as blobs of color with no definition. I wiped them with the back of my hand and knelt next to each body individually. None of them was Freuchen, but I recognized Denise. She lay on her back, her sightless eyes staring up at the silver *Brimstone* high overhead as though she were captivated by its grace. The shaft of a wooden spear protruded from her chest, and blood still trickled from the wound, soaking into the dirt.

Another gunshot jerked me back to reality. I was a sitting duck out here. I began crawling on all fours toward the forest, which was nothing but a swirling mass of colors to my smoke-stung eyes. When I reached the edge of the forest, I got to my feet and began to run, only to trip over what must have been a root of a tree. Crashing into the carpet of leaves, I stayed there a few moments, catching my breath, trying to orient myself. I rubbed at my eyes, which only made them sting more, but after a few excruciatingly long seconds of pain, I opened them again.

My sight was back. Or at least, enough for me to quickly assess where I was in relation to where I needed to be. I was on the opposite side of the pit from where we had initially arrived the day before. Across the pit's open mouth, I saw the two cabins Freuchen and I had passed between when we had surrendered to the guard—what was left of them, anyway. They were now flaming ruins. If someone didn't tend to them, the fire would surely take hold of the forest and potentially burn everything to the ground.

"Meredith!"

I squinted, scanning the opposite side of the pit, then felt my heart lurch in my chest as I spotted first Chou, an arm raised above her head waving to attract my attention, then the golden form of Silas as he strode into view. I heaved a sigh of relief.

"Hello, dearie," a woman's voice, husky, with a distinct English accent said.

I spun around, straight into the barrel of a rifle pointed at my head. My right hand began to move to grab the barrel.

"Uh, uh, uh," the woman said, taking a step backward, sensing what I was about to do. "Put your hands up."

I did as I was told, unable to move my eyes from the black hole of the rifle's barrel to see who held it. Then, fingers were in my hair, and my head was pulled sharply back.

A man's voice said, "Is that her? It's her, right?"

The woman said, "Yeah, that's gotta be her. That one in white just called her Meredith."

There was a metallic click, and the man's voice said, "Baroness, Jean-Pierre here, I think we have her for real this time."

This time? What does he mean this time? I thought.

There was a momentary hiss of static, then a woman's voice said, "Excellent! *Bring her on board.*"

A deep rumbling ululation—a cross between a whale's call

and feedback from a subwoofer—rolled across the sky from the airship above us. It repeated once more.

The man named Jean-Pierre yelled, "Move out. We got what we came for. Back to the *Brimstone*... now." The command was echoed by other voices, both male and female.

"Move, now," he ordered, prodding me painfully in the small of my back with the barrel of his rifle. "I said, move. Faster!"

I stumbled off in the direction he indicated, just as thirteen more grim-faced and smoke-smeared men and women, all armed with rifles or spears emerged from the pit. Some paused to point their rifles back down into the pit and fire off a couple of rounds covering their comrades' retreat.

"Stop!" Jean-Pierre ordered. I did as I was told but managed to steal a glance across the open mouth of the pit. I spotted Chou and Silas through the smoke, sprinting toward me. They were still several hundred feet away.

"Watch your heads," someone called out.

I looked up and gasped when I saw that the airship, the *Brimstone*, was now only about thirty feet above us and descending rapidly. It was easily two hundred feet long. Attached to the bottom of the balloon was a gray gondola that ran almost its entire length. At the front of the gondola was a large glass canopy where the pilot sat. There were two doors, one at the front, the other at the rear. Two rows of portholes, one above the other, ran between them, suggesting there were at least two levels. Four large propellers, two at the front and two at the rear, jutted out from the sides of the gondola. The actual balloon was built from some metallic-looking silver material, but the top half was covered in something like solar panels.

As the *Brimstone* descended, the attackers backed up, occasionally firing at anyone from New Manhattan brave enough to pop their head up.

Beneath the gondola, ski-pad-like feet ran its entire length. The moment they made contact with the ground, the two doors on the side of the gondola closest to us flew open. The men and women around me surged forward, and I was pushed along with them.

I needed to buy myself time— time for Chou and Silas to reach me and... what? There were at least fifteen heavily-armed men and women on the *Brimstone*. What could anyone here do against them? All I could do was trust that they would do *something*, because if my kidnappers got me inside the airship and it lifted off... that would be it. Game over.

Jean-Pierre pushed me toward the gondola door. "Get in," he ordered.

A surreptitious glance in the direction I'd last seen Chou and Silas showed me that they were now only a matter of seconds from reaching me. In what I knew was probably a futile attempt to delay them, I threw both hands against either side of the door opening and locked my elbows in place.

"No!" I yelled, "I'm not moving."

"What the hell is that thing? Is that a... it's a *robot*?" someone screeched behind me. Their voice was a mix of surprise, fear, and awe. There was no doubt they could only be referring to Silas.

I allowed myself a smile. If they thought Silas looked scary, just wait until Chou got ahold of them.

Jean-Pierre's head swiveled in the direction I'd last seen Chou and Silas approaching from. The man yelled into the open door, "Baroness, we got a problem. Starboard side. Coming in hot and sweaty." Then he turned his attention back to me. "I said get inside."

I gasped in pain as his fist connected with my kidneys. It wasn't a wild punch or particularly violent, but it was delivered with the precise amount of force needed to buckle my knees.

My body suddenly turned to jelly. My fingers slipped from the doorway, and I collapsed onto my back, half-in, half-out of the airship. From this new vantage point, I saw that on the other side of the door was a corridor running the entire length of the gondola. Several doors lined the one side as well as three other corridors that bisected the main one. There was a stairwell a few feet from my head with a neatly-painted sign that read UPPER DECK and PILOTHOUSE.

A broad-shouldered muscular man came down the stairs taking them two at a time, struggling to negotiate a large metal object which he cradled in both arms through the narrow stairwell. It was some kind of multiple-barreled weapon, I realized as he stepped over me—like something out of an old Western.

"Well, don't offer to help," the man spat at Jean-Pierre.

"Wouldn't dream of it," came the reply, followed by a bout of laughter. "Better hurry up or that robot's likely to screw us all up."

The big-man grunted as he hefted the machine-gun onto a large L-shaped metal spindle fixed to the gondola's inner wall. He popped a latch on the wall and pushed open a four-by-three section of the gondola, then swiveled the multiple barrels of the weapon out through the opening. He took hold of the two metal handles at the opposite end, then swung the weapon in Chou and Silas' direction.

I managed to squeak "No" before the machine gun opened up, but my words were lost to its deafening roar. Tracer bullets spat from the multiple barrels and arced through the air splitting trees apart where they hit. Chou and Silas zigged away, diving for cover as the barrage of lead sought them out.

And that was the last I saw before I felt myself lifted by the scruff of my sweater and dragged inside. The door closed behind me as the man swung the machine gun back and forth. His face was a mask of ecstasy as he continued to fire, hundreds of spent cartridges hitting the floor like metal rain around his feet.

My stomach lurched suddenly as the airship began to ascend. The machine-gun-toting man continued his barrage until the last round was fired. Then he reversed the process, disassembling the gun and closing the window.

"Did you get 'em?" Jean-Pierre asked.

The big man turned and looked in my direction for the first time and smiled. "Pretty sure I nailed both of them." His grin grew wider when he saw my obvious despair.

"Oh, don't be sad," Jean-Pierre said with mock sympathy, as he grabbed me by my arm and jerked me to my feet. "You're about to make a whole bunch of new friends." He shoved me toward a door at the end of the corridor.

When we reached the door, Jean-Pierre pointed at my backpack and, snapping his fingers, said, "Give me your backpack." I undid the fasteners and handed the pack to him. He tossed it into an alcove adjacent to the door.

"Now, turn around and put your hands against the wall."

I did as he said and tried not to react as he ran his hands over my clothing and checked all my pockets.

"Wait," he ordered as he pulled out a key and unlocked the door. "Inside, now."

As I stepped inside, I felt a hand push me hard between my shoulders, and I stumbled across the threshold, falling face-first onto the bare wooden floor. The door slammed behind me, and the key turned in the lock with an efficient sounding *thunk*.

I lay there for a while, trying to process what the hell had happened to me. I stood and looked around. The room was about eight by six with no windows and no furniture other than a disgustingly filthy plastic bucket for a toilet in one corner. There was no bed either, just a worn gray blanket crumpled in the corner.

I grabbed the blanket. It smelled of mildew and other things I didn't even want to try and identify. I sat back down and pulled the blanket around my shoulders, not because I was cold but because it offered me just a little comfort.

These people had swooped in and kidnapped me. And if their comments when they captured me were anything to go by, they had been *specifically* looking for me. Which meant only one thing: they were agents of the Adversary.

I felt my spirits sink even further when I remembered that the woman who'd been firing the machine gun when I was being dragged onto the airship seemed convinced that she'd hit both Silas and Chou. I couldn't bear the idea that my friends might be hurt or... worse.

I pulled the blanket tighter around me.

I'd lost Freuchen in the smoke. Hopefully, he was okay. But what about Albert? If Silas and Chou had been injured trying to rescue me, who would look after the boy? I consoled myself with the knowledge that Albert was a smart kid. He would get to *New Manhattan*. Emily and her people would surely look after him. Assuming Emily was still alive. I pushed that thought from my mind. What I needed to worry about now was how I was going to get off this airship and back to my friends.

And how exactly I was supposed to do that, I had no idea.

EIGHT

I SETTLED into the corner of my cell, wrapped the smelly blanket around me like a shawl, and tried to form a plan. At some point, my kidnappers were going to come for me—it was surely only a matter of time. I had no idea what it was they or the Adversary wanted from me, but they had not killed me outright, so that meant they needed *something* important. I took a few deep breaths to try and make my thumping heart slow, but it wouldn't. I kept seeing the machine gun flash and the heavyset man's gleeful delight when he said he thought he'd hit both Silas and Chou. I wasn't worried about Silas so much; the Nazis we'd encountered back on Avalon had shot him multiple times to no effect. But Chou was, in the end, only human. If she'd been hit... No! I just couldn't think that way. The best thing I could do right now was try to conserve my energy. That way, I would at least have some of my wits about me when my captors did show up. I pulled the blanket tighter, leaned my head against the wall, and closed my eyes.

Time passed. How much I don't know, there was no way to even guess at it in this tiny cell. I repeatedly slipped in and out *of* consciousness, dreaming of my kidnapping and the attack, of Chou and Silas and death.

My morbid thoughts were interrupted by the scrape of a key in the door lock. It opened, and Jean-Pierre strutted in.

"On your feet," he ordered, but before I could react, he grabbed my elbow and pulled me up, tore the blanket from my shoulders and tossed it to the floor, before pushing me out the door into the corridor. "Get a move on," he demanded, his hand against the small of my back, pushing me along the hallway toward the stairwell then up the steps to the upper deck. "To the right," he ordered when we reached the top.

I did as I was told and found myself in a large room filled with bunks, chairs, and a couple of sofas that looked like they'd seen better days. Most of the men and women I'd seen raiding *New Manhattan* lay sprawled on them. Some talked and laughed amongst themselves. Others rested on bunks, eyes closed, apparently asleep. Those that were awake eyed me with curiosity, others with suspicion.

"Go on, that way." Jean-Pierre pushed me toward a door at the front of the airship. Painted in red on the door were the words: PILOTHOUSE.

"Stop," Jean-Pierre ordered. He swallowed nervously, then knocked three times.

"Enter," a woman's voice called out. Jean-Pierre opened the door wide and nodded for me to step inside.

A man, his back to me, sat in front of a horseshoe-shaped console that extended almost the entire width of the room. It was covered with dials, lights, switches, and a couple of computer screens, which he was studiously monitoring. Except for the one behind me, the rest of the room's walls were all made of glass, giving an unparalleled view of the world beyond as the *Brimstone* soared rapidly. Glowing green lines of information were displayed on the glass like a fighter pilot's heads-up display.

A large black leather chair sat in the center of the pilot-house, its back to me, obscuring whoever occupied it. Now it swung around to face me.

A woman in her fifties—judging by the wrinkles on her fore-head and the crows-feet around her eyes—eyed me up and down. She wore a sky blue, single-breasted frock coat that stopped just above her knees. Intricate military-style gold epaulets crested each shoulder, and she wore equally elaborate gold cuffs. Black pantaloons and brown knee-high boots. A scar, white and puckered against her deeply tanned skin, ran from the top-right side of her hairline across her forehead and right eye, down over her nose and left cheek, and ended in an upside-down-**Y** just before her jaw. She wore a red patch over her right eye, and her hair was styled in a utilitarian bob.

Pirate, I thought. *She's a freaking pirate.*

"Well now, so, *you* are Meredith Gale," the woman said with such firmness that I knew it was pointless to argue.

I'd learned that those sent by the Adversary had received a very specific psychic picture. Strangely enough, it was of me winning a presidential election. If she'd really been sent by the Adversary, then it was logical to expect she would have received it, too. The woman eased herself out of her seat, smiling broadly, not in a friendly way, more like a shark greeting its dinner. "My name is Captain Isabella Teresita Galindez," she said. "But in the time I am from, I am known as the Red Baroness." She offered me her hand. I stared at it until I felt a prod in my back from Jean-Pierre's rifle, and reached out and shook it limply.

"What do you want?" I asked bluntly.

The Red Baroness tilted her head, smiled. "Straight to the point. I like that. It's okay," she continued, returning to her seat. "I completely understand. If I were in your position, I don't think I would be too talkative either." Her eyes drifted to the forest visible through the sizeable plexiglass-glass bubble. "This world is so very beautiful. Not like the version of Earth we came from." She paused dramatically, "I assume you know that we are all refugees from different dimensions?"

I nodded. She said it so casually, and I guess it was normal now.

"Good, good," she continued. Her voice grew unexpectedly wistful. "Now, why we were all transported here to this planet so like our own and yet so very different—I do not know. But what I do know is that it's a thousand times better than the hell-hole we called home. So much land. So much green. So much potential."

Interesting, I thought, she seemed unaware that this was actually just another version of Earth. I saw no harm in trying to gently pump her for any information. Truth was, I was more than a little curious about the kind of world where airships might be a common mode of transportation, and she struck me as the type of personality that would enjoy having her ego stroked.

"So, what's your story, Baroness? How did you get here?" I was right. Her face immediately softened; her chin tilted upright as she cleared her throat.

"On September 26, 1983, *our* world came to an end. Some say it was the Americans who launched first, others that it was the Russians. Some even say it was just a big misunderstanding, a computer glitch. Whoever is right or wrong doesn't really matter; the results were the same. Our world became a radioactive wasteland in less than a day."

There a small part of me that felt some sudden sympathy for the Baroness and her crew, but that quickly evaporated as she continued to tell her story.

"Survivors no longer had access to petrochemicals, so we

had to find other ways to power our societies." She waved her hand to encompass the *Brimstone's* cabin. "And so, the great age of airships was born. Those first few years were brutal beyond anyone's imagination. But with so few resources available, we quickly learned that the only way to get what you needed to survive was to take it by force." She leaned forward and snatched at the air with a fist. "And I am very happy to say that we were the best, most feared crew in all of what was left of our world."

"That's... incredible," I said, honestly amazed. Her world, a virtual radioactive graveyard, was so very different from mine, from *anyone's* that I'd met so far on my journey. I decided to push my luck a little and see if she would bite. "So, I guess you were brought here like all the others, by the *Voice*."

She simply dipped her head in acknowledgment.

I continued, "And before you were brought here, you were in some kind of life-threatening situation, yes?"

"Ah," the Baroness sighed, "therein lies the tale of our doom and our salvation. During one of our raids, an unanticipated storm blew us off course and into the badlands of what had once been Poland. We were mere seconds from crashing and burning at best, or if any of us had survived, dying a horrendous death by radiation."

"And that was when the *Voice* asked if you wanted to be saved, right?"

Her look soured. "This... voice, as you called it, only promised us that in return for our lives, we were to use any means necessary to locate you."

"But why?" I said. "What could I possibly know that would be of use to you or whatever it is behind all of this."

The Baroness stood again. She approached me and cupped my chin in one calloused hand. "Oh, you really don't know, do you?" She gave my head a gentle shake then let go. "You, my dear, are apparently the key to everything. You are the one who knows the location of Candidate 1."

Shit!

So, there it was, confirmation that the Baroness and her band of killers were not just some random group of marauders but instead were sent to find me by the Adversary. And the Baroness knew about Candidate 1, which meant that the Adversary knew about them too. The one thing they did not seem to know was where Candidate 1 was located.

The Baroness continued, "In the time that we have been searching for you, Meredith, we have had numerous 'guests' who have told us a similar story to your own, although they made no mention of being 'candidates.'"

"What do you mean by 'guests?'" I asked.

"You'd be surprised at just how many red-headed women who look like you there are on this planet." She turned to look at Jean-Pierre. "How many did we find up to today?"

"Twenty-seven, Baroness."

"Yes, that's right. Twenty-seven. Lovely young women, all of them. Unfortunately, for all parties concerned, none of them were you, and we had to... part ways."

I didn't even want to think what that meant.

"Now, as wonderful as it is to chat with you, I really do think it's time you gave us something in return, don't you?" The Baroness glanced at Jean-Pierre. "Is Abernathy ready to receive our guest?"

Jean-Pierre nodded. "He is, Baroness."

"Then please escort Meredith to him." She dismissed me with a wave of her hand. Two pairs of hands grabbed me by my elbows and pushed me through the door, back past the crew area, and into another room.

Inside, a tall, gaunt-featured man was waiting.

"Where do you want her?" Jean-Pierre said.

The man said nothing but pointed to one of two plastic chairs facing each other in the center of the room. I gave a little gasp when I saw his right hand. A second thumb sprouted from the joint of his first. It was almost as large and jutted out at a forty-five-degree angle.

I was manhandled into one of the chairs, my wrists tied to it. My guards stepped back but didn't leave.

"My name is Thomas Abernathy," the man said, leaning back against a cabinet. "I have been tasked with gathering as much information from you as I can. Now, this can be easy for you, or it can be hard. The choice really is up to you, Meredith."

I held his gaze and said, "I have no idea what it is you think I know, but I can tell you right now, I know nothing."

Abernathy raised his eyebrows. "I thought that might be your answer. Now, let's prove which of us is correct, shall we?"

He took a single step closer to me and leaned in.

"All we want to know," said Abernathy, "is where Candidate 1 is. Just tell me, and we can dispense with any of the unpleasantries."

"And then you'll kill me, right?" I spat back.

Two-thumbs slowly shook his head. "No. Much as I might enjoy that, we're under strict instructions to keep you alive. But make no mistake about it, you're ours now. We own you. But things will go a lot easier for you if you tell us what we want to know. Who is Candidate 1?"

"I don't know," I said.

"You don't sound convinced," said Abernathy, sarcastically.

"I don't know why, because I have no idea what you're talking about."

Abernathy took a step back, his hands still clasped behind his back. "You are Meredith Gale, are you not? You have lived so many lives successfully, but here, you are just a... suicide." He spoke that last word with such disdain.

I felt anger well up inside me. "You don't get to judge me," I spat, straining against my bonds.

He laughed—cackled more like it. "You have such spirit." He stepped in closer to me, finally unlocking his hands to place them on my shoulders. "You have probably been wondering why the crew refers to me as Tommy Two-Thumbs. No? Let me explain." He slipped his right hand from my shoulder and held it in front of my face.

He slowly moved the hand with the extra thumb in front of my eyes, as though he were showing it off.

"Hold her tight," Two-Thumbs said. Then, before I could resist, he drove the extra thumb into my left ear and twisted it back and forth like a corkscrew.

I screamed as the thick nail gouged skin from my inner ear. I felt a trickle of warm blood running down my neck.

Two-Thumbs pulled out his digit and cleaned it with a handkerchief from his pocket.

"While it works with weaker souls, I do believe that you will take some extra convincing before you give up your secrets." He opened a leather case. Inside, I saw knives and scalpels and hammers and tongs and saws and shears. Abernathy ran his hands lovingly over the glistening tools as though they were faithful pets.

"You... you're going to torture me?" I said, unable to keep the fear from breaking my words apart.

Abernathy turned to look at me over his shoulder. "You? Oh no. We are, as I mentioned, restrained from doing you too much harm."

I let out a silent sigh of relief.

Abernathy turned his body fully toward me, planted his hands on his hips, and allowed a huge grin to spread across his face. "However, that rule does not extend to others. Please bring in our guest."

From somewhere behind me, I heard a door open, and a man yell, "Bring 'im in." The sound of something being dragged across the deck reached me. I struggled to turn to see, but my bonds held me tightly in place.

Abernathy placed the second chair in front of me. He smiled. As he leaned with one hand against its high back. "I believe you know each other?" he said, nodding.

I gasped in shock as the two men dragged an almost unconscious and badly-beaten Freuchen to the chair and dropped him into it. Freuchen toppled sideways.

"Whoops!" said Abernathy, grabbing Freuchen by the shoulder and propping him back up.

"You bastard!" I yelled through gritted teeth. I tried to leap at him, but the two guards were ready for me, and they forced me back down into my chair.

Abernathy ran his hand through Freuchen's hair. "One of our men had the forethought to mention that he'd seen the two of you trying to escape together. Lucky for us... not so lucky for you. Worse for him."

The Dane's face was a bloody mess; his eyes swollen shut, several teeth missing, bloody drool running from the side of his mouth. His nose was skewed to one side. Blood still ran from it over his chin to form an ugly semi-congealed slick on his shirt.

"He put up a wonderful fight—killed two of our men before we managed to subdue him. Quite extraordinary... quite extraordinary." Abernathy walked to the box of blades and blunt instruments. He paused and tapped an index finger against his lips. "Decisions. Decisions. Ah! I think we'll start off with... this, yes?" He plucked a large pair of serrated shears from the box and dramatically snapped them open and closed twice. "Snip, snip."

I hissed an expletive at him, then yelled it at him a second time as he walked over to Freuchen's unconscious body, snipping the air with the shears.

"Tsk! Tsk! Such language," he said mockingly. "Did your mother not teach you *any* kind of manners, young lady?"

I thrust my chin out and snarled at him.

Abernathy made an exaggerated sad face, lifted Freuchen's left hand, and before I could scream "no," cut Freuchen's thumb from it. The severed thumb fell with a wet smack to the floor while Abernathy regarded me with raised eyebrows and a childish look that said *Oops! How did that happen?*

Freuchen shifted in the chair, groaned, his head lifting from his chest. His swollen eyelids parted slightly, and he sucked in a huge gasp of air. He raised his injured hand to his face, his head moving back and forth as though he were trying to focus. His good eye grew wide, and then he howled.

The two who'd dragged Freuchen into the room leaped to his side and grabbed hold of his shoulders and wrists, pinning him to the chair. Freuchen tried to struggle, but he was simply too weak. After a few seconds, he slumped forward, slipping back into unconsciousness.

Blood poured from where his thumb was supposed to be.

"No, please," I pleaded. "Help him."

Abernathy's head tilted to his left shoulder. "Now, why on —" he raised his hands and waved them "—wherever this is, would I want to do that?"

I felt the anger well up in me again but fought it back. If I didn't tell Abernathy what he wanted to know, then he would surely continue to torture Freuchen. And in the end, what did I know? All I had was a location from a vague message. I didn't even know if it was the *right* collector. Was any of it worth my friend's life? I knew what both Chou and Freuchen's answers would be, but *I'm* not *them*.

"Okay," I said, "I'll tell you. But only if you help him first."

"Information first, help after."

My mind was a whirlpool of panic. I needed *something* I could give them that wouldn't give our destination away. I remembered a phrase Freuchen had once used, *If you want a dog, first ask for a pony*.

"The robot," I blurted out.

"What?" said Abernathy, suddenly interested. "The one that tried to rescue you? Tell me about him."

"I... it gave me a message," I said.

"What message? Tell me now," Abernathy demanded.

"It was from the person we call the Architect... the one that brought us here.

"And this robot, he knows who Candidate 1 is?" Abernathy said, eagerly, his face so close to me, I could smell his bad breath.

I was about to tell him Silas had even less idea than we did but decided Two Thumbs didn't need to know that. I had to buy time for me and Freuchen.

"Help my friend, and I'll tell you who it is you're looking for."

"I don't believe you," Abernathy said, standing upright again.

I shrugged. "I've already told you more information than anyone else on this planet knows. What else do I have to lose by telling you who Candidate 1 is?"

Abernathy stared wordlessly at me for what felt like minutes. I stared him in the eyes, willing myself not to blink. God, I hoped this bluff would be enough.

Then Abernathy gave a wave of his malformed hand and said, "Take him to the sickbay."

Freuchen's guards put a hand under each of Freuchen's armpits and dragged him out of the room, leaving a trail of blood behind him.

"Now, tell me what I want to know," Abernathy said.

I shook my head. "Not until I know you're looking after him. If you kill him, you won't get another word out of me, and I'll make it my priority to kill myself at the first opportunity. I've done it once already, and I'll have no problem doing it again." At this point, I was only partly bluffing.

Abernathy stepped quickly to me and leaned in until his nose was almost touching mine. "Do not test me, girl," he hissed.

I stared back, resisting the urge to clamp my teeth onto his nose and rip it off his face. "When I know you're keeping your end of the bargain," I hissed, "then, I'll tell you the rest of what I know."

He sucked air in through his teeth and stepped back. "Take her to her cell," he said, turning away from me.

I was yanked to my feet and dragged back down the corridor toward my cell. They threw me inside and locked the door behind them. I leaped to my feet and rushed to the door, hammering it with my fists.

"What have you done with Freuchen," I demanded. "You're not going to get another word out of me until I know he's safe."

I heard movement beyond the door and took a couple of steps back at the sound of the key turning in the lock. The door opened, and I breathed a sigh of relief when I saw Freuchen held between the same two men who'd dragged him away. They stepped inside my cell and dropped him to the floor.

I skated on my knees to his side. Freuchen groaned when I placed a hand against his cheek. "Peter," I said. "Peter, it's me, Meredith. You're okay. I'm here." His now thumb-less hand had been bandaged, and his cuts and bruises had been cleaned up, but he was still only semi-conscious. I took the blanket from my shoulders and threw it over him.

Freuchen's eyes fluttered open, took a second to focus on me. He groaned, grimaced, then said, "Ver are ve?" His voice creaked like uneven floorboards.

"We were captured by the people who attacked *New Manhattan*. We're on their airship, the *Brimstone*, heading for God-knows-where." I paused to let that sink in. "They beat you up and tortured you, which is why you're in such a state."

He raised his injured hand and stared at the bandage. "They took my thumb?" he said, incredulous.

I nodded.

"Vat time is it?"

I guessed it was somewhere around three-ish in the afternoon. "Not too long to wait." I knew he was gauging how long it was until the aurora would sweep across the sky and repair him.

Freuchen nodded. He sat up, flinching.

"You're not in any shape to be moving around," I told him.

Freuchen worked his jaw like he had something caught in his teeth. He spat blood and a piece of tooth into his good hand then wiped it in his already bloody trousers. He was beginning to regain some of his faculties, and I couldn't help but wonder at how tough this man actually was. If I'd taken the kind of beating he had, I'd be laid-up in hospital for months, or dead.

He turned to look at me. "Who did this to me?"

My eyes dropped to the floor. "A man, Abernathy, but everyone calls him Tommy Two-Thumbs because he has an extra thumb."

"Two extra, if he kept mine," Freuchen croaked, and laughed, his dark humor apparently undamaged by the beating the rest of him had taken. He motioned for the bucket, which I brought to him. He spat a gobbet of blood into it. "Sorry. Go on."

"Like I was saying, this Abernathy guy, he brought you in after his thugs beat you up, and he cut your thumb off. He had the tools to do it, too."

"Vy? Vy vould they vant to do that to me?"

I held my breath for a second. "They're agents of the Adversary. They were looking for me, but Abernathy says the Adversary has told them not to hurt me, so they tortured you instead."

Freuchen's brow furrowed. "Vy?"

"They wanted to know what we knew about Candidate 1," I said.

"And? Vat did you tell them?" I heard the resignation in his voice.

"I don't know if they're listening." I leaned in and whispered, "Just that Silas had given me a message."

Freuchen nodded slowly that he understood.

"I saw Chou and Silas when they grabbed me. Did you see them?" I asked, trying to change the subject.

"No," Freuchen said. "After I lost you in the smoke, I headed up to try and find you again, but I vas ambushed. I think someone hit me from behind and knocked me out, because the next thing I remember I vas vaking up tied to a chair. That's ven the two goons vent to vurk on me. Damn cowards. I vould have broken both of them in two if it had been a fair fight. I vill have their guts for garters by the time ve are through."

I had absolutely no doubt that he could have made good on his boast. In our time together, I'd learned that Freuchen was, at heart, a gentleman. But he also came from a time when violence —whether it came from nature or his fellow man—was everywhere, and his life as an adventurer had more than prepared him to take on almost anything that was thrown at him.

"I think ve need—" Freuchen was interrupted by the sound of the cell-door unlocking. It swung open, and the two men who had beaten Freuchen stepped into the room. My heart lurched, expecting them to go to work on Freuchen again... or maybe me this time. Instead, they stepped aside just enough to allow a woman into the room. She held a plate of bread and some kind of meat, and a large plastic cup of water.

"Any funny business and I'll 'ave my two pals here deal with you. Understood?" she said, pausing between the two men and eyeing us with the feral suspicion of a junk-yard dog.

Freuchen and I both nodded that we understood, but I could see in Freuchen's eyes that he was already planning his revenge. I surreptitiously reached out my right hand and squeezed his elbow. Now was most definitely not the time for him to try and break us out of here. We needed a plan.

The woman stepped closer and laid the plate and cup on the floor, nudged it closer to us with the tip of her shoe, then stepped out of the room, followed by the two men. The door slammed shut.

We split the bread and mystery meat between us. Freuchen winced as he slowly chewed his food. The water we decided to ration as well as we could. After we'd fed ourselves, I suggested that Freuchen try to get some rest. It seemed pointless putting him through the pain of any more explanation until after the aurora had worked its magic. He concurred, and within a few minutes, I found myself alone with my thoughts again while my friend slept fitfully, his head resting in my lap while I gently stroked his blood-tangled hair.

———

I woke with a start. Freuchen was already awake, his back against the cell wall watching me. The room was completely dark save for a sliver of light beneath the door... and the hundreds of tiny white dots that now coated my friend's body.

It was weird experiencing the aurora without actually seeing it. Even in the Everwood, light filled the tree-tops, but in here, there was just the pixie dust. The nanobots swept silently over Freuchen, seeking out his wounds while he sat calmly as they worked their miracles on him, restoring his broken body bit by bit. Then the room grew warmer as a wave of heat emanated from him, as though he were suddenly racked by a fever, but Freuchen seemed perfectly comfortable. He reached across and unwound the bandage from his mutilated hand. I watched in absolute wonder as the digit slowly grew back again: first the bone, then the muscle and arteries, building upon each other like I'd seen things being made in 3-D printers. Finally, a layer of skin, pink and new and fresh.

"Just like your arm," Freuchen said, flexing his new thumb as though it had always been attached. "Vunderful."

I felt my own stress, aches, and pain fade. When the pixie dust finally faded away too, the room fell back into darkness. I scooted across the floor to where Freuchen sat and squeezed his arm.

"Ve need to discuss how ve are going to get ourselves off of this airship," Freuchen said, his voice just loud enough to hear. "How many people did you see ven they brought you on board?"

"At least fifteen," I said, thinking back. "That includes the raiding party that captured us."

"Too many for us to fight unarmed. Did you see ver they kept their veapons?"

I shook my head, realized he couldn't see me, and said, "No, sorry."

"Blast! Vell, ve shall just have to find another vay off of this thing. The vun thing ve cannot allow to happen is for them to get any more information out of us." I heard the rustle of his clothes as he shifted position. "Now, I think it's time ve both get some rest. Ve are going to need all the strength ve can muster tomorrow."

———

We were startled awake by the cell door being flung open.

Wordlessly, the two goons swooped into the room, grabbed Freuchen, another two men right behind them for me. They dragged us both out into the corridor. I expected Freuchen to put up a fight. Instead, his head hung low as though he had completely given up.

Through the portholes lining the corridor, I could see the *Brimstone* was moving along at a leisurely pace. Not more than a hundred feet or so above the forest canopy, the view was beautiful—which was an odd thing to think under such duress.

"Watch 'im," the man on my right said, nodding at Freuchen. "He's not one to give in so easily."

The two goons apparently thought otherwise, and that was a mistake. As we approached the door I had seen the day before, Freuchen suddenly tensed, he took a fast step backward and used that momentum to bring the guards on either side of him careening into the other. There was an unpleasant crack as the two men collided face-to-face, blood spurting from one of their noses. The other staggered away, clutching a hand to his right eye.

I tensed, readying myself to fight out of the grip of the two who held me, then stopped as I felt something sharp pressed into my ribs. "Don't think about it, love," said the man on my left, a long-bladed knife held firmly in his hand.

Freuchen dove for the exit door, which was just a few feet away, grabbed the lever and pulled it upward, then slid the door along its tracks. Instantly, wind and rain whipped into the corridor. He grabbed the man with the broken nose by the scruff of his neck and with one mighty heave, tossed him through the opening. I don't think Broken-Nose even knew what had happened because he didn't even scream as he plummeted toward the ground.

The second man, seeing his comrade thrown to his death, ducked low and rushed Freuchen, hitting him square in the belly. He threw his arms around my friend and lifted him off his feet, carrying him backward, slamming him into the bulkhead. Freuchen gasped, then raised his right arm and brought his elbow down hard on the back of the man's skull. The man fell face-first to the deck, and Freuchen delivered a swift kick with the heel of his boot to the side of the man's head to make sure he stayed down. He turned to face me and the two men who held me.

"Uh-uh, where's your manners, mate? You take another step, and I'll slit your girlfriend open."

"No, you von't," said Freuchen. "She's vorth too much to you and whoever it is you vurk for. But you, on the other hand, are disposable."

Freuchen walked toward us, almost casually raised his fist, and delivered a short jab to the face of the man holding the knife. He collapsed like a sack of potatoes. My remaining captor pulled his own knife and brandished it, swiping the air in an **X**-shape. Freuchen deftly grabbed him by the arm, dragged him to the lip of the doorway, and as I stood there open-mouthed, pushed him out too.

His scream echoed through the corridor.

Freuchen quickly checked the two remaining men's pulse, then moved to me. "I don't like to hurt people, but I vill make an exception for anyone who tries to kill us." He began to drag one of the unconscious men toward the door by his feet.

"Peter, no!" I hissed.

Freuchen stopped and looked first at me then down at the unconscious man. He paused, then shrugged and dropped him. Now Freuchen's attention switched to the taupe-colored back-packs that lined the opposite wall. He moved to them, quickly undid the straps securing them, and brought them to me.

"Are those parachutes?" I asked, suddenly realizing what he had in mind. "I can't jump. I've never parachuted in my life."

"Neither have I," Freuchen said with a grin, "but I don't see any other vay of getting off this damnable sky boat."

I looked out through one of the portholes, shading my eyes against the rain. The canopy of the Everforest stretched out all around us. It couldn't have been more than two hundred feet below us.

"I don't think we're high enough for the chutes to work," I said.

Freuchen stood at my side and looked down and shrugged. "Eh, ve don't have a choice."

"But there's nowhere for us to land. Even if the parachutes open, we're going to just hit the tops of the trees. Then what do we do?"

Freuchen turned me to face him. "Ve don't have any choice, Meredith. You must understand that. Now turn around."

Reluctantly, I did as he said and turned to face the wall. Freuchen slipped the parachute over my shoulders, clipped the safety harness together, then tapped me on my shoulder. "All done."

I turned to face him just in time to see a sudden flurry of motion behind Freuchen. "Look out!" I screamed.

Freuchen started to turn, but he wasn't quite fast enough. Perhaps he was wondering why his two prisoners had not been brought immediately to him, but while Freuchen had been helping me into the parachute, Abernathy had snuck up behind us. Holding a metal cylinder in his right hand that glinted in the overhead lights, he thrust it into Freuchen's side. There was an electric buzz, and Freuchen jerked, stiffened, then collapsed to the floor.

I started to move toward Freuchen.

"Stay there," Two-Thumbs ordered, taunting me with the tube. "If you move, I'll throw your friend out that door. Now, take off that parachute."

I did as I was told and dropped the parachute at my feet.

His eyes on me the whole time, Two-Thumbs checked the still-unconscious men. Two-Thumbs slapped them hard across their faces until they groaned, and their eyes fluttered open.

"Get up, you idiots," Two-Thumbs said, kicking one man in the ribs with the tip of his boot. The men dragged themselves to their feet, teetering uneasily. Anger shone in both men's eyes. One took aim at Freuchen's head with his foot as though he was going to kick a soccer ball.

"Stop!" Two-Thumbs ordered.

He paused, looking as though he might just ignore the order then thought better of it when Two-Thumbs began smacking the metal rod he had used to zap Freuchen into the palm of his hand.

"Now," Two-thumbs continued, visibly relaxing. "You two fools, if you would be so kind as to remove Mr. Peter Freuchen from the *Brimstone*."

"No! Please don't," I pleaded as the men grabbed Freuchen by both hands and began to slowly drag him toward the opening. "I'll tell you everything you want to know."

The men stopped and looked at their boss,

Two-Thumbs didn't even look in my direction when he replied, "Oh, I know you will, but I can see it is going to take some... subtler measures to ensure that I get everything I want from you. And as such, I no longer have any need for Mr. Peter Freuchen, here." He nodded at the men to continue.

The men dropped Freuchen and began to roll his huge body toward the lip of the door. They were close to the edge when a violent shudder vibrated through the *Brimstone*. My ears popped, and I reached for the wall to steady myself as the airship began a rapid descent. A second later, a klaxon, shrill and loud, sounded throughout the ship, and a red bulb in the ceiling blinked on and off.

All three of our captors froze. Two-thumbs seemed to be considering his options, then said, "Get them both back into their cell. Then meet me in the pilothouse." He moved toward the exit door and slid it shut.

The two thugs grabbed Freuchen under both arms and dragged his limp body down the corridor while Two-Thumbs took me by the arm and wordlessly pushed me along after them.

Crew ran past us, concern on every face. Even with the chaos playing out around us, I couldn't help but notice that some of the cockiness had gone out of Two-Thumbs.

NINE

FREUCHEN LAY QUIETLY GROANING on the floor of the cell, his eyes tightly closed. A few minutes later, they flickered open at the same time the emergency klaxon stopped. I could still see the red light blinking through the gap at the bottom of the door, so whatever the emergency situation was that had saved Freuchen's ass from being kicked out of the airship was still ongoing.

"Vat in God's name did they do to me this time?" Freuchen asked, slowly sitting up.

"They Tazered you," I said, then, realizing he possibly couldn't know what a Tazer was, added, "They hit you with an electrical shock that knocked you out. They were going to throw you out of the airship, but something must have happened because an alarm went off and we started to descend."

In the time since we'd been taken back to our cell, I'd heard numerous people rush back and forth past the door. Now someone stopped and began talking with the guard stationed outside. I put a finger to my lips and slid quietly across the floor, placing my ear as close to the gap as I could.

"—thought there was supposed to be a fail-safe on the inner balloon," a gruff male voice said.

He was answered by a much younger-sounding man. "There're four compartments, each cut off from each other. If one leaks, the others are safe, but somehow all four of them were sliced open. Engineering's trying to patch 'em up right now, but the boss is taking us to land just to be safe."

"How the hell did all four of 'em burst?" the gruff-voiced man said.

"Has to be sabotage. No other explanation."

The gruff-voiced man said, "Who would be stupid enough to do that? We're in the middle of bloody nowhere. If the boss catches 'em, they're gonna get strung up by their balls."

"She thinks it's a stowaway; someone from that village we hit yesterday."

There was a brief burst of laughter from the gruff-voiced man. "I wouldn't want to be them when the boss catches 'em."

"Yeah, it's going to—"

The gruff-voiced man suddenly interrupted his friend with a sharp, "Hey! You! Stay right where—"

The sound of a brief struggle was followed by a couple of short, painful-sounding gasps, two thuds... then nothing. I smashed my ear to the door, trying to hear what was going on. Something metal jingled just beyond it, and I skidded back to where Freuchen sat.

After the sound of a key being slid into the locked door, it eased open a crack, then swung wide. A figure dressed all in white backed into the cell dragging the body of one of the guards who had been stationed outside our cell.

"Chou!" Freuchen and I said in unison.

"Obviously," Chou replied matter-of-factly, turning and nodding at us. "Please, help me with the other man."

Freuchen and I jumped to our feet and grabbed the body of

the second guard who lay sprawled across the floor, his eyes staring sightlessly toward the ceiling. As we dragged him inside, I tried not to pay attention to the way his head lolled unnaturally from side to side. We dropped him next to the body of the first guard while Chou stuck her head back into the corridor, before closing the cell door behind her.

"You are a sight for sore eyes," Freuchen said. "But how in God's name did you get on board?"

"Later," Chou said. She accepted the hug I offered, then took a step back.

"Wait, if you're here, where's Albert?" I asked, concerned that the boy might have found himself alone if anything had happened to Silas.

"We instructed him that if we did not return, he was to approach the people of the village when he thought it safe to do so."

"New Manhattan," I said. "The woman who's in charge— her name is Emily Baxter—seems like she has a good head on her shoulders, so I know he'll be okay. My main concern is how they will react to Silas, especially after the attack."

"The tin-man is more than capable of looking after himself," said Freuchen.

"I know, but I have his slate. It's still in my backpack, which the Red Baroness' people took when they captured me. Without the slate, Silas isn't going to remember anything or anyone," I said.

Freuchen exhaled a sharp, "Damn!"

"Do you know where they took it?" Chou asked.

I nodded and quickly described where they'd tossed my bag.

"Stay here," Chou said. She moved to the door, cracked it open, then disappeared. Several minutes later, she slipped back into the room with both Freuchen's and my backpacks, my sword and armor, and Freuchen's ax.

I took my stuff from her and breathed a sigh of relief when I pulled out Silas' undamaged slate, then slid it back in again.

"Now, ve at least have a fighting chance."

"Let's get to the exit now," Chou said.

"Wait!" I said. "Shouldn't we wait until we've landed. What if we're seen?"

Chou shook her head. "They'll have the crew ready to set the mooring lines as soon as we land, especially in this weather. Come on." Chou moved to the door, checked the corridor for movement, then the three of us moved out of the cell, closing the door behind us. We jogged quickly to the exit Freuchen had used to try to escape.

"It's impossible to see anything through this damn rain," Freuchen said, straining to see beyond the rain-slicked porthole. "Vait a second... get ready... here ve go." He slid the door open, and we were instantly buffeted by a sheet of icy wind and rain. Freuchen leaped through the doorway a second before a long shudder ran through the deck that was followed by a gentle thud as the *Brimstone* landed.

Freuchen stood outside, beckoning me to jump. "Come on, be quick about it."

I leaped to the ground, Chou right behind me. I had an instance to take in my surroundings; the *Brimstone* had landed in a large clearing. Tall grass, a good three feet or so high, grew everywhere. It swayed and rustled, battered by the downpour. Within seconds, we were all soaked.

My breath caught as from within the *Brimstone*, I heard the sound of approaching voices.

"Keep low," Chou whispered. Single file, we followed Chou, hunched low so the grass would help camouflage our escape. We headed toward the edge of the clearing, which was nothing but a vague watery mirage barely visible through the sheets of falling rain. I'd expected to see the usual forest that seemed so ubiquitous to this future Earth, but instead, as we approached the edge of the clearing, I saw a jungle. Creepers hung between the branches of huge trees, creating a spiderweb effect. Monkeys, hiding from the storm beneath broad leaves, chattered in the tree limbs, stunned by the strange invaders that had descended from the sky like some ancient god.

We'd almost reached the jungle when a loud yell from behind us cut through the thrum of the rain. I turned back toward the *Brimstone* in time to see several vague human shapes descending from the gondola, pointing at us and shouting. There was a bright orange flash, then what sounded like a bee zinged past us and hit a nearby tree. Several scale-like pieces of bark exploded from it.

"Run!" Chou hissed, and we plunged into the jungle.

TEN

"THIS WAY," Chou yelled, grabbing my hand and dragging me off to the left. I looked back toward the clearing where the *Brimstone* rested and saw ten or so of the crew moving through the forest toward us.

"Eyes forward," Freuchen said.

We continued to run for another minute, then Chou pulled me again, directing me to the base of a steep embankment that led up to a hill. She paused for a second and looked back.

"If ve can get higher, ve might be able to break our pursuers line of sight and double back behind them," Freuchen said.

I was panting heavily, and my back and my leg muscles had begun to take on that heavy feeling of fatigue.

"Won't they be able to follow our tracks?" I gasped as I took three deep breaths.

Freuchen shook his head. "No, I don't think so. The floor of the forest is so cushioned vith leaves ve aren't leaving much in the vay of tracks."

"Now's not the time to talk," Chou said. "We need to keep moving." Without another word, she began to power up the embankment at a forty-five-degree angle. I followed after her, trying as hard as I could to keep up.

Someone yelled behind us, and I turned in time to see a man step into view between two trees. He beckoned to some unseen other behind him, then raised his rifle and let off three quick shots. The rounds zinged past us, kicking up spouts of dirt and leaves in the embankment that separated me from Chou.

An angry woman's voice shouted, "Stop firing, you idiot. We want her alive." I saw the Red Baroness step into view and deliver a vicious blow to the man with the butt of her pistol. He dropped to one knee, his hand cradling his head as the Baroness and the rest of the search party streamed past him in our direction.

The embankment grew steeper, and I began to slow, almost entirely depleted.

"Here," Chou said, reaching a hand to me. I grabbed it, and she pulled me up and onto a four-foot-high wall of earth, then continued to drag me stumbling along with her, heading straight up now, trying to put as much space between us and the Baroness and her crew as she could. "You must keep going," Chou said over her shoulder. "The summit is close."

"Not... sure... I... can," I panted back at her.

"I will carry you if I must, but I'd prefer not to."

"Under... standable... I... guess."

"Almost there," she said, her grip on my hand tightening. I looked up in time to see Chou reach the rough rolling plateau that was the top of the embankment. She turned, beckoned for my other hand while her eyes searched the forest below us. "Quickly," she said.

I grabbed her outstretched hand and allowed her to pull my exhausted body up next to her. Dropping to my knees, ignoring the rain pounding at my head and the cold streams running down my back, I somehow resisted the urge to simply lay down and not move.

"Come on," Freuchen urged. "Ve must keep on."

I pushed myself to my feet. I had time to suck in a huge gulp of the cold, wet air before we were off again. We side-stepped our way down the opposite side of the embankment. When we reached the bottom, Chou said, "This way."

Rather than simply running into the woods, she followed the bottom of the embankment to the left, leaping over roots and boulders, pushing her way through bushes as though they were nothing.

But now, even Freuchen was starting to tire. While whatever process had brought us to this version of Earth had certainly made us healthier than we'd ever been on our original Earths, it hadn't given us superpowers. We were still human— even Chou, who had been bred to be fitter than any human that had ever existed in my time. On top of it all, Freuchen and I hadn't had a thing but the measly chunks of bread and a few sips of water for the past twenty-four hours.

"Ve need... to find somevhere... to rest," Freuchen said a few minutes later, his breath coming out in great clouds of steam.

Chou looked back, slowed, then came to a stop. I could see that she was frustrated that we couldn't keep up with her, and once again, I was thankful that she didn't simply abandon us to fend for ourselves. She scanned the trees for a second, then said, "Come on. This way," before taking off at a ninety-degree angle into the woods. She slowed her pace to more of a fast jog, enough that Freuchen and I could keep up with.

For the next ten minutes, we zigzagged our way between trees, doubling back, then heading off in a totally different direction. Their voices had faded, so I knew we had at least put some distance between us, but I didn't know if we'd managed to throw our pursuers off our tracks. My eyes were fixed on the ground most of the time, trying to avoid tree roots and anything else that might cause me to trip or break a leg.

Chou stopped suddenly, and Freuchen and I pulled up alongside her, my hands resting on my knees as I tried to catch my breath.

Ahead was a large clearing easily as big as the area the *Brimstone* had landed in. Very little lived here; what few trees left were either nothing more than broken trunks or blackened and dead. Younger trees had sprouted up, but they were sickly, wilted.

But that wasn't what had made Chou stop.

It was the enormous rusted and broken robot that lay just ahead of us. I could see more huge, vague shapes through the mist-like rain, scattered around the clearing.

"What happened here?" Freuchen whispered, his voice low out of either respect or fear.

Perhaps it was Edward's recent influence on me, rekindling my old love of poetry and the sense of melancholy which inevitably came with it, but when we passed the first metal behemoth, its rusted verdigris-covered skin hidden behind decades of growth of moss and vines and thicket, I was struck with the most profound sense of abandonment.

This first rusted hulk stood thirty feet tall, with a squat box-like body sitting on two articulated tree-trunk-thick legs. Two equally large arms hung from either side of the body, one with a claw-like hand, the other with some kind of corkscrew tool that could have been used for mining, perhaps. That may have been the original intention of those tools, but not how they'd last been used—judging by the hundreds of broken and dismembered parts of other machines that lay scattered all around it. This machine had done a lot of damage before it, too, had finally succumbed to whatever madness had overtaken it.

"There's another over here," said Freuchen, pulling at a clot of thick brown vines that had grown over another relic.

"And over here," I said, parting a sickly bush to expose the back of yet another mechanoid lying face down in the forest's detritus.

"There are more there," Chou said, pointing to a group of three machines frozen in a violent embrace.

"It's almost as if they ver in some kind of a battle," Freuchen said.

I guess Howard Carter must have felt the same range of emotions when he broke the seal on Tutankhamen's tomb and felt the dead breath of three-thousand-year-old air exhaled from within. This place held a power in the frozen metal statues hidden behind the vegetation that had grown around it. It was a glimpse into some distant cataclysm, and this robot graveyard still held a deep resonating power.

"Listen!" Chou said, throwing up a hand. "They've found us." From somewhere in the jungle behind us, I heard the voices of our pursuers drawing closer.

"Damn it!" Freuchen said.

Wordlessly, Chou took off again, and Freuchen and I ran behind. We passed by more and more machines. Some were little more than rusted metal skeletons, decayed beyond ever being recognizable, others had fared a little better. But it was evident that the fifty-or-so machines we found in that short time were only part of a much more extensive collection of dead robots. And they had been there for a very, very long time. Perhaps longer even than Silas had been trapped beneath the rockfall at the tower back on Avalon before we had found him.

We ran between the machines, looking for somewhere to hide.

"There!" said Freuchen, pointing at a massive machine with

thirty-plus articulated legs. It lay on its side and looked like its design had been based on some kind of beetle.

We ran toward it, and that was when I spotted something even stranger. Across from the giant mechanical beetle, floating several feet off the ground was a giant ball of what looked like oil. It was perfectly spherical, opaque, but a translucent outer skin gave it a wet sheen that partially reflected its surroundings. I felt a shiver of unease rattle down my spine. Staring at it, I couldn't help but feel like it *knew* we were there, like it saw us. We weren't even close to it, but I felt something gathering around it, an invisible energy, dense and electric. I shook off the feeling of unease and managed to splutter, "What on Earth is *that*?"

Both Chou and Freuchen stopped momentarily and looked to where I pointed. The ground directly beneath the levitating sphere, and for twice its circumference beyond it was dead, leaving nothing but mud that looked as black as the sphere itself. Not a single thing grew within that semi-circle.

"Is it... rotating?" Freuchen asked, leaning toward it as if he might see through the sheets of rain that still fell.

"I think so," I said.

Chou looked back the way we'd come. "They are coming," she hissed. "We must hide."

We sprinted to the back of the huge beetle-like machine. Its legs seemed to be pointing toward the weird rotating sphere as if in warning. The main body of the juggernaut was now nothing but a mass of torn and jagged shards of metal that faced outward as though something had exploded deep within it. Or some*thing* had opened it up like a rusty-can, judging by the mass of broken wiring, gears, and other unidentifiable stuff that hung from the hole like spilled guts.

"Inside," Chou said, parting a curtain of vines and pointing to the cavity within. We climbed in, carefully avoiding the sharp edges and pointy bits. Chou followed us in then let the vines slide back into place, obscuring us completely.

Inside the dead machine, it smelled like cut grass and motor oil. The outer shell was sliced and torn in multiple places, but the wounds were small enough that no one outside would be able to see us huddled together in the darkness, but they were also big enough that if we stood close to them, we had a pretty good view of the area.

"What *is* that thing?" I whispered to Chou, as I stared at the slowly rotating ball of blackness. Chou's reply was to lightly touch my arm and with a subtle nod, direct my attention toward the path we'd taken through the robot graveyard.

Five men walked cautiously into view, and I felt my anger rise when I recognized Tommy Two-Thumbs amongst them. The men were dressed in shiny yellow rain slickers that covered their uniforms. They didn't look happy. One of the men stopped suddenly and pointed in the direction of the black orb. The rest of the group came to an abrupt stop alongside him. A full minute passed as they talked amongst themselves, obviously debating what they should do next. Then Abernathy started toward the slowly rotating orb. One of the men—a big muscular guy, who stood a full six inches above the rest—stepped forward, obviously trying to dissuade Two-Thumbs. But Two-Thumbs just waved him off and continued to cautiously advance through the mud. As Abernathy got closer to the orb, I saw a ripple, like a wave, pass over the ink-black surface.

"Is he mad?" Freuchen whispered.

Yes, I wanted to say, *yes, he is.*

Two-Thumbs stood less than ten feet away from the orb. He turned to look back at the other men, nervously shuffling their feet in the pouring rain. He gestured for them to join him.

This time I clearly saw the ripple pass over the orb's skin. Two-Thumbs, his back to it, saw nothing and continued to angrily gesture at the men to join him. Reluctantly, they began to edge closer.

A third wave, this one tsunami-like compared to the first two, washed over the orb's surface. Then another and another. The advancing men saw it and stopped in their tracks, but Two-Thumbs still had his back to the orb. He yelled something at them I couldn't hear. The big man yelled something back and pointed at the orb. Two-Thumbs slowly turned. The orb's surface was a mass of movement now, wave after wave pulsing across its oily surface.

Two-Thumbs took a single step away from the orb... and froze as a shiny black tendril extruded from its surface and snaked through the air toward him. His face was frozen in a mask of shock as the tendril moved first from one side of him then to the other, as though it were drug dog sniffing him. Then, it drew back and with a whip-like crack, flew at Two-Thumbs. He tried to dodge out of its way, but he was simply too slow. The black tendril struck him on the right side of his abdomen, attaching to it like some kind of glue.

"Oh my God," I stuttered, throwing a hand to my mouth.

Two-Thumbs staggered backward, then stopped as the tendril drew taut. His back arched to the point I thought he might snap in two, while his mouth hung open in a silent scream of agony. I gave an involuntary jump when both of his arms flew out on either side of him as though he were being crucified. Then, his whole body convulsed as wave after wave passed over the surface of the orb and down through the tendril.

Three more snake-like tendrils flashed through the air and attached themselves to Abernathy.

"Look!" Freuchen hissed. "It's getting smaller."

Freuchen was right. The orb was rapidly shrinking with each passing second, like a deflating balloon. It had started out about the size of a large wide-screen TV but was quickly becoming smaller and smaller.

"It's transferring itself to him," I said, realizing with horror what was happening and unable to keep the disgust out of my voice. But I was right; the black orb was oozing over Abernathy's body. Several new tentacles had extended from the larger mass covering Abernathy's abdomen. They slithered up his chest and oozed their way into his open mouth, his Adam's apple pulsing as they forced their way inside him.

It was a vomit-inducing sight. I hated this man and would never mourn his death for a second, but this was excruciating to watch.

The orb, still suspended above the ground by some unseen force was now the size of a tennis ball and continued to shrink by the second, until finally, only the tendrils hung in the air. A second later, they too slipped themselves around Two-Thumbs' face and merged with the rest of the mass, expanding across his paralyzed body. He remained in the same rigid crucified pose for several excruciating breaths, the black oil moving over his skin. Then, he crumpled to the ground with a splash of water and mud and lay still.

Steam or smoke, I couldn't tell which, rose slowly from Two-Thumbs' body. I was sure he was dead. Whatever that orb was, whatever it had done to him, it had surely killed him.

Throughout all of this horror, the four men who had accompanied Abernathy had remained rooted to the spot. Now the big guy mustered the three others, and slowly, ever so slowly, they took one tentative step after the other toward Two-Thumbs. The big man leaned over his body then gave a quick step backward when he saw the covering of black oil-like substance that coated his torso. He took a deep breath, moved to Two-Thumbs' legs, and picked up one of his feet. He yelled something to the other men, but they remained where they were, regarding each other with wide, frightened gazes. It was obvious none of them wanted to touch Two-Thumbs and risk contact with the black oil. The big guy dropped Two-Thumbs' feet, reached into his rain-slicker, and pulled out a pistol, which he pointed at the three men. There were a few moments of heated discussion between them all as the big man moved the gun to each of them, one after the other. His threat was clear: help him pick up Two-Thumbs, or he would shoot them on the spot. His companions must have been convinced he would carry out the threat because they immediately—but reluctantly—bent and hefted Two-Thumbs.

"He must be dead," I said to Chou as I watched them carry his limp body toward the *Brimstone*. "Right?"

"Perhaps," Chou answered.

"You think he's still alive?" I said, disbelievingly.

Chou nodded.

I let that sink in.

Freuchen, ever the optimist, said, "Vell, at least that's vun of them ve do not have to vurry about. I vould have liked to have dealt vith him myself but..." He shrugged and allowed his words to taper off.

I started to part the curtain of vines, but Chou stopped me.

"I think it might be a good idea to rest here for a little while. It's dry and relatively comfortable, and I don't think they'll be sending a search party back here. Not after what just happened."

"Thank God." I sat down, feeling some of the tightness leave my tense shoulders. Freuchen eased himself down next to me while Chou remained standing at one of the slits, watchful as ever.

A minute passed, then I looked up at Chou and said, "How did you get onboard the *Brimstone*?"

She answered without looking at me. "When we heard the

gunfire, Silas, Albert, and I made our way to the outskirts of the village. We saw the marauders attacking and that you had been captured and were being dragged to the airship. We hid Albert, then Silas and I ran to try to help you. When they fired on us with the heavy weapon, I became separated from Silas. Still, I managed to sneak close enough to the airship to use an emergency access port and gain entry just as it took off. I hid until the ship quieted then began to try to locate you while avoiding the crew. I did not realize that Freuchen had also been captured until I observed him being dragged to the room where you were being interrogated."

"What?" I said, loudly. "You knew Freuchen was being tortured?"

Chou looked down at me. "Please, keep your voice low. We do not know if there are any other search parties close by. Her head turned back to surveilling the world beyond our metal sanctuary and continued. "There was nothing I could do to help him. If I had revealed my presence, I *might* have managed to free you, but it was unlikely I could have overwhelmed the entire crew—not with the number of weapons they had and the tight quarters. And at that point, Freuchen was in no condition to help me."

"So, you let Two-Thumbs take Freuchen's thumb?" I said, a little flabbergasted.

Freuchen placed a reassuring hand on my arm and laughed gently. "I do not blame her, Meredith. It vas the right thing to do."

Chou turned again to look at me, the displeasure in my voice finally getting her full attention. "I had no doubt it would grow back," she said. "The alternative would have meant all three of us either being captured or losing our lives."

I huffed. Chou was right, of course. Still, I couldn't help but feel a little betrayed on Freuchen's behalf.

Freuchen gave my arm a squeeze and said, "You know, that airship vould make our journey to the collector much faster and more comfortable."

I did a double-take. "What?"

Freuchen slowly nodded. "If ve could gain command of it, ve could travel a hundred miles or more a day, rather than the veeks it takes us now."

"We'd have to be crazy to try and get back on board the *Brimstone*. They'd kill us in a heartbeat," I said. I looked up at Chou for support.

"Peter is correct," she said. "It *would* cut our travel time down substantially."

"Oh, come on," I said. "Even if by some miracle we managed to take control of it, no one here knows how to pilot an airship."

Chou raised her eyes to mine and smiled. "In the event my husband was incapacitated, I was trained extensively in how to pilot my vessel, the *Shining Way*. I do not believe it would be too difficult for me to master the controls of the *Brimstone*."

"The problem vill be how do ve convince the Red Baroness and her crew to give up control of it?"

I was beginning to get the feeling they were serious about all this. I exhaled a long breath. "Maybe we could kidnap the captain. Hold her hostage until the crew surrenders?"

Freuchen shook his head. "I traveled vith enough sailors ven I hunted vales to know that ve cannot trust them any further than I could throw them. Their loyalty to their captain vould extend only as far as it vas in their best interest."

"What do you mean?" I asked.

Freuchen looked at me and said, "I believe there are several individuals who vould seize the opportunity to take control of the *Brimstone* by killing us *and* any hostage ve might take, including the captain. Her type rule by fear. Remove that fear and vat do they have to lose?"

"I concur," Chou said. "The *Brimstone's* crew appears to be held together more by dread than by loyalty. We will have to find another route."

A silence of several seconds followed.

Chou said, "I have a plan that I believe will work."

Freuchen scooted closer.

"The *Brimstone* achieves its lift by using solar cells on its outer skin to generate energy. That energy is stored in fuel cells that power the ship, but they are also used to extract hydrogen from water, which gives the *Brimstone* an inexhaustible amount of fuel. Theoretically, it could stay aloft forever. The hydrogen is stored in bladders within the main balloon. I caused a distraction by making a small slit in several of those bladders that would allow enough hydrogen to escape out over time to trigger one of their leak alarms."

"Wait a second. Isn't hydrogen really dangerous?" I said, remembering a grainy black-and-white video I'd seen on *Youtube* of an airship crashing to Earth in flames.

Oh, the humanity, I thought, or at least what was left of it.

"You are correct, Meredith. It is very flammable. But the *Brimstone* has many safety features to ensure that if there is a hydrogen leak, it will be quickly identified and sealed by the crew. But there is another quality hydrogen gas possesses that I believe we can use to our advantage." She paused dramatically. "If enough is released into the main gondola, it will displace the oxygen and incapacitate everyone in several minutes. I have calculated that emptying one bladder into the crew's quarters will be more than sufficient to render them... ineffective."

I just stared at her.

"So, let me get this straight," I said eventually, "you want us to somehow sneak on board the *Brimstone*, avoid the guards, release a gas that is not only going to knock everyone out but could also, quite literally blow up in our faces."

"As I said, the *Brimstone* has numerous safety features such as non-static surfaces that will greatly decrease the chance of ignition when the gas is released."

I looked to Freuchen, who had remained suspiciously quiet through this whole crazy conversation. He just raised his caterpillar-eyebrows as if to say, *Who am I to argue with her.*

"But there's only three of us, and at least fifteen of them." I continued, desperately looking for a way to convince my friends that this was an insanely bad idea. "*And* they have guns. Oh, and did I mention there's only three of us! We can't just walk onto the *Brimstone* and hijack it. And you two aren't exactly going to blend in with the crowd." I ran my eyes up Chou's six-foot frame and Freuchen's bear-sized bulk. "They'll spot you from a mile away."

"Meredith is correct," Freuchen said, finally chiming in.

"Thank you!" I hissed, feeling like sanity might actually be restored to the world.

"But..." he continued.

"Oh, great," I sighed.

"But *you*..." Freuchen allowed his words to hang in the air for a moment. "You vould be able to blend in successfully. The search party is looking for three people dressed exactly like us. They vill not be looking for one of their own."

Chou nodded in agreement, but I didn't follow what Freuchen meant and said so.

"Ve will have to obtain vun of their uniforms for you."

"How are we supposed to do that?"

Chou said, "I will identify a suitable candidate of your approximate size, then we will have to isolate him and relieve him of his clothes."

"You mean kill them?" I said.

Chou nodded.

"Ve do not have the luxury of taking prisoners," Freuchen added. "Ve cannot risk them escaping and alerting the rest of the crew."

The rain was coming down heavily again, big drops hammering against our hideaway's metal skin, the constant thrum blocking out all other sounds.

"Vat's the matter?" said Freuchen, sensing my hesitation. "It's okay to be afraid, but you vill be fine."

"No, I'm not afraid... well, yeah, of course, I'm afraid. I'm going to have to lie my way aboard an airship where everyone wants to capture me. But it's not that, it's—"

"What?" said Chou.

"I made a promise."

"A promise?" Freuchen said. "To who?"

"To me. And Silas, and, I guess to everyone. I promised that I would try to be more like the version of humanity the Architect expected us to be. It brought us here because of our potential to be something better than we were, not to repeat the same mistakes of our past. And that means doing my best to find a way to avoid hurting anyone, and definitely not killing anyone."

Chou regarded me with cool eyes for a very long moment, sighed deeply, then said, "There will be no room for error on your part. The effects of the gas will render the crew unconscious within three to four minutes. If we can remove all the personnel from the *Brimstone* within another *five* minutes of them falling unconscious, I believe the majority, if not all will survive. At worst, they may suffer some brain damage, but I expect the aurora will take care of that."

"Ve vill need to restrain them," Freuchen said.

Chou nodded. "There are four nylon mooring lines keeping the *Brimstone* anchored. When you are sure that the crew is incapacitated, cut one of them, and we will use the line to secure the crew. The remaining three lines and the loss of buoyancy should ensure that the airship remains stable on the ground."

I thought about it. They were right, we had no idea how far we were from New Manhattan. It might take us weeks to make our way back there on foot, and there was no guarantee we would even find the place again. We could walk right past it. We had none of our supplies, other than what was in our backpacks, having left everything of real value back with Silas and Albert. And if we could, by some miracle, steal the *Brimstone* out from under their noses, it would make our journey much easier.

"Okay," I said. "I'll do it."

"That's the spirit!" Freuchen exclaimed, patting me gently on the back.

Chou parted the vines, checked the coast was clear, then ushered Freuchen and me out into the rain again.

ELEVEN

CHOU LED us out of the robot graveyard back along the path we'd taken when we fled the *Brimstone*. I wouldn't have had any idea where we were or how we had gotten there, but Chou unhesitatingly maneuvered us through the trees, stopping every now and then to look and listen for any signs of the search parties we were sure were still out looking for us.

A few minutes later, she stopped suddenly then slowly dropped to her knees. Freuchen and I did the same, huddling close to her. We waited silently for over a minute, the rain smacking and popping all around us.

"What is it?" I whispered.

Chou threw a finger to her lips, then whispered back, "Listen."

I strained to hear over the thud of the rain.

"I don't hear any—"

The unmistakable crackle of radio static followed by a muffled voice filtered through the trees ahead of us.

Freuchen tensed.

I began to say we should hide, but Chou reached out a hand

and covered my mouth. She nodded to a thicket of bushes between a tightly packed group of trees.

Two figures—a woman and a man—emerged from behind the bushes. Both wore *Brimstone* uniforms: gray jackets and pants, and gray baseball caps. They were facing away from us, but I instinctively pushed myself closer to the tree trunk we were sheltering under.

The man held a walkie-talkie in his left hand, an ax tucked into his belt. The woman had a large knife attached to her belt. The man pressed the walkie-talkie to his mouth and said, in what sounded like French-accented English, "Charlie-party responding; no sign of the missing prisoners."

"*Roger Charlie-party. The captain says take another thirty minutes, then head back here before it gets dark. Copy?*"

"Copy," the man said. He clipped the walkie-talkie back onto his belt. It continued to chatter as the radio operator back on the airship reached out to other search parties. They began walking in a diagonal path that would bring them close to where we hid.

The woman said, "I'm going to die of pneumonia before we find them in this rain. What a waste of time. I'm soaked to the skin."

The man replied, "Which would you prefer: dying of pneumonia or going back, empty-handed?"

The woman grunted. "I suppose you're right, but we weren't the ones who allowed them to escape in—"

Chou leaped from our hiding spot. She hit the man in the side of the temple with her elbow and sent him sprawling to the ground, unconscious already judging by the way he collapsed face-first without trying to break his fall. The woman had time to turn in surprise, giving me a moment to see she was about my age, her green eyes wide in astonishment before Chou threw an arm around her throat and proceeded to choke the life out of her. When it was over, Chou allowed the woman's body to fall to the ground then turned her attention to the unconscious man. Before I could object, she dispatched him with a brutal twist of his head. I jerked when I heard the crack of his neck breaking.

Chou stood, looked at the body of the dead woman, then at me. "She is about your size."

A white name tag was stitched onto the left breast of the woman's jacket. "Miller," I said, reading it while trying to avoid the woman's reproachful dead eyes. The man's name was Dupuis.

"Help me get her out of her clothes," Chou said, unbowed as far as I could see by any kind of regret or sentiment. We quickly stripped Miller down to her underwear. I swapped my soaking wet clothes for hers while Freuchen, his back to me, made an exaggerated scene of relieving the dead man of anything he found useful. Chou dragged Miller's body back into the underbrush we'd hidden in and covered her with some fallen leaves, then Freuchen did the same.

Chou stepped back and eyeballed me. "A good fit," she said.

She was right; the pants were a little too long in the leg and a little too big around the waist, but otherwise, it was a passable fit. I fastened the belt around my waist, pulling it tight. Then I picked up the man's baseball cap from where it had fallen, pulled my hair up into a bun, and slipped the bill down as far as I could to try and hide my face. Chou tucked in a few stray strands of hair, then bent over and scraped away a layer of leaves to reveal the soaked earth. She scooped up a large handful of mud and began to smear my new clothes with it.

"What the hell?" I said.

Chou talked while she continued to pick up more mud. "When you get to the *Brimstone*, if anyone asks, tell them you slipped down a hill and got separated from your partner." She spread a handful of mud across my face, then applied a final streak across Miller's name tag, hiding most of it.

"There," she said, taking a step back to admire her handiwork. "Done."

Freuchen stood with his hands on his hips, nodding appreciably at Chou's camouflage skill. "I vould never know it vas you, Meredith," he said, chuckling quietly.

"You should head back to the *Brimstone* now," said Chou, "while most of the crew are still looking for us and before the rain washes the mud off you." She told me where I would find the access hatch that would take me up into the balloon of the *Brimstone*. Made me repeat the directions back to her, just to be sure.

"What about you two?" I asked. "Where will you be."

"Don't vurry about us," Freuchen said. He pulled the radio I'd seen Dupuis use earlier from his belt. "Ve'll be nearby and listening on the radio. Vhen you're done, come to the starboard exit and flash this three times."

He handed me a flashlight he had taken from Dupuis. I took it from him and clipped it to my belt next to Miller's confiscated knife.

"Don't forget, try to avoid contact with the crew as much as possible," Chou said. "Get up into the balloon and hide. Wait until you are confident everyone is asleep, then use the release valve on the bladder nearest the hatch. Do not forget to put your emergency oxygen mask on *before* you start."

I nodded that I understood.

In the ten minutes or so between stumbling across the two crewmembers and now, darkness had begun to descend over the forest. To my right, through the trees, I saw a row of lights that roughly matched the *Brimstone's* portholes.

"Wish me luck," I said to my two friends, then turned and made my way through the trees and underbrush toward the lights of the *Brimstone*.

TWELVE

GUARDS ARMED with machine guns were positioned at each of the two entrances to the *Brimstone*. I held my breath as I trudged across the uneven ground from the forest into the clearing, trying my best to look like I belonged. Suddenly, the beam of a flashlight illuminated me, and I almost froze. Instead, I forced myself to keep moving, raising a hand in greeting.

"You're gonna break a leg if you're not careful," one of the men called out, while he illuminated the path ahead of me.

I was about thirty feet away when the second guard yelled, "What the hell happened to you?"

I shrugged and mumbled, "Slipped on the way back." I hung my head as if in shame, trying not to let them get a good look at my face.

"Well, getcha self inside and cleaned up. Cook's got hot food waiting in the galley. And don't let the Cap'n see you like that; she's as pissed off as I've ever known her, and she'll have your guts for garters if she catches you in that state."

I nodded my thanks and climbed up into the *Brimstone's* gondola, pausing to listen for a second. The sound of voices from upstairs filtered down, but the corridor leading to the stern of the airship was deserted. The portholes were all open, which Chou had told me I would have had to open myself to allow the airship's air-conditioning to pull the hydrogen throughout the vessel and force the air out of the *Brimstone*. Otherwise, the gas would simply sit in the balloon. That was one less thing to worry about, at least.

I followed the corridor to the stern of the airship. Chou had explained that there was an access ladder I could use to get up into the *Brimstone's* balloon. I found it exactly where she had told me it would be, and I had my foot on the first rung when I looked behind me.

"Shit!" I hissed under my breath. A line of muddy footprints followed me. Anyone who saw them would know exactly where I'd gone and might start wondering why one of their own had come in from the search and immediately taken the ladder. I had no way to clean up my tracks, so instead of using the ladder, I followed the corridor another ten feet past it around another corner and stopped outside a door. I put my hand against the wall to steady myself and slipped first my right shoe off, then my left. I knotted the laces together and slung them around my neck, so they hung down on my chest, then I retraced my steps back to the ladder, checked that the corridor was still clear, and began to climb. At the top of the ladder, I eased the trapdoor open an inch and looked cautiously through the gap. There didn't appear to be anyone up there, so I pushed the trapdoor all the way and climbed up and out onto a narrow gantry, slowly lowering the trapdoor behind me. I quickly undid my shoes from around my neck and slipped them on again. The gantry was fastened to huge ribs that made up the superstructure of the *Brimstone's* balloon. The ribs were made of the same material as the gantry, some kind of hardened plastic-like material rather than metal, which reduced the ship's weight and the chance of a static discharge, which could, in the event of a leak, cause an explosion. Standing here almost at the aft-section of the balloon and looking forward, it was like I was standing in the belly of a mechanical whale. The gantry extended along the whole length of the airship's balloon, curving around the front and then coming back again on the opposite side. It encircled four huge bladders that reminded me of the Mylar balloons you could pick up at the store. The bladders took up almost the entirety of the space inside the outer skin of the *Brimstone's* balloon. At four points, the gantry crossed between each bladder, connecting with the opposite side. Reached by two ladders, a second gantry ran around the top section of the balloon, allowing the airship's personnel full access to the bladders from top to bottom. Along the bottom gantry, at the mid-point of each bladder, was a small recessed area. Each recess had a raised console and a flat computer screen that intermittently displayed large numbers and graphs. Below each computer screen was a control panel with a selection of knobs, switches, and dials, which I assumed were used to monitor the gas in the bladders.

Chou had told me that I needed to find an emergency respirator that she was certain would be up here somewhere. If I released the hydrogen without wearing one, it would take just a couple of minutes to render me unconscious, and a few more minutes before it killed me. I walked along the lower gantry but found no sign of anything resembling a respirator. Frustrated, I headed back toward the main ladder and found four of them hanging from hooks in a slight recess just at the top of the ladder. I'd missed them because I'd had my back to them when I climbed up from the gondola. Above the four respirators was a large plastic box. Inside were several cellophane-covered packs of the same material the bladders were made from folded into neat packages with the words EMERGENCY PATCH stenciled across each package. There were also tubes of what I presumed must be glue used to fasten the patches to the bladders in the event of a leak. I took three of the respirators from their hooks and laid them next to the hatch—one for each of us.

Chou had told me where to find the leak sensors, and I quickly tracked them down and did as she'd told me to do. The sensors relied on a gas-permeable membrane to detect any hydrogen leaks, not particularly advanced. Chou had explained they could be fooled simply by covering the membrane with a sock, of which Freuchen and the two dead crew members had supplied enough to do the job. I fished the socks from my pockets and worked my way to each of the eight sensors, then disabled them.

Now, all I had to do was wait for everyone to come back to the ship.

———

I waited next to the hatch, listening impatiently as the next forty-five minutes seemed to drag into an eternity. The men and women who'd been searching for us returned to the *Brimstone,* wet, bedraggled, and disillusioned—judging by the snippets of unhappy conversation I heard from those passing beneath my hiding place. Then gradually, the hustle and bustle began to fade away as the crew, exhausted from their fruitless efforts to recapture us, made their way first to the ship's commissary for their dinner, then after several hours had passed, to their bunks.

I gave it another thirty minutes after the ship went silent before I lifted the hatch enough to see down into the corridor. The interior lights had all been dimmed, and I slowly eased the hatch up... then froze as a shape, his shoes almost silent against the anti-static flooring, stepped around the corridor, and made his way toward the ladder.

It was Jean-Pierre, the man who'd initially captured me. I froze. If I closed the hatch now, he would almost certainly sense it. Still, if I remained here with it open six inches and he looked up or, even worse, if he decided to climb up the ladder, it would be game over. He walked casually, a rifle slung over his shoulder. It must be his turn for sentry duty—something we'd not anticipated. He strolled up to the bottom rung of the ladder and placed a boot on it.

I held my breath. *Don't look up! Don't look up!* My mind raced to come up with some kind of a plan to get out of this. I was still covered in dried mud from head to foot; Maybe he wouldn't recognize me. But then how was I supposed to explain why I was up here when everyone else had showered and headed to bed?

But instead of climbing the ladder, Jean-Pierre leaned his rifle against the wall and proceeded to tie a bootlace that had come undone. When he was done, he arched his back, cracked his neck, then stifled a loud yawn before picking up his weapon and continuing on his way.

I exhaled.

This was a new problem. If all this guy did was wander the hallways of the *Brimstone*, then he would be passing under this same spot every few minutes or so. The hatch was going to have to be wide open for the *Brimstone's* AC units to pull the hydrogen down into the gondola. If he wasn't exposed to the gas for long enough, he might be able to sound the alarm. Or worse, he might decide to take a shot at me and ignite the gas, and that would be it for all of us. I was going to have to delay and see how long it would take him to pass under the hatch again. I lowered the lid down, so only a sliver of light made it through, enough so I could see into the corridor, then started counting off the seconds in my head. I'd almost reached three minutes when Jean-Pierre's shadow approached.

Was that going to be enough time? I didn't know. But I couldn't wait any longer. It was now or never. I started the count again as I slowly lifted the lid of the hatch, then picked up one of the emergency respirators and slipped it over my head. Instantly, the plastic eyepieces began to fog, limiting my vision. Nothing I could do about it now.

I moved to the first bladder. A tightly rolled ribbed-pipe that reminded me of air-conditioning ducting was coiled neatly around a spindle fixed to the recessed gantry. The pipe had a clamp of some kind at the end that matched a similarly shaped receiver attached to the skin of the balloon. The other end was connected to the bladder. I quickly unfurled the pipe and ran it over to the opening, threading a couple of feet of it down through the ladder's rungs. I ran back to the bladder and tried to turn the large red knob of the bleed-valve.

It wouldn't budge.

"Shit! Shit! Shit!" I mumbled under my breath, the words dulled by my respirator like I was at the bottom of the ocean.

I grabbed the knob with both hands and heaved with all the strength I could. It moved a little, then finally, with a creak that I was convinced was loud enough to wake the entire crew, spun smoothly in my hands. I kept turning until it would move no more.

I ran back to the opening, realizing as I did so that I had completely lost count of time in my head. According to Chou, hydrogen is odorless and colorless, but I thought I sensed a subtle movement of the air around me as the bladder gradually deflated, but that could have been my imagination for all I knew.

A minute passed.

By now, the hydrogen should be making its way through the ship. In theory, it would force the oxygen out through the open portholes and, if Chou actually knew what she was talking about, render the crew unconscious in under four minutes.

Hopefully faster, if I was to escape being discovered by Jean-Pierre.

Time passed even more slowly as I sat crouched by the opening. I jumped suddenly when I heard someone in the corridor singing at the top of their lungs. They sounded drunk.

"Six hellish months have passed away, on the cold Kamchatka Sea. But now we're bound from the Arctic ground, rolling down to Old Maui." It was followed by a childish high-pitched giggle, then laughter, and then by another badly-out-of-tune line of what must be a shanty. This time it sounded like Alvin and the Chipmunks; the voice was so high-pitched.

Jean-Pierre staggered around the corner. He was barely able to stand, reeling from one side of the corridor to the other, his head lolling back and forth while he mumbled the chorus of the shanty to himself. He bounced off one wall, then the other, then lurched forward until he grabbed hold of a rung of the ladder. He looked straight up into the hatch where I was hidden, staring down at him. For a moment, he seemed to sober up enough that I could almost hear the cogs whirring in his head as his addled mind processed what he was looking at.

"Hey!" he shouted, "you're not supposed to be up there." His words were slurred, like a drunk's. "And why... why... why are you wearing a mask? It's not Halloween." He blinked three times in a row. Then he unslung his rifle and pointed it at me. "Take it off."

I felt every molecule in my body suddenly stop as I became stone. If he pulled that trigger, the *Brimstone* would be turned into a huge fireball, and everyone on board would burn with it. I remembered the video I'd seen of the *Hindenburg* as it burned and fell to the earth; people running, scattering as they tried to escape the fiery ball of death dropping from the sky. I did not want to die like that. It left me with no choice. I sucked in one last gulp of air, then slipped the mask off my face.

Jean-Pierre gave me an exaggerated stare. "I don't recognize you," he mumbled. "What are you doing up there." His words were melding into one long, slurred sentence now.

If I said something, I'd have to exhale the breath I'd just taken. I smiled down at him instead.

Jean-Pierre shoved the barrel of the rifle up at me, his finger caressing the trigger.

Well, shit! I let out the air and said, "I was just checking the... ummm..." It wasn't going to be long before the gas did its thing to Jean-Pierre, but I could already feel the gas working on me. I was becoming lightheaded. Jean-Pierre's face seemed to grow bigger, then smaller. My tongue felt ridiculously large in my mouth.

Jean-Pierre swayed, blinked a couple of times. "Get down here. I need to wake the Baroness," he said, the barrel of the rifle just inches from my face now.

"No. No need to wake her. I... I'm here because..." I tried to think of anything, something, but my brain was already too cloudy to come up with an excuse even remotely believable. In a final gasp of desperation, I started to sing the first song that came to mind.

"I've been drinking, I've been thinking." I gulped as I tried to force the rest of the words of Beyoncé's *Drunk in Love* past my rapidly numbing lips. "Why can't I keep my fingers off you, baby? I want you, na na." My voice sounded like it was an octave louder than usual, and I tried to resist the urge to giggle. I knew inhaling helium made your voice sound weird, but I hadn't realized hydrogen would have the same effect. Thanks for the warning Chou!

Jean-Pierre stared wide-eyed at me, then broke out in a smile. "You sound like an angel," he squeaked.

I found myself smiling back at him. "Thank you," I said and sang the lines over again, slower this time. My head was swimming like I'd downed half a bottle of cheap Chardonnay. The gas was beginning to really take hold of me. If I kept my mask off much longer, I was going to be too far gone to care what happened next.

Jean-Pierre stumbled to the base of the ladder. "I... think... you..." He stopped talking, blinked several times at me, then collapsed, his rifle slipping from his hands and clattering to the floor. I closed my eyes and waited for the fireball I knew was surely going to sweep over me... but nothing happened. When I opened my eyes again, he lay face down on the floor, unconscious.

I fumbled the mask back over my face and cinched the straps tightly, breathing in long deep breaths, and rolled onto my back, staring up at the top of the balloon. A minute passed, then my head began to clear, but a residual headache throbbed behind both of my eyes.

"Come on, get up. Lives are at stake," I said to myself. I staggered to my feet and, still wobbly, climbed down the ladder. A quick glance at Jean-Pierre told me he was still breathing. I crouched next to him for a few seconds, listening for anything that sounded out of the ordinary, but the entire ship was silent. We'd made enough sound that someone would surely have heard and come to check, which meant, fingers-crossed, that everyone else was out too.

Quickly, I jogged to the door, flung it open, pulled the flashlight Freuchen had given me from my pocket and flashed it three times toward the woods. Almost instantly, I saw the beam of another flashlight cut through the darkness. I jumped down onto the sodden grass, dropped Chou and Freuchen's emergency respirators, and ran toward the nearest mooring line.

There were four in total. I was going to have to cut one and then slice that into smaller segments to use it to tie up the *Brimstone's* unconscious crew. Chou had assured me that the remaining three lines would be more than enough to keep the airship on the ground, especially after I'd let the hydrogen out of one of the bladders.

I quickly found the mooring line and sliced it from the peg it was tied to, then rolled the line up as far as it went back to the gondola and sliced it again. Throwing the rope over a shoulder, I sprinted back to the *Brimstone*, aware that time was not on my side if I wanted to save the crew.

According to Chou, prolonged exposure to the hydrogen would eventually cause permanent brain damage, seizures, and finally, death. But since we'd landed on this other world, those rules had changed, and every injury other than full-on death could, apparently, be reversed by the aurora.

I climbed aboard again and cut as many two-foot-long pieces I could from it. I'd reached five when I heard the door at the end of the corridor click closed and the sound of someone moving toward me.

"Welcome aboard," I said, turning to look back over my shoulder to where I knew Chou and Freuchen would be.

Instead, I froze in horror at the sight of Thomas Abernathy standing midway between me and the door. Or more accurately, what had once been Thomas Abernathy, because this warped and twisted *thing* was no longer a man.

Whatever the orb had been, it was now a part of Abernathy. In the time between our little group watching from the hulk of the dead robot while the orb seized him and now, terrible changes had been inflicted on Thomas Abernathy. What was left of his clothing hung in tatters from his malformed body, exposing almost every part of him. From his midriff to his left shoulder and down his left arm was coated in the same oily substance as the orb. It clung tightly to his skin, almost like it was made of rubber, but it was moving too, shifting along the edges, slowly but inexorably spreading over what remained of his body, transforming him from a man into something... else. Something that, to me, seemed more machine than human.

It was Abernathy's face that kept me pinned to the spot in horror. It was a mass of scars run through with thin black veins. His nose was a misshapen globule, more like a dog's snout than a human nose. His head, almost completely hairless with only a few wispy tufts left here and there. He glanced back over his shoulder, and I saw that the three raised, bony protrusions that pushed up from beneath the skin of his forehead ran back over his mottled skull and appeared fused to his spine just beneath the nape of his neck.

Our eyes met again.

Only a small part of his upper lip still remained. The rest was just two thin lines, like the mouth of a fish. And when he parted those lips, I saw two rows of pointed teeth where his own should have been. His eyes were sunken pits with a black copy of the orb that had performed these perverted alterations to him in each socket. Within each of those orbs, blue rings of light burned like St. Elmo's fire where irises should be.

"Whash haff... haffening true me?" he slurred from between the thin lines of his lips.

"I... I don't know," I said. I took one tentative step backward.

Abernathy shuffled toward me. His left leg and half of his right were coated in the same midnight-black oil. I stared hard, unable to shake the terrible fascination I felt as it shifted and moved over him, expanding inch by inch across what was left of his human skin.

"You did thish too meeee," he mumbled, burning with inhuman hatred.

I took another step back toward the ladder that lead up into the balloon.

"No," I spat at him. "You brought this on yourself."

The oil spread across the last human parts of Abernathy's

face, completing its work on his lips. With the transmogrification now complete, his slurred voice became almost human again.

"You should have just given us what it wants," Abernathy said. His voice carried an electronic resonance to it now, as though it was being synthesized rather than spoken by a human.

"What?" I said, honestly confused. "Given who what it wants?"

Abernathy took another step toward me. "What was it your people on Avalon called him... the Adversary? Yes, the Adversary. You should just have given the Adversary what it wanted."

I felt my mouth fall open in astonishment. How on earth could Abernathy know any of this? He hadn't been there... no, *he* hadn't been on the island with us, but the Adversary's deadly mechanical bugs had been. Which meant only one thing: it had been listening to us all that time. But it couldn't have heard everything because then it would have no need for me. Which meant it still didn't know about the collector or Candidate 1.

The oil shifted across Abernathy's chest, spreading bit by bit over his shoulder. It was mesmerizing to watch as this man was slowly subsumed by whatever mysterious substance the orb had been made of. And terrifying beyond belief.

Abernathy made a grab for me. I squealed and leaped back... and felt my heel kick against the body of the unconscious Jean-Pierre. I spun around and grabbed the rifle he had been carrying from the floor, then turned back to face Abernathy.

He was just four feet from me now. "If you pull that trigger, you will destroy us all," Abernathy snarled.

"Maybe it'll be worth it?" I said.

Abernathy stopped mid-step.

I didn't want to die, but I also wasn't going to let this thing get its hands on me.

"But then, who said anything about shooting you, asshole?"

I yelled. I flipped the rifle around, gripping it by its barrel, then lunged at Abernathy's head, hoping to any gods that might still be listening that I didn't accidentally fire the thing. The wooden butt struck him right between his glowing eyes. It landed with a loud crack against the mask of black oil covering Abernathy's face. The mask broke apart momentarily, and, this close, I could see it wasn't oil. It was made of tiny spider-like creatures. Machines. They had to be machines—like the nano-clusters that floated unseen through the air. These things were larger, but they were definitely machines, I was sure of it.

Abernathy staggered back down the corridor. I leaped across the space between us and caught him again with the rifle butt. He staggered backward, his hands reaching for the wall to steady himself.

Behind Abernathy, Freuchen's huge form pulled itself up into the corridor, followed by Chou. Both had their respirators on. They froze for a second when they saw Abernathy.

Abernathy must have seen my distracted glance toward them and turned. Then, just as he returned his gaze to me, I jabbed the rifle at his head again, but this time he ducked, snarled something indistinguishable at me, then barged past me. His shoulder caught me and sent me spinning to the floor. I looked up in time to see him race back down the corridor.

"Are you okay?" Chou said, suddenly at my side.

I nodded, allowing Freuchen to pull me to my feet. "Vas that...?"

"Abernathy? Yes, what's left of him anyway."

"Come on," I said, and we raced after him. I rounded the corner just in time to see him throwing open the second exit. He jumped to the ground, looked back at us one final time, then vanished into the darkness.

Chou raced to the open door, leaned out, but after a few moments, she stepped inside and locked the door behind her.

"I'll tell you about it later," I said when she looked at me. "Right now, I want to get the crew off this thing before they asphyxiate. If they aren't already dead."

I could tell by the way Chou's eyes narrowed behind the visor of her respirator that she still wasn't happy about letting the crew go.

"A deal's a deal," Freuchen rumbled. "Now, let's get on vith it."

———

We opened all the portholes we could between the exit and the crew's quarters to help the AC system force the remaining hydrogen out of the *Brimstone*. The crew lay in disheveled heaps around the room, some still in their bunks which were stacked three high, others on the floor. Many were bloodied—presumably injured during the delirium caused by the lack of oxygen.

"Excuse me," said Freuchen and pushed past me. He picked up two crewmembers, both women and carried them out, one under each arm. I grabbed one of the men by his boots and dragged him into the hallway and then out to where Freuchen had lain the two women. The rain had stopped, but the ground was like quicksand and sucked at my boots. Chou followed behind me, carrying a woman under one arm while dragging a man by his ankles.

"They will start to recover quickly now that they have access to fresh air. Tie them up securely and make sure they have no weapons," Chou said.

For the next couple of minutes, I went about doing just that while my two friends brought the remaining crew out. I felt a wave of relief wash over me when Freuchen carried the Captain out and laid her next to the rest of the crew, announcing that she was the last. Every one of them was breathing, cloudy puffs of warm air drifting from their mouths in the cold night. One of the women we had brought out first was starting to moan and move against her bonds, but the rest were all still unconscious.

"We can't just let them sit out here in the cold and rain," I said as Chou approached me.

She pulled the respirator from her head and tossed it back toward the ship. Freuchen and I did the same.

"Yes, we can," Chou said. "It is more mercy than they showed the people of New Manhattan that they killed without compunction."

Freuchen wiggled his formerly lost thumb at me. "And don't forget vat they did to me, eh?"

They were right, of course. Still, I felt as though I was letting Silas down, but I couldn't see any other way to help them. And I knew that if any of our prisoners got free, they would kill all of us if they had the chance.

"What we need to do now is refill that empty bladder and get airborne so these fools cannot cause us any more harm. Peter, will you watch over them, please?"

Freuchen nodded. "It vould be my pleasure."

"And watch out for Abernathy," I said, as I followed Chou back into the *Brimstone*. "He could be lurking out here somewhere."

———

"The air should be fine to breathe by now," Chou said, "but if you feel even slightly nauseous, let me know." We walked to the access ladder and climbed up into the balloon.

Chou moved to the control panel next to the bladder I'd deflated to gas the crew into unconsciousness. "It is actually a very clever design," she said with a hint of admiration in her voice. "The photovoltaic skin of the *Brimstone's* balloon captures energy and charges those batteries." She nodded at a bank of black boxes toward the front of balloon. "They power the amenities and electronics on the ship, but they also allow the engineers to create their own hydrogen." She nodded up to the large tank suspended from the top of the balloon by thick cables. "That contains water, and using the process of electrolysis, the *Brimstone* can create as much hydrogen as it needs, giving us almost unlimited fuel." She flipped a couple of switches on the console. There was an electrical humming and what sounded like a jacuzzi bubbling to life above our heads. A ripple passed through the almost empty bladder, and it began to inflate. Chou tapped the screen with her finger. "It should take about an hour to fill back. Then we are on our way."

I smiled broadly, threw my arms around her, and gave her a squeeze. Surprisingly, Chou hugged me back just as tightly.

"I am proud of you," she said, releasing me and taking a step back. "What you just did was very brave. And your insistence on keeping the crew alive, while I believe it to be somewhat foolish, was also commendable." She paused for a long moment as though she were searching for the right words to say next. "I will strive to live up to your standards more often," she said eventually. Then she turned and made her way back to the ladder, leaving me to watch her in shocked silence at this unusual show of emotion. The smile didn't fade as I ran after her.

———

"Anything going on?" I asked Freuchen. He was sitting on the lip of the exit, his legs dangling over its edge, moving his flashlight over the *Brimstone's* former crew as they sat in the orange glow of the airship's lights. Most had returned to consciousness, but three of them, including the Red Baroness, still lay in the mud, their chests rising slowly. At least I knew they were alive. The conscious crewmembers watched us silently, but their eyes conveyed the fear they all felt. And if the roles had been reversed, I'd feel the same way, too. I'm sure they all expected to be executed at any moment; after all, that's what they would have done to us. And I was quite happy to let them keep thinking that too if it kept them quiet and submissive until we were ready to leave. Jean-Pierre sat next to his unconscious captain, his eyes focused exclusively on me.

"No sign of Abernathy?" I said, keeping my voice low so our prisoners would not hear.

Freuchen shook his head. "None. I think he is long gone."

"Okay, well, Chou says we can expect to be ready to leave in about forty minutes or so."

"Ver is she?"

"Up in the pilothouse, familiarizing herself with the controls."

"Do you know vat—"

Light splashed across the sky, and the air was lit with the twinkle of pixie dust as the aurora finally arrived. I felt the tension drop away, only to be replaced by a welcome feeling of wellbeing. I exhaled a deep sigh of relief when I saw the three crewmembers who had, until now, still lay unconscious. They sat up, confusion evident on their faces as they, no doubt, began asking their fellow captors what had happened. They fell silent again when they noticed us watching them from the airship's doorway.

———

It took longer than Chou had anticipated for the bladder to fill, and by the time she announced that we were ready to leave, it was close to dawn. I followed her out of the cabin, where I had just taken a shower. It felt amazing to have washed all the mud from me and change into some fresh clothes. We joined Freuchen, where he still stood guard over our prisoners. Our band of captives sat in the mud, their heads down, all resistance now beaten out of them by the rain and cold.

"I'll untie the mooring lines," Freuchen said, handing me his rifle before dropping to the ground. Moving from line to line, he untied the rope from the pegs, then heaved the pegs from the rain-soaked ground with his bare hands. Chou pulled the lines aboard and stored them again, then rejoined Freuchen and me at the doorway.

I jumped down and walked to the Red Baroness, who sat at the end of the line of captives. I pulled a knife I'd taken off of one of the guards and threw it into the mud about ten feet from her.

"If any of you tries to get to that knife before we are airborne, my big friend over there will shoot you dead. Once we are in the air, you can use it to cut your bonds. Do you understand?"

"You can't leave us here," Jean-Pierre yelled at me. "We'll die with no food or any way to defend ourselves."

I turned and looked at him, then nodded in the direction of the tree line. "We've left food and water in the woods over there. There's at least three days' worth, more if you ration it properly. We're confiscating all of your firearms and ammunition, but we've left your knives and swords. You won't be defenseless."

I made my way back to the airship but stopped and turned to face the prisoners again.

"Oh, and one last thing. If any of you should get the bright idea to come looking for revenge, understand that we will be ready for you, and next time we won't be so forgiving. This world has plenty for all of us, go live your lives. You've been given a second chance you did not deserve. There won't be a third."

I took Freuchen's proffered hand and climbed back inside the *Brimstone*, closed and secured the door behind me, then followed Chou to the pilothouse while Freuchen stood guard at the door and made sure the prisoners kept up their end of the bargain.

———

The *Brimstone's* wheelhouse was a glass bubble that gave us a two-hundred-degree view of the area immediately around and below us. That included the airship's former crew, their dejected faces watching us as we made our preparations for takeoff.

A large black panel placed all of the knobs and levers needed to control the airship in front of the leather pilot's chair. A second co-pilot's chair sat next to it. I stood to Chou's left, watching her flip switches, turn a couple of knobs, and pull down on three overhead levers.

"I do not like to fly," Freuchen said, joining me at the window.

I laughed. "But to be fair, you haven't experienced it when you're not a prisoner."

He nodded. "This is very true. Still, I do not—"

The *Brimstone* lurched, and I felt butterflies in my stomach as the ground began to recede. Freuchen's eyes grew wide, and he grabbed hold of a stanchion with one hand and my shoulder with his other. For such a big tough man, he really was easily frightened.

We rose slowly above the tops of the trees, their boughs transformed to bronze by the early morning sun. Through the plexiglass bubble, I watched the Red Baroness scramble through the mud to retrieve the knife. She moved to Jean-Pierre and got to work on the rope that bound his hands together. When he was free, he did the same for her.

Our ascent slowed then stopped, and we hung motionless in the air, about seventy feet above the ground.

"I need your help, Meredith," Chou said

"What's up?" I said, parking my butt in the co-pilot's chair.

Chou pointed to the three computer screens in front of her. "Your translative ability does not appear to work on the written word and numbers. Would you please translate these for me?"

"Sure." I began reading the headings at the top of each display aloud for her. It seemed to work as she nodded each time I spoke.

"And these," she said, pointing to a bank of switches.

"Those control the landing and traveling lights," I explained, reading each aloud too. "And these over here—"

"Meredith! Chou!" Freuchen snapped, his voice laced with panic. "Something is... my God... vat is he doing?"

Chou and I wasted no time joining Freuchen at the window.

"What are you—" The words stuck in my throat. Below, a figure dressed entirely in black ambled toward the *Brimstone's* crew. The Red Baroness lay face down in the mud a few feet behind the figure, her body convulsing as though she were being electrocuted. She'd managed to free three others, and now those men and Jean-Pierre were cautiously approaching the black-clad figure, their fists raised.

"Abernathy!" I hissed.

It was difficult to make out too much detail from where we hovered, but it was obvious that whatever change Abernathy had gone through after the orb had grabbed him was now fully complete. Now, he resembled his previous human form in shape only. His head was covered by what I thought was a cowl like

Chou's, but when he looked in our direction, I saw that it was more like the hood of a cobra, two black fleshy extensions on either side of his head where his ears should have been. His face was a point-down-triangle, his features too far away for me to make out with any clarity, but his eyes... they burned with such intensity I could feel the hatred emanating from them. The rest of his body looked mostly human, except that his limbs had all grown more muscular, and longer, suggesting a newfound strength. He alone would have been terrifying enough, but something *else* was moving at Abernathy's feet.

At first, I thought it was just his shadow, but that couldn't be because the sun was in the east still. Whatever this was, moved in the same direction as Abernathy, toward Jean-Pierre and the other men. The men began patting at their bodies as the shadow-thing separated, flowed up their legs, over their chest, and into their mouth and nose. The two men fell to the ground, writhing like the woman.

Abernathy reached the first of the still-bound crew and, like a priest giving the benediction, covered the man's face with his hand. The crewman's back arched violently, and he fell backward. He started convulsing too. The other crewmembers struggled, wriggling and rolling from his touch as he made his way up the line, trying to get away from Abernathy. Still, the restraints did their job—the restraints *I* had tied on at least half of them. They didn't stand a chance. In my attempt to ensure their safety, I had doomed them all to whatever it was that Abernathy was doing to them.

"We've got to help them," I said, turning to face Chou.

"No!" Freuchen said. "Look." He pointed down to where Abernathy's first victim, the woman, lay in the grass. Except now, she was sitting upright. She rose slowly to her feet and stood, staring directly ahead of her, wobbling slightly from side to side.

A man got stood up and waited silently just like her, slowly swaying like a branch in a breeze while we watched in horrified silence as Freuchen worked his way down the line. He sent his shadow after those that managed to roll or crawl away.

"He's creating a fighting force," Freuchen said when there were only three people left.

I shuddered and said, "What do you mean?"

Freuchen turned to me. "Why else vould he do this? He's creating a small army to try to stop us... to stop you. It is the only thing that makes any sense."

"That's absurd," I said, but deep down, I suspected he was right. Below us, the thing that had once been Tommy Two-Thumbs released his final victim. The woman toppled sideways, shivering and trembling, what looked like black foam bubbling from her mouth.

As if he had been aware of our presence all along, Two-Thumbs turned and raised his head skyward. I felt his electronic eyes burning through the space between us. Then, one after the other, the men and women he had changed turned and stared skyward at us too. The eighty feet or so separating us from him no longer felt as safe as it should have. A terrible thought came to me: If Abernathy was able to send whatever that shadow-thing was made of across the ground, who was to say it couldn't fly too?

"We need to get out of here. Now," I said.

Chou leaped into the pilot's seat. A moment later, the propellers were whirring again, and we were ascending. Fast.

I watched Abernathy grow smaller and smaller. Only when I couldn't see him anymore did I start breathing again.

THIRTEEN

FOR THE NEXT FIFTEEN MINUTES, we traveled in complete silence while Chou urged the *Brimstone* ever higher. But the horror of what we'd just witnessed couldn't keep us silent for long.

"What *was* that?" I blurted out. "I mean, what the hell was that?"

Freuchen stared at the western horizon, saying nothing.

"I think it was a trap," Chou said.

"A trap?" Freuchen rumbled. "Set for who?"

"Us?" I asked.

Chou shook her head. "Perhaps, but I don't think so. Whatever created that sphere seems to have taken over Abernathy with a very clear purpose."

I tilted my head questioningly.

"To transform Abernathy into something capable of changing people. Changing them into... whatever *they* were."

It wasn't too much of a leap to imagine exactly what was behind it. "You think it was the Adversary, don't you?"

"That would be the most logical conclusion, I think."

I turned my attention to Freuchen. "You said you thought he was creating a fighting force."

"Yes. Vat other reason vould he... *it* have to do vat he did to those people? He could have just slaughtered them and been done vith it."

I thought about that for a few moments. "But why would he need to build an army? Why not just come after us himself?"

Freuchen shrugged. "Perhaps he knows something ve don't."

"Well, considering how little we actually know, that's not too high a bar to set," I replied sarcastically.

Chou said, "Right now, Abernathy is the least of our worries. Look." She nodded ahead of us.

Where the early morning sky had been clear just minutes ago, black thunderheads now crept insidiously across our path, obscuring the horizon completely. Lighting flashed within the billowing gray and black clouds. Chou slowed the *Brimstone* to a halt, but still, the clouds crept closer, pushing closer to us by the second.

"Can we outrun it?" I asked.

"No, I don't think so," Chou answered. "We're going to have to try to get above it."

A sudden gust of wind buffeted the *Brimstone*, rattling the airship's superstructure. Ahead, the canopy of the Everwood whipped, leaves flew into the air, dancing, and whole branches were ripped from trees and flung about like they were nothing.

"Hold on!" Chou said through clenched teeth. Freuchen and I grabbed onto anything that we could as Chou raised the nose of the *Brimstone*, and we started to ascend. I squealed as a streak of lightning flashed across the sky to starboard, then I jumped again as a peel of thunder crashed over us.

Chou let out an expletive that even my translating ability seemed incapable of understanding. She pushed a set of levers all the way forward, and I could just make out the sudden rise in the struggling engine's thrum over the roaring of the storm.

"What's wrong?" I yelled.

"Strong headwind. It has slowed us almost to a stop. She leaned forward and cursed again, the sky above us blocked by the huge balloon. A violent gust of wind smashed into the *Brimstone's* gondola, swinging us like a pendulum. I was flung toward the cockpit window and would surely have cracked my head open if it wasn't for Freuchen's quick reactions. He grabbed me by my arm with his free hand, the other holding onto an **I**-shaped stanchion that ran from the floor to the ceiling. He reeled me into him like he was landing a fish. I grabbed his belt, then staggered to the co-pilot's seat and fastened the safety harness around my shoulders.

Another bolt of lightning flashed so close to us it seared my eyes, leaving a white ghost of itself on my eyelids.

"Vat happens if ve are struck?" Freuchen asked nervously.

"I don't know," Chou said, her lips barely moving as she fought against the controls. "We will probably explode, I suppose," she added.

"Vunderful. Just vunderful."

"Can I do anything?" I asked.

Chou shook her head. "No. I just need to get—"

I screamed as we were swept suddenly sideways, swatted like a fly by a violent gust of wind. Memories burst into my mind; of the F-150 and the car crash that had killed my best friend. Of the depression that ultimately led me down the road that brought me to this place. Lights began to blink on the console accompanied by an insistent alarm. Chou flipped a switch, and the alarm stopped. The blinking red light did not.

"What's that mean?" I said.

"We have lost one of the engines."

"Oh, great."

"Not to vurry. Ve have three more."

A second light began to flash next to the first.

I started to say something but instead screamed a warning as something about ten feet long flew through the air toward us and smashed through the cockpit side window. A tree branch, the pithy white interior exposed, passed through the narrow space between Chou and my head and struck the stanchion behind us. A few inches either way and one or the other of us would have been instantly dead. Freezing wind and rain ripped through the hole it had made. I glanced over my shoulder, half expecting to see a disemboweled Freuchen. But instead, he lay on the floor, eyes wide in surprise, staring back at me as the *Brimstone* shook and rattled like it was a runaway freight train. The gondola swung left and right, a prisoner of the ever-changing wind.

Why is this world always trying to kill us? I wondered.

A sudden swirling updraft grabbed ahold of us, and we began to rotate like a corkscrew. Chou's hands were off all the controls; she'd given up on fighting the storm. We were utterly at its mercy. I felt my stomach surge as we spun faster and faster. Freuchen groaned in discomfort behind me. The world beyond the gondola was nothing but vast globules of smoky grays and blacks like we were trapped in some nightmarish '70s lava lamp. The truth was, I didn't know which way was up or down. For all I knew, we could be spiraling toward the ground.

Chou lolled in her seat. I tried to focus my eyes on her chest, the spinning making it almost impossible; she was breathing, I was sure of it.

I heard someone let out a long panic-filled, "Arrrrrghhhh," and only realized it was me when another violent buffeting slammed my mouth shut and cut me off.

The nose of the *Brimstone* dipped violently until my harness was the only reason I didn't fall out of my seat and end up face-first against the cockpit window. Then we swung upward just as dramatically... and the chaos stopped. The clouds surrounding us thinned and dissipated, replaced by a brilliant blue sky. Gradually, the spinning slowed, then ceased altogether. The sound of the storm faded, replaced by a chaotic warble and trill of numerous alarms.

I was panting like I'd just outrun a pack of wolves.

A hand touched my right shoulder.

"Meredith, are you alright?" Freuchen asked, breathing hard too.

I don't know. Am I? I thought. "Yes, I'm okay," I said after a quick self-assessment.

Below us, the thunderstorm whirled and circled like a pack of starving wolves. Chou had done it, I realized. She'd managed to save us all, again.

"Chou!" I said, suddenly remembering that she was hurt. I unbuckled myself and dropped to my knees in front of her. A thin cut ran from the middle of her forehead just above her right eye and extended back past her ear, exposing red raw skin where the branch had caught her with its glancing blow.

"Chou! Can you hear me?" I said as calmly as I could, shaking her knee.

Chou shifted against her restraints. Her head lifted from her chest, and her eyes fluttered open and focused on me.

"Ugh. What happened?" she groaned.

"You literally got hit by a tree," I said, unable to keep the awe out of my voice as I pulled a quarter-inch splinter from the skin of her neck. She did not flinch. There were a bunch of smaller fragments embedded deeply around the wound that I'd need a needle and tweezers to get out.

"We are alive?" Chou asked.

"Yes. Thanks to you."

Chou looked out over the storm raging beneath us. We were

at least a thousand feet above it now and still ascending. She reached out and silenced the alarms, then with the flip of a couple of switches, she halted our ascent. Her eyes moved over the control panel.

"Two of our engines are down," she whispered.

"Blast!" Freuchen said. "That cannot be good."

Chou shook her head slowly. "Not as bad as it sounds. I was running them at full power, and I think they just shut down to ensure they did not burn out."

Her eyes moved over the panel again, lingering on a set of large illuminated buttons. Two of them were blinking red, the others were all green. "I think if I just—" She pressed each blinking button in turn. "Yes, that's it." The flashing lights turned green one after the other. She eased forward on the throttles, and the *Brimstone* began moving forward again.

"Here, let me check your injury," Freuchen said, ducking under the tree limb to get close to Chou. He'd found a first-aid kit somewhere and began slathering an antiseptic cream onto her wound. I showed him how to apply a large Band-Aid to it. Despite the detour, we were making good headway again. The storm still raged below us, but it was continuing its erratic course inland, and we could see its furthest most edge approaching. A little over an hour later, the storm was well behind us, replaced by a thick layer of white cloud that looked like an almost perfect layer of freshly dropped snow.

"Ve are not going to be able to spot New Manhattan from this altitude," Freuchen mused.

Chou nodded. "We are going to have to descend below the cloud base," she said. She slowed the *Brimstone* to a crawl, then began to gradually take us down.

The world beyond the windshield became white.

"Meredith, I need you and Peter to be my eyes. Tell me if

you see anything below us. I don't want to fly us straight into the side of a mountain."

I nodded and moved myself to the left side of the cockpit while Freuchen took the right.

Slowly, almost painfully, Chou allowed us to drop through the layer of cloud. We could see nothing beyond a few feet, and I felt my old nervousness return. But the cloud finally began to thin, and then we were out of it. Hundreds of feet below us loomed the canopy of the Everwood, still glistening from the downpour that must have washed over it just a short while earlier. The *Brimstone* continued to descend until it was a hundred feet above the forest canopy. Peeking just above the western horizon was the mountain range we'd crossed when we first landed. Hundreds of streams of smoke rose into the air, scattered across the thousands of square miles of forest between us and the range.

I felt my heart drop.

"There are so many camps," I said. "How are we ever supposed to find New Manhattan?" I was growing more nervous by the minute, wondering what had happened to Albert and Silas after Freuchen and I had been kidnapped.

"Ve might have to take a best guess," Freuchen said, his eyes scanning the forest.

"That will be too time consuming and dangerous," Chou said. "We need to remember that the *Brimstone* probably raided many of these camps looking for Meredith before they found New Manhattan. We could be met with violence before we even land and explain ourselves."

"Vell, vat other option do ve have then?"

"I have an idea," I said.

I'd been watching the mountain range we'd had to climb over as it grew larger with every passing second. "We need to locate the bay where Captain Joel dropped us off. Then we can just retrace the route we took over the mountain. That'll put us in the best position to spot the camp."

"Ha!" said Freuchen, smacking a fist into the palm of his other hand. "You are a very smart human, Meredith."

"That's why they pay me the big bucks, I guess."

Chou must have thought it was a good idea too because she gradually increased the speed of the *Brimstone's* engines and began to take us up higher.

————

I'd made us all a meal from the *Brimstone's* galley. It was surprisingly well-stocked with canned food and wild-picked fruit and vegetables. There was a decent-sized freezer that held a stock of fresh mystery meat I thought might be venison but could have been wild boar for all I knew. There was even an electric stove, and what I thought might be a microwave. I settled on pears and apples. Sliced them all up, sprinkled some sugar over Freuchen's, and took the three bowls back to the cockpit. We ate in silence, watching as the mountain range, now just a few miles away, drew closer.

"How fast can this thing go?" I asked.

"It has a top speed of about sixty miles an hour, assuming there is no headwind to fight," Chou said. "Faster still if we have a tailwind to aid us."

"That's awesome," I said. This was seriously going to help our journey. I couldn't guess how far away the collector was, but the *Brimstone*—God, I was really starting to hate that name— was going to be a huge asset for us.

"Look here," Freuchen said, drawing our attention to the view beyond the windshield. "We are passing over the mountains."

Chou and I both stood and stared down at the craggy gray

rocks. When we first encountered it, we'd thought it probably ran for a few hundred miles at least, but now we could see it was much further than that. Beyond the mountains, the sea glistened and scintillated. Somewhere out there, beyond the misty horizon, was Avalon. I wondered how Edward, Wild Bill, Evelyn, Bull, and the rest of our friends were doing. I felt a strong pull of homesickness for them and almost suggested it might be worth taking a quick detour to pay a visit, but I thought better of it.

"There!" Freuchen said. "Those are the same outcroppings ve saw ven ve first arrived. I'm sure of it, vich means that the cove must be in that direction."

Chou adjusted our direction to take us south. From this height, we had a fantastic view of the terrain for miles and miles, and it wasn't long before I excitedly yelled, "There! There's the cove."

The horseshow-shaped cove looked tiny from all the way up here, but it was the only similarly-shaped landmark within sight. It had to be ours. Chou drew parallel to it, then swung the *Brimstone* around to head back in the direction we had come.

"That outcropping looks familiar," Chou said, pointing at a low-lying section of the mountain.

"Yes," I agreed. "I think that's it."

Freuchen pointed at a thick column of smoke rising through the branches of the Everwood just a few degrees off to our left. "Vich mean that has to be New Manhattan."

I threw my arms around Freuchen and hugged him hard. He stepped back, laughing, and gently swung me around then released me. I took my place in the co-pilot's seat and watched as the plume of smoke gradually drew closer.

FOURTEEN

CHOU STARTED A GRADUAL DESCENT, intending to land the *Brimstone* in the same clearing as I'd been abducted from.

"Listen! Do you hear that?" Freuchen asked, cocking his head.

"It's a bell," I said after a few seconds. "Someone's sounding a bell."

Outside, I saw people running.

"What on Earth are they—oh, shit!" I yelled when I saw numerous fires spark to life around the edge of the forest. About twenty men and women stepped from the trees armed with bows and lowered the tips of their arrows into the flames before aiming the arrows right at us.

"If vun of those pierces the balloon, it could ignite the hydrogen," Freuchen said. That chance was pretty high, judging by the number of flaming arrows pointed at us.

We were still fifty or so feet above the ground. I had no idea how accurate the archers were at that range, but after what had happened to poor Phillip in those first days on Avalon, I knew that they could be incredibly precise and deadly in the right hands.

"Hold us here," I said to Chou and sprinted from the cockpit. I skidded around the corner and ran toward the exit facing New Manhattan.

"Come on. Come on," I mumbled as I undid the lock of the door and slid it open. Standing in the opening, my hands holding onto either side of the doorframe, I leaned out into the cold air and looked down. I saw faces staring back up at me from behind their bows. I searched those faces for anyone that I recognized but saw none. Then, from the tree line to my right, a figure lowered the bow it held and began to walk out into the clearing toward me.

"Emily!" I yelled, recognizing her lithe form, long blond hair, and her malamute, Thor, walking confidently at her heel. "It's me, Meredith." I let go of the door with one hand and waved.

Emily looked up, a hand guarding her eyes against the hazy sunlight reflecting off the thick cloud.

"It's okay," I yelled, not really sure if she could hear me. "We hijacked the airship. The people who attacked you are... gone."

Emily looked up at me for a few more long moments, and I started to suspect that she hadn't heard me after all. Then she looked first to her left, waving her hand to her people, then her right. One after the other, the archers lowered their bows but kept their arrows nocked and at the ready. Well, it was better than nothing. I waved to her, slid the door closed then ran back to the cockpit.

"Take us down, Chou," I said, then made my way back to the door and waited until I felt the *Brimstone* bump against the ground. I slid the door open and started to move toward the first mooring rope to secure the airship.

"Stop right where you are." Emily, flanked by three large men armed with swords and bows, was striding across the open ground toward me. The bows were aimed at me. Thor clomped along at her feet, his big brown eyes focused on me, his tail swishing.

At least someone's happy to see me, I thought.

One of Emily's bodyguards suddenly switched their bow from me to the *Brimstone's* exit. I turned to see Freuchen and Chou standing in the doorway.

"You two, get down very carefully, and keep your hands in the air," Emily ordered.

Chou and Freuchen did as they were told.

"Emily," Freuchen said, "if ve do not secure the airship, it could be damaged beyond repair. Or verse, if it drifts into vun of those fires, there could be vun hell of a big bang." The *Brimstone* was already drifting toward the line of fires at the edge of the forest. "It puts all our lives at risk."

Emily thought for a second then called out to her people, four of whom came running to her side.

"Show them what they need to do," she told Freuchen. "But if you do anything stupid, it'll be the last thing you do."

Freuchen and Chou walked with the New Manhattan people and began to secure the remaining mooring lines while Emily walked toward me and stopped a few feet away. "Make sure there's nobody else on board," she told two of her bodyguards. They nodded and climbed into the *Brimstone*. One of her other men began to pat me down. He stepped back and shook his head.

"You haven't been at all honest with me, have you?" Emily said.

"That's not entirely true," I said. "We told you as much as we could."

"You just left out the part about your three other friends.

One of whom just happens to be a robot with a penchant for repeating himself and calling us' Candidates.'"

She seemed mildly amused, which I took as a good sign.

"Albert and Silas?" I asked. "They're okay?"

"They're fine," Emily answered. "A little weird, but fine."

I felt a weight lift from my shoulders. "Can I see them?"

She ignored my question. "So, you were working with those... pirates?"

"What?" I said, astounded that she would think that. "No! No way."

"So, why did they come here. Why did they single you and your big friend out?" She nodded in the direction of Freuchen and Chou who were being escorted back to where we stood.

"We weren't working with them. They were *looking* for us. For *me*."

"Why?"

"It's a long story," I said.

"I've got all the time in the world, apparently."

"Listen. Emily," I took a step toward her. Her bodyguards' blades rose and pointed at my gut.

Emily pushed the blades down. "Let her talk."

"Thank you. I know we're not in a position to make demands, but if you let us see Albert and Silas, I promise you we'll tell you everything that we know. It might not make sense —God knows most of it doesn't to me—but you'll know as much as we do." I paused for a second, my eyes locked with hers. "Please."

"Take them to my cabin," Emily ordered. Then to another guard, "You go get the boy and the robot and meet us there, too."

————

Emily sat behind her desk, her fingers steepled as she watched us. Chou, Freuchen, and I stood and waited, two armed guards on either side of us.

Five minutes later, the cabin door creaked opened, and I turned just in time to see Albert appear, spot the three of us, then run straight to me. He threw his arms around my waist, hugged me, then did the same to Chou and Freuchen.

"I thought... you weren't... coming back," the kid said between barely suppressed sobs.

Freuchen swept him up in his arms and said, "Ve vill alvays come for you, little man."

The light from the doorway dimmed as Silas eased his giant form into the room.

He regarded each of us in turn. "*Welcome, Candidates 13, 20078, 207891. I know that you are confused and have many questions. I am here to help you assimilate into your new surrou—*"

Albert said, "These are our friends, Silas. The ones I was telling you about this morning... again." He turned and looked at me. "You took his slate with you, so he forgets everything each night."

I said, "We'll figure that out as soon as Emily lets me have my backpack back. Now, tell me, are you okay?"

He nodded. "When the airship came, Chou and Silas told me to stay hidden and that they would be back. But only Silas came back. Silas wanted us to turn ourselves in, but I told him we had to wait for you to come back."

Emily interrupted. "A group of my people out looking for fresh berries discovered Albert and Silas. Came as a bit of a shock to them." She laughed, pleasant and bubbly. "They brought these two back to camp, which caused a pretty big commotion, but it didn't take too long for us to figure out that

Silas was not a threat. Now Albert, on the other hand..." She flashed a wry grin and a wink at the boy, who blushed tomato-red.

"Thank you for looking after our friends," Chou said.

Emily acknowledged Chou with a dip of her head. "I've heard an awful lot about you, Weston, from young Albert."

"Call me Chou."

"He said that you are a pilot... of a starship?"

"The *Shining Way*, yes."

Emily nodded slowly and said, rather enigmatically, "And I thought my story was a strange one." She got to her feet. "I've done as you asked and reunited you with your two friends. Now it's your turn. Give me the truth."

Chou, Freuchen, and Albert all looked silently at me.

"Okay, I guess I'm nominated," I said. I took a deep breath and began to tell her the story of everything that had happened to us from the day we'd all dropped out of the sky into the ocean. As I talked, Emily paced slowly back and forth on the opposite side of the table, her head cocked slightly to one side, her eyes moving to each of us as if I was narrating a story, and we were all its characters. When I was done, she pulled out her chair and sat again, her forearms flat on the table.

Albert broke the long silence. "You believe us, Emily, don't you?" he said.

Emily's eyes moved over all of us one final time, and to my relief, she said, "Yes, Albert. For some reason I can't quite understand, because—and let's be honest here, this is the weirdest sounding shi... *story* I've ever heard—I believe you. And believe *me*, I know weird."

I felt some of the tension leave the room.

Emily stood again. "So, this Architect brought us all here because—why exactly?"

"Don't know," I said.

"What about the robot? How much does he know?"

"He doesn't remember anything really," Albert piped up.

"He just knows that we were supposed to work toward a common goal," I said. "But what that goal is... or was..." I shrugged. "Your guess is as good as mine."

"But I thought you said the robot—"

Albert interrupted. "Silas. His name is Silas."

"I thought you said *Silas* had given you some kind of a message from the Architect. To travel to the collector to find this Candidate 1?"

"He did give us that message, yes, the night we first found him. But then he forgot it."

"And then the Nazis who captured your friends. And the raiders who came on the airship—they're all agents of this other... entity. The Adversary."

I nodded.

"And he wants you captured, but you don't know why."

I nodded again.

"And we're all from different dimensions, right?"

"Yes."

"Well, that explains a few things, I guess."

"Like what?" Chou asked.

"Like how you and Meredith existed after 2012."

Chou and I looked at each other. Then we both looked at Emily. "I don't follow."

Emily leaned in closer. "Because in my world... my version, there were only two humans left alive after that."

———

"Aliens?" I said, still unable to believe the story Emily had just recounted.

Emily shrugged. "I'm not really sure. All I know is that after the red rain killed everyone but me, their bodies were... repurposed, turned into something else. Weird crab-like creatures that assembled themselves into these giant trees. I was traveling to Alaska—there was a group of scientists alive on an island—when I was attacked by these other creatures in the forest. That's when Thor here showed up and tried to save me and got brought with me when the voice asked if I wanted to be saved."

"An amazing story," Freuchen said. He had sat enthralled while Emily spoke.

"So, what's your plan?" Emily asked.

Good question. I had no idea what the answer was. "We haven't had a chance to talk it through yet."

"We will need your help with something," Chou said.

"What?" said Emily.

"Crew," Chou said. "We could use two or three people—people you trust—preferably with some experience of working aboard a ship or piloting an aircraft. Maybe someone with military experience who we could use as security to protect the ship."

"I'll ask round," Emily said. "See if anyone wants to volunteer."

"Thank you," I said.

"Anything else?"

"Our backpacks. May we have them back?"

Emily nodded.

We each retrieved our packs. I opened mine and dug around until I found the memory slate. I took it to where Silas stood near the door and held in front of his face. His eye-bar quickly scanned the code. Silas suddenly tensed, standing erect, his metal arms straightening, his eye-bar moving quickly around the room.

Emily's two guards jumped to their feet, their weapons at the ready.

"Meredith? Where are we? How did I—"

"Silas, it's okay. Something happened, and you've lost a couple of days. Let me explain."

FIFTEEN

"IT'S BEAUTIFUL!" Albert whispered when he saw the *Brimstone* for the first time. "Can I go onboard?" he asked, looking up at Chou and me.

"Of course, little man," Freuchen said. "Come on, I vill give you a guided tour, and you can pick out a cabin for yourself. How does that sound?"

"Really?" Albert replied, his eyes as big as baseballs.

"Really," Freuchen smiled back before lifting the boy up and disappearing into the airship.

"*It really is quite beautiful,*" said Silas. He stood next to Emily, towering over her. Thor seemed to have taken a liking to the giant golden mechanical man. He sat between the robot's legs while Silas stroked his head. "*You said the original owner came from a world devastated by nuclear war? And yet, they were still able to create such marvels. Humanity has never stopped amazing me.*"

"If there is one thing I have learned since arriving on this planet," Chou said, "it is that humanity's drive to survive seems more than capable of overcoming almost any obstacle that presents itself. We are a tenacious species."

Just then, Bartholomew and a woman I didn't recognize approached us.

"Hello," Bartholomew said, grinning broadly. "We heard you were looking for volunteers to help operate this wonderful machine."

"We are," I said, eying the woman who stood just behind him. She looked somewhat familiar, but I couldn't place her. She was taller than me, close to six feet, I guessed. Her hair was thick and looked permanently tussled, covering her ears and highlighting her slim, almost elven face and features. She wore a brown leather jacket that came down to just below her midriff, and light green pants with several large pockets built into each leg.

"We'd like to volunteer," the woman said, every word pronounced with a precision I'd rarely heard before.

I stepped in closer to her and held out my hand. "Hello, I'm Meredith. That's Chou, and the big golden guy is Silas."

Both said hello.

The woman nodded at each of us, still smiling. "It's a pleasure to meet you all. I've heard a lot about you."

"And you are?" Chou asked.

The woman flushed red, dipped her head in embarrassment before raising her eyes to look directly at me. "Amelia," she said. "My name is Amelia Earhart."

————

For the rest of that day and the next two, Chou taught Amelia how to pilot the *Brimstone*, launching practice flights around the canopy and eventually joy-rides for some of New Manhattan's residents. To a one, those who took part in the flights came back with a deeper understanding and respect of just how vast and beautiful this version of Earth was.

We left the next day, Chou and Amelia occupying the pilot and co-pilot seats of the newly repaired pilothouse. Emily and a large collection of her citizens waved us off, and we watched them grow gradually smaller until, finally, Chou swung the nose of the *Brimstone* toward the monolith. The engines revved to max speed, and we began our journey again.

SIXTEEN

THE NEXT THREE days felt like more of a vacation than anything. Chou and Amelia seemed to hit it off and spent most of their time in the cockpit, switching shifts so the other could get some rest. Albert seemed in a permanent state of excitement, and when he wasn't in his cabin, he was in there too, in the cockpit, happily providing a running commentary on the different trees and animals he spotted. Meanwhile, Freuchen and Bartholomew were becoming fast friends, spending their days playing cribbage and bridge in the crew quarters. They invited Silas in on a couple of games, but after he repeatedly thrashed them, he was promptly disinvited. Bartholomew also turned out to be a hell of a cook and kept us fed better than we'd been since we arrived.

Like I said, it felt more like a vacation, but each day, the collector drew closer and closer, and with it, a sense of unspoken disquiet.

———

It was at the end of the fourth day that Chou used the ship's intercom to call all of us to the cockpit. I was the first to reach it, closely followed by Freuchen and Bartholomew. We stopped dead when, through the darkness, looming like some ancient giant, we saw the collector.

"My God," Freuchen whispered, his voice vibrating with awe. "It's beautiful."

Goosebumps broke out along my arms. The hair on the nape of my neck rose, and I was rendered momentarily speechless.

We were about five miles from the collector. It glowed with dim white incandescence against the backdrop of the night. Amelia was in the pilot's seat, and she angled the *Brimstone's* nose slightly away from the collector so the airship's balloon wouldn't obstruct our view. We crowded to the window, our eyes tracing the side of the structure up and up and up, until it vanished into the sky, miles above us.

"One cannot help but feel insignificant in the presence of such a terrible feat of engineering," Bartholomew said.

I silently agreed. It was unimaginably huge.

Chou threw a couple of switches, and the *Brimstone's* forward spotlights flashed on, illuminating the land around the base of the collector. A mountain range stretched for miles on either side, encasing the bottom portion of the edifice in gray rock.

"Incredible," Chou said. "The foundation must be buried deep in the mountains, secured by the bedrock itself."

"Yes," Amelia said, "but look at the ground around the mountain." There was no forest around the base of the collector. Instead, extending out in a perfect circle for what I estimated was two miles or so was what looked like a gray landscape of... nothing. No trees, no brush, no grass—just gray nothingness. It might just as well have been the surface of the shattered moon whose glow was barely perceptible in the night sky.

Amelia allowed the *Brimstone* to hover in place.

I estimated we were a little over two miles from the collector now, its faceted walls taking up the entirety of our view. Chou used a small joystick to point the spotlights at the very edge of the circle of dead ground, about half a mile away.

"Look at the trees around the edge of the circle," she said. "They're all dead or dying."

Chou was right. Where the dead-land met the forest, the trees closest to it looked sickly, burnt, or charred, dead or dying. But only the first couple of rows. Everything beyond that looked just as healthy as the rest of the Everwood.

"Radiation?" I asked.

"Perhaps," said Chou. "But until Silas is awake, we have no way to gauge whether that's true or not. I think a more probable answer is the aurora."

I checked the clock on the airship's instrument panel. It was after midnight. The aurora was due soon.

Chou continued, "I think, perhaps the prudent thing to do would be to put some distance between us and the collector until after the aurora. In the morning we can—"

A pulse of light spread out from the tower across the tops of the Everwood.

"Crap!" I said. "Better get us out of here."

The pulses grew stronger and more frequent with every passing moment, each of the collector's facets throbbing with a quickly-growing intensity. Amelia fired up the engines to max and began to swivel the *Brimstone* in the opposite direction of the collector, but the thing was so huge, it was going to take a minute or more to swing us around.

"Come on, come on," Freuchen whispered, egging the *Brimstone* to move faster.

A roar, deep and thunderous, like the approach of an enormous freight train rattled the *Brimstone*. I swear I felt the vibration right down to my bones. I saw rocks tumbling from the side of the mountains. I almost laughed out loud when I saw the hair on Chou's head begin to rise, even as I felt the sudden buildup of static electricity coursing over my own skin.

The *Brimstone* reverberated suddenly as a deafening boom ripped the silence of the night apart, louder than any thunderclap, stunning me.

"Oh, sh—" I began, but the words froze in my mouth as I was thrown backward, colliding hard with the fuselage. For a thousandth of a second, reality was replaced by a furious wall of color bursting from the collector as it unleashed the power of the aurora into the world. An excruciating bolt of pain lanced inside my head as the raw, primal energy crashed over us, blindingly bright.

The *Brimstone's* superstructure shook violently with every wave of energy that passed over it.

"Faster!" I said as the aurora's light spread across the land, filling the cockpit with a blinding flash, the pixie dust lost in the brilliance.

Amelia continued her slow turn, blocking more of the light as she repositioned us, so the nose was facing away from the collector.

And then it was done. The light faded, allowing darkness to claim the land again, and for a few moments, we all just stood there, catching our breath.

"Ve need to find a place to land," Freuchen said.

We all agreed.

Chou flipped a couple of switches and turned on the *Brimstone's* powerful searchlights, then quickly began moving them over the ground below us.

"There!" Albert said after a few minutes of searching. He was pointing to a plot of open ground about a quarter-mile away from the edge of the dead-land surrounding the collector. "We can land there."

My stomach lurched as Amelia turned the airship in its direction and dropped us rapidly toward it.

We landed and quickly tied off the *Brimstone*.

Just within the range of our landing lights, a dead redwood lay moldering on the forest floor. Not for the first time, I wondered at the amazing biodiversity of the Everwood. While the redwood had crashed to the forest floor many years before we set foot here, in death, it had become a kind of coral reef of the forest, allowing new life to flourish. Lichen covered the thick, armor-like bark and here and there I saw the ghostly white shape of mushrooms and toadstools. Birds had built nests in some of the remaining branches and squawked low warnings to their neighbors at the approach of these strange visitors.

In time, all would pass and return to the ground, passing on the life-giving nutrients to new plants. This endless cycle had stretched on for billions of years and would likely continue to do so until the sun became a red dwarf and swallowed the planet whole. A sad end to all of our memories, I supposed.

My eyes rose to the clear night sky and the shattered moon, looming huge and bright. The moon was full tonight—or as full as it could get, at least—its tail of broken rock trailing behind it like a comet moving across the sky. And in the distance, visible even through the forest that separated us from it, the collector glowed dimly, like a beacon... or a warning, perhaps.

In a strange spell of introspection, I wondered what had happened to the version of me that had existed in this reality. Had it *been* me, perhaps? Is this what became of *my* version of the world? Or had this planet belonged to some better version of me? Had my alternate-reality-sister led a happy, productive life? Maybe she'd gone on to be some great lawyer. I'd never know.

Somewhere out there, buried deep in the fertile soil, if I dug deep enough, would I find the fossilized bones of that other me? Had I even existed here? No way to tell. And that was okay. But I hoped that I... *they* had. Hoped that their life had been long and blissfully happy; I would have chosen that for myself if I could have.

The one thing this place had gifted to us was more questions than I suspected any of us could ever have answered in tens of lifetimes.

Come one, come all, it's time to take the adventure of more lifetimes than you could possibly know what to do with.

I laughed, drawing Freuchen's attention.

"Vat is so funny?" he asked, his voice lowered to a respectful whisper.

"Oh, nothing really," I said. "I think this world is bringing out even more of the poet in me."

My eyes drifted back up to the moon. Its tail consisted of several large chunks that must have been tens of miles wide, numerous smaller ones that also must have been a mile or more in diameter, and tail of debris that followed behind it like baby ducklings.

I'd watched the moon travel across the sky on other nights when it had been difficult to sleep, but none of those nights had been as clear as this one, and none had given me such a crystal clear view of the Earth's damaged sibling in such glory.

A new thought struck me.

"Hey, Freuchen," I whispered, stepping closer to him and nodding at the moon. "Doesn't the debris field of the moon seem like there's more than there should be? I mean, I've been doing a jigsaw puzzle in my head for the last few minutes, and I just can't seem to fit all of those pieces back into the space it came from." In my mind, there was at least thirty or forty percent too much debris left in the moon's tail once I had pieced it all together again.

Freuchen looked skyward. "I had not given it any thought," he said. His eyebrows furrowed, and his head cocked back in a child-like manner of interesting surprise. "But now that you have mentioned it; yes, there does appear to be more debris than vould seem to fit that.

"Weird," I said, unable to come up with any solution.

"Perhaps there is more destruction that ve cannot see," he said.

"On the dark side of the moon?" I said.

"Perhaps. That vould account for it."

"You're too damn smart for your own good," I said, smiling at him.

Freuchen blushed, a rare enough event that it elicited a bigger smile from me.

"So many questions," I said quietly, still unable to lay to rest the idea that I was missing something with the moon.

"At least it isn't raining," Freuchen said as we made our way back to the crew quarters where everyone else was already waiting for us. I lay down on one of the beds and looked at my friends, both old and new.

Nobody seemed to want to start the conversation off, so I jumped in.

"Well, we've made it," I said. "Now, what are we supposed to do?"

"It would be a mistake to leave before sunrise," Chou said, "but we are going to have to time our trek to the mountains very carefully. We do not want to get caught in the aurora."

"The dead-land," I said.

Chou nodded. "It would be a mistake to be caught within the confines of that area."

"Thank goodness it only happens once a day," Albert said, sitting cross-legged on the bed next to mine.

"Ve have to decide how ve are going to get across the dead-land. If ve valk, ve are going to eat up valuable time," Freuchen said.

"Yes," I said, "but if we use the *Brimstone,* we risk it being caught in tonight's aurora. Maybe we should use it as an Uber; take us there, drop us off, and then return here to wait for us."

"That sounds like the safest option," Bartholomew said.

"Vat is this... Uber?"

I laughed, though I thought I might be the only one who truly knew what I was laughing at.

"But that would also mean someone would have to stay behind to pilot the airship back to us," I said.

Freuchen leaned forward. "Ve vould also need someone else to act as security, just to be on the safe side."

It was obvious who those two people should be: Bartholomew and Amelia.

"Are you agreeable to that?" Chou asked, looking at both of them.

With some reluctance, they both nodded, but their disappointment was palpable.

———

We slept. And when dawn arrived, we woke Silas and filled him in on what we intended to do.

"That sounds like a good plan. Would you like me to stay behind with the Brimstone *too?"*

"No," Chou said, "we're going to need you for this."

"Very well."

We'd already resupplied our backpacks with enough water and food for forty-eight hours. While Freuchen had been taking inventory of the airship's supplies, he'd found a long length of rope, binoculars, and some cold-weather gear. We added it to the rations, and we were ready to go.

"If ve have to climb those mountains, ve should be prepared."

Chou gave us all a silent once-over. "I believe we are ready," she said.

I agreed.

"Then let's begin."

SEVENTEEN

THE *BRIMSTONE* skirted slowly around the base of the mountains for almost an hour, looking for a visible entrance, but we found nothing.

"We do not have any more time to waste," Chou said eventually and directed Amelia to land the airship near the base of the craggy mountains. Before we disembarked, I handed Bartholomew a walkie talkie I'd taken from a rack in the crew's quarters and showed him how to use.

"We'll signal you when we're ready to be picked up," I said.

We said our goodbyes and good lucks then watched as the *Brimstone* took off again.

"My God," Freuchen said, eyes following the collector skyward, his voice hushed as though he'd stepped into a grand cathedral. "I could never have believed such a marvel of human imagination could exist unless I had seen with my own eyes."

I had to agree with him. Nothing mankind had ever built in any of our lifetimes had even come close to the sheer immensity of this. The view from the *Brimstone* last night had been something. But now, from where we stood, there was nothing between us and the collector except fifty feet of empty dead space and the occasional dust devil that danced and pirouetted across the dead-land.

I felt a small hand take mine and looked down to see Albert, his eyes wide with either wonder or fear.

"I don't like it," he said. "It scares me."

"Yeah, I know what you mean, kid," I whispered, squeezing his hand tightly. I was fighting an urge to simply turn and walk away, overwhelmed by the heart-stopping immensity of this structure dominating the world. It was a Titan, frozen forever.

I allowed my eyes to roam up the faceted sides and instantly regretted it. I was overwhelmed by a sensation of imminent danger, like I was standing on the edge of a cliff, and at any moment, gravity would switch and I would fall upward, vanishing into the permanent halo of clouds that swirled slowly around the vanishing point a couple of miles or more into the crystal blue sky.

"Are you feeling alright?" Chou asked me.

"Huh? What?" I shook my head and turned to look at her, only then realizing that I had grabbed onto her arm with my free hand. I exhaled loudly, then sucked in a deep breath, smiled at my friend, and nodded. "It's a bit of a sensory overload."

Chou, her eyes fixed squarely on mine, raised her eyebrows and deadpanned, "Meredith, in the time that I have known you, I have learned that you have a propensity for understatement. You have just outdone yourself."

I couldn't help myself; I laughed loudly.

"Silas," Chou said, "you will lead us. We need to find an entrance to get inside the collector."

"*Very well*," he said.

We started out across the dead-land, our feet kicking up little puffs of the dust that, presumably, had been trees and plants and animals but which the aurora had destroyed.

"How are we supposed to climb those?" I said when we

reached the base of the mountains. The sheer immensity of the collector had created an illusion of scale, I realized. The mountains looked tiny in comparison, but this close, I realized we'd underestimated the mountains' size. They had to be at least fifteen-thousand feet high.

I hadn't really given our situation enough thought. What had I expected? To show up and there be a door with a sign telling me that this is where Candidate 1 waited? Hardly. But I hadn't expected this.

"I have some experience mountaineering," Freuchen said, "but even if ve had the correct equipment, I do not believe any of us are experienced enough to make it even halfvay up."

Chou summed up the growing sense of frustration I felt. "It does not make sense that we would be sent here for there not to be some way for us to gain access."

"Assuming this is the *right* place," Freuchen said, a hint of pessimism creeping into his voice.

I shook my head adamantly. "No, this has to be the place. Silas' message was very explicit. This *has* to be it."

"I know. I know," Freuchen said, "but ve do not even know if this is the right collector. There are three others that ve had to choose from."

"It *has* to be here," I repeated, "we're just not seeing it."

I tried to ignore the sense of doubt I felt nibbling at my confidence. It *could* be any of the other three collectors that had been visible from the mountain back on Avalon, but they just didn't feel right.

"We were all put on the island for a reason," I said. "That's where Silas was. That's where the message was waiting for me. Why put us there in plain sight of the closest collector and not expect that this would be the logical one for us to choose. No, this *is* the right one. We just have to figure out how to get in."

Freuchen glanced skyward. "Vell, ve had better do it soon,

because ve have less than fifteen hours before the aurora triggers again."

I took out the binoculars, raised them to my eyes, and began searching the craggy, inhospitable side of the mountain. Like I said, I wasn't expecting there to be a sign saying 'Candidate 1— this way,' but maybe there was some hint that we were in the right place, a path or a building or... some*thing*. Ten minutes of searching turned up nothing.

The mountains seemed to simply sprout out of the ground, clutching the sides of the collector so perfectly, rising so steeply skyward that there was no hilly area leading up to them, no gradually-rising escarpment. They just *were*.

"It's almost like they were formed specifically to anchor the collector," I said. "Would that even be possible?" I asked Chou.

She shrugged. "I think such a feat of geo-forming would be only a minor project to any intelligence capable of creating such impressive engineering accomplishments as the Dyson Sphere surrounding this sun, the translocation of almost so many humans through time and space, or the collectors themselves."

I avoided allowing my eyes to travel up the outside of the collector. This close, the sense of panic I felt each time I happened to glance at it was magnified tenfold. I huffed a couple of times to clear the anxiety then said, "Well, I guess we have to decide which way we're going to go."

"*Meredith?*" Silas said, his eye-bar following the mountains north.

"What's up?" I asked.

"*I believe I am picking up some kind of low-frequency radio emission. It is coming from that direction.*" He raised an arm and pointed north."

"What? You mean like a message? Someone's trying to contact us?"

Silas' eye-bar rotated to look at me. "*No, not a message, it does not appear to be modulated. It is more a series of pulses occurring every two seconds."*

"Couldn't it just be some spurious emission from the collector?" Chou asked.

"I do not believe so. The signal is weak, but it comprises of a series of numbers."

"Vat numbers?" Freuchen said.

"1 4 4 2 3 3 3 7 7 6 1 0 9 8 7..."

"Okay," I said, "I have no idea what any of that means."

Both Chou and Freuchen shook their heads. Albert, however, seemed to be deep in concentration. With his index finger, he'd traced the numbers in the dust at his feet.

"What're you thinking, kiddo," I said, kneeling down until I was at his eye level.

He ignored me for a few seconds, continuing to stare at the numbers instead, then began to add commas after some of them until it read 144, 233, 377, 610, 987.

"It still makes no sense to me," I said.

"Those are Fibonacci numbers," Chou said.

I turned my attention to her, "The Fibonacci what?"

"Each number is the sum of the two numbers that came before it: 144 plus 233 equals 377. 233 plus 377 equals 610."

"Oh, wow! And 610 plus 377 is 987," I said, suddenly understanding. Math wasn't exactly my strong point, but the idea was simple enough for me to grasp.

Albert nodded enthusiastically.

"You amaze me sometimes," I told him. "It's like we have our own personal Google."

Albert just smiled sweetly, despite him having no way to know what Google even was.

Freuchen stepped closer to us. "You think this is some form of a message?"

Chou said, "It could be, or perhaps it is more of a beacon."

"But how vould anyvun be able to pick it up vithout a radio receiver unless..." Freuchen paused, looked at Silas then looked at me before continuing, "...Silas."

"Right!" I said, beaming. "When the Architect left the message for me with Silas, he must have guessed that I'd take Silas with me. It *has* to be a message specifically for us."

Chou did not look convinced. "It is possible, I suppose..."

"Look, we can either stand around here, debating it, or we can let Silas lead us to where the numbers are coming from," I said. "What do we have to lose?"

For two hours, we followed behind Silas as he led the way, skirting the base of the mountain, the sun crawling higher and higher into the sky.

"*Here,*" Silas said, stopping suddenly. "*The source of the radio signal is coming from there.*" He pointed toward a section of the wall of rock that looked exactly the same as the miles of similar limestone and granite that we had already passed.

"You're joking, right?" I said.

"*No, Meredith. The radio signal is coming from somewhere within.*"

I walked up to the side of the mountain, careful to avoid the scattering of loose rock and boulders. There was nothing to discriminate this part of the mountain from any other part of it —gray, dirty, craggy. I reached out with the flat of my hand to touch it... and stopped.

There was faint shuddering coming from it, like a low power hum.

"Is everything okay?" Chou called out.

I nodded. "Yup!" Then I placed the flat of my hand directly against the rock.

EIGHTEEN

"GET BACK!" Freuchen yelled just as I felt him grab my sleeve and yank me backward.

The rocks were falling away, dropping… and vanishing.

"An illusion," I said.

"An advanced hologram of some kind," Chou corrected.

Behind the fake rockface, two enormous metal doors were opening wide, rumbling slowly apart. Whatever was beyond them was hidden in darkness and shadows.

I said, "Do you think we should—"

The darkness within the tunnel was replaced by a cool blue illumination that revealed a perfectly semi-circular-shaped tunnel as wide as the huge doors. The walls arced high over our heads and were covered in a mosaic of randomly shaped pieces of glimmering glass, as smooth as a layer of ice. The floor was a checkerboard of ever-changing blue hues, creating the illusion that we stood on the edge of a lake. The tunnel was completely empty. It stretched far into the mountains in a gentle curve toward the base of the collector, obscuring whatever lay at its end.

"It's beautiful," Albert gasped. He stepped across the

threshold and knelt to touch the softly-glowing floor. A ripple of pale blue light spread out where his fingertips brushed against it, adding to the illusion that the floor was water. Albert looked back at us, his lips transformed into a massive grin of wonderment.

We all joined him, our shoes causing similar ripples to expand out in intricate patterns across the floor. Chou reached out and laid the flat of her hand against the wall, then jumped back as a ripple of light expanded upward, and a sound, like someone humming a single musical note, rose from all around us. A second later, it began to fade. Albert rushed to her side and placed one of his own hands against the wall. A new note sounded, a little higher in frequency than the first. Chou turned back to look at us, trying but failing to keep the smile of enchantment from her face.

"Silas, what is this?" she asked.

Silas did not immediately answer. Instead, he reached out a hand and drummed his fingers against the wall, setting off a cascade of ripples and notes.

"*The Architect was concerned that the effects of the translocation on Candidates would induce mass-panic. While certain chemical alterations were made to you to reduce that possibility, every effort was made to ensure your environment was as calming as possible. I imagine this is a simple attempt to ensure that whoever passed through this tunnel remained tranquil.*"

"Though it is enchanting," Freuchen said, apparently immune to the desire to touch the wall, "ve do not know if this area is shielded from the negative effects of the aurora. I vould suggest that ve make our vay to vatever lies at the end of this tunnel as quickly as possible."

"Peter's right, we really should keep moving," I said. I adjusted my backpack and began walking again.

Albert skipped ahead of us, jumping left then right as if the enormous tunnel was his own personal hop-scotch board.

We adults walked abreast of each other.

"Vy so big, do you think?" Freuchen asked, swinging his head back and forth as he took in the cathedral-sized dimensions of the tunnel.

"Perhaps it was used to transport parts of the collector or other machinery," Chou said.

"Or maybe they just expected a ton of people," I added, then said, "Silas, got any ideas?"

"I'm *sorry, I do not have any information on why these tunnels were built to such specifications,*" he said.

We had only gone a hundred steps or so when a rumbling echoed behind us, causing all of us to stop. The two huge doors were closing again. They were still thirty feet from meeting when a screech of grinding metal called out to us... and the doors shuddered to a stop.

"Well, that can't be good," I said.

"Nothing ve can do about it. Ve must carry on."

I agreed, but until the curve of the tunnel finally blocked the route back from our sight, I could not shake a nagging sense of worry that periodically drew my attention over my shoulder to the two stuck doors and the open space between them.

NINETEEN

FORTY-FIVE MINUTES LATER, we reached a second set of doors identical to the first. At least we assumed they were identical because only the left one was in the closed position, the other still in its recess.

Freuchen looked at Chou, his eyebrows raised questioningly. He didn't have to say a word. It was obvious we were all thinking the same thing. Here was just another indication that this place had fallen into disrepair. And that did not bode well for us finding anyone alive within.

"Ve need to be careful," Freuchen said, edging along the door toward the gap where the other should have been. "Ve have no idea vat—"

"Albert! No!" I hissed as the boy happily skipped his way past the door right into the gap. Albert stopped, started to turn back to me, and froze, his eyes fixed on whatever lay beyond. He turned to face us, his eyes full of awe, and waved eagerly to us to join him.

I ran to his side, my back toward the gap. "You have got to stop running off like that," I said, pulling him back in the direction of the door, but he refused to budge. "Albert, you have no idea what—"

"Look, Meredith," Albert said, pointing one small finger past my head. "*Look!*"

I heard a duo of simultaneous gasps.

Chou and Freuchen both stood rooted in place.

Slowly, I turned to face the same direction as my friends... and felt my words disintegrate as my tongue sucked all the saliva from my mouth. And that was okay, because I was beginning to run out of adjectives to describe the almost constant flood of mind-melting sights that bombarded us on an almost daily basis, and I wasn't sure there were any that would truly sum up the grandeur of what I was now seeing.

I settled on, "SHUT. THE. FRONT. DOOR."

We stood on the edge of another world. One that was, at once, both familiar yet alien. Fields of green grass stretched out for miles and miles. Sprinkled here and there was the occasional plot of what must be wheat or barley, I couldn't quite tell. It created a quilted pattern of yellow against the backdrop of green. A river, a quarter-mile wide at the point closest to us, bisected the landscape, meandering serenely through the fields, past copses of willows and oaks, and other more exotic-looking trees.

And, *oh!* the scent was heavenly.

This microcosm of Eden was contained beneath a dome of some barely visible energy. Shifting blue hues moved over its surface, and puffy white clouds — *actual clouds* — scooted across the counterfeit sky.

And sitting in the center of it all, rising up to almost touch the apex of the dome, was the most beautiful building I'd ever seen.

Five jade green flute-shaped glass spires soared toward the uppermost reaches of the dome, each one a different height from the others, but all connected by what I thought were covered walkways. I saw stained-glassed windows and balconies with ornate metal railings that must have given an even better view of this land than we had. The spires rose up from a five-level ziggu-rat-like glass-sided building that was as large as any cathedral I'd ever encountered. Five other buildings were scattered across the landscape, all as large as a big city museum and with the same beautiful architecture as the cathedral.

What I took to be a monorail connected each of the build-ings. It, too, had fallen into disrepair in places, with large chunks either missing or lying in piles of debris.

"In Xanadu did Kubla Khan, a stately pleasure-dome decree: Where Alph, the sacred river, ran through caverns measureless to man down to a sunless sea," I whispered, quoting Coleridge's most well-known poem.

"Are those trees in the buildings?" I said, pointing toward the cathedral.

"Fascinating. Each level appears to contain a different biome," Chou said.

She was right. On each level of the ziggurat were trees and flowers, each level representing a different environment: deep forest, jungle; rainforest; tundra.

Beyond the energy dome covering this place, set back perhaps a mile or so from it, the gray and black face of the mountain this idyllic space had been carved out of rose up around us. Distorted, as though I saw them through a haze of hot air, giant tightly wound corkscrew-shaped protrusions that must have been miles long, extended out of a circular opening. They stretched out on all sides, their tips buried deep into the walls of the mountain. Further into the opening were what looked like colossal milky-white pyramids, each as wide as a jetliner, they're apexes pointing downward, forming a crys-talline ceiling.

"We must be directly under the very center of the collector," Chou said, pointing up at the corkscrews. "Those anchors must help secure it in place."

As if by some psychic agreement, all five of us stepped into the amazing landscape and began walking toward the nearest building, about a mile or so away. We had walked less than a hundred feet when, from behind the buildings to our left, I saw movement. Freuchen must have noticed it too because he let out a gasp of surprise. Something rose quickly into the air above the building's alabaster walls. It stopped, hovered momentarily, then accelerated in our direction.

It was a machine, I realized... and it was enormous. Its body was orb-shaped, the diameter of a Greyhound bus. Hanging from beneath its bottom sections was a cluster of long articulated tentacles that made it look like a giant metal jellyfish as it sped toward us.

Chou frantically searched the nearby landscape for anywhere that we could use as cover, but there was nothing nearby. I looked back over my shoulder toward the doorway we'd come through, hoping we might have time to run back to it. However, when I turned to look again at the thing flying toward us, it was already closing faster than even Chou could run.

We were caught out in the open. Proverbial sitting ducks.

With less than a hundred feet left between us, Silas took several steps toward the fast-approaching machine and said, "*Hello. I am Standard Instruction and Learning Servitor 762. You may call—*"

There was a white flash of light from an aperture at the top of the machine. Silas' eye-bar snapped back into his head with a loud crack. His eyes blinked out, and he collapsed motionless in a heap on the ground, like a marionette that had had its strings sliced.

"Silas!" Albert yelled and took two steps toward our friend

before Chou caught his wrist and swung him in one fluid motion into her arms. Freuchen growled and placed himself in front of us, his shoulders so broad he blocked my entire view. I had to step to the left to see the machine as it slowed to a stop, with less than ten yards separating us. Around the circumference of the orb was a recessed trough; lights, all of them blue except for a single red one that was obviously fixed on us, glowed brightly. As I stepped out from behind Freuchen, the red light that had been focused on him turned blue, and the one to its immediate right changed to red... its focus now me. I couldn't help myself; I took an involuntary step back. This thing was hugely intimidating.

The machine dipped lower and covered the distance between me and it in the blink of an eye, its tentacles rattling like wind through metal trees. At the end of each tentacular limb were various blades and drill bits, saws and pincers, scissors and hammers. They could be tools... or weapons, for all I knew. All I did know was that everything the Architect had placed in this world was designed to aesthetic perfection. Silas, the collectors, the graveyard of dead robots, all had been *meticulously* constructed. Even the ruined tower where we'd found our metal friend back on Avalon, despite its state of disrepair, had still retained its elegance. This machine had none of that finesse. It looked like it had been cobbled together out of spare parts.

Its outer casing looked to be made of copper that had long ago lost its luster. It was scratched and gouged in places. Here and there, blue flakes of paint still clung to it like scabs. Four steel panels of varying sizes had been fastened to it in places across its surface, the welds that held them in place, severe and ugly scars. This close, I could see that what I had taken for lights in the recessed area running around its middle were actually lenses, similar to telescopic lenses of a camera. At least three of them were broken, shards of glass still visible in the housings.

Compared to every other machine I'd seen or met on this planet, this one looked like the machine equivalent of a bum who called a cardboard box in the back of a liquor store his home.

It drew close enough that I could feel the slight disturbance in the air caused by whatever kept it aloft, could smell the scent of oil and grease. The red lens whirred as it extended in then out again, as though it were having trouble focusing on me. One of its appendages flashed through the space between us, the pair of scissor-like blades snapping together just inches from Freuchen's head.

"Who are you?" the machine demanded, in a disarmingly feminine voice. "How did you get in here?"

"My... my name is Meredith Gale," I stuttered. "We were sent here by the Architect to find Candidate 1." I paused, then added, "Are *you* Candidate 1?"

The machine pulled back ten feet as if I'd slapped it. Its appendages, which until now had been held like fists, cocked and ready to strike, relaxed.

"I am not," it said, then, "Give me your hand."

"What? Why?" This time, I pulled back.

The machine advanced menacingly toward me.

Freuchen and Chou both made to block its path, but an appendage flashed between them, knocking Freuchen aside, and grabbed me by my right wrist.

I screamed, "Let me go, you—" I winced as I felt something sharp pierce the palm of my hand. The machine let me go, and it withdrew its tendril. There was a small spot of blood on the palm of my hand. "What did you just do to me?" I yelled.

The machine remained silent for a few moments, then it said, "A blood sample to ascertain that you are who you say you are. I apologize, but I had to be absolutely sure."

"Well, did I pass your damn test?" I snapped.

"You did. Now, please follow me," the machine said, its

voice so gentle it simply did not fit with the sheer, ugly, utilitarian design of its body.

"What did you do to Silas!" Albert suddenly yelled, wriggling out of Chou's arms and running to my side. His face was flushed with anger, and I felt a sharp pang of guilt tinged with a sudden surge of anger at myself that I had forgotten my friend so easily.

"He is an unauthorized SILAS unit, and I have deactivated him until I can ascertain his allegiance," the machine said.

"Allegiance?" I said. Now I took three long steps forward until I was face-to-face with the sultry-voiced monstrosity, angrier than I could remember being in a long time. "Silas saved all our lives. He led us here. I demand that you release him, right now, or I swear to God I will fu—"

Freuchen wrapped a hand around my left bicep and squeezed hard enough to distract me. He leaned in and whispered, "Perhaps, it vould be a good idea to remember that ve are guests of this... entity."

I got the point, took a deep breath, then backed up, but the desire to pull one of this thing's tentacles off and shove it right up its—

"Hello," Chou said, stepping forward. "Do you have a designation?"

The blue light I was staring into turned red as a lens closer to Chou gave her the once over. "Who are you?" The machine's focus shifted from Chou to Freuchen to Albert.

"They're with me," I said, suddenly terrified that it... *she*... might decide to permanently 'deactivate' my three friends like it had done with Silas.

I was its center of attention again.

"I am Blue Alpha," it said matter-of-factly.

"Well, Blue Alpha, it's good to meet you," I lied, forcing

down my still swirling anger. "Now, will you reactivate our friend Silas. Please."

"As I have already said, that will not be possible until I have ascertained his allegiance. Once that has been determined, I will choose to reactivate him or recycle him."

"What do you mean 'recycle?'" I asked.

Blue Alpha ignored me, its attention switching to a lens that seemed focused on something behind us.

"The security doors," she said, a note of alarm in her voice. "How long have they been opened?"

"I have no idea. They were that way when we arrived."

The robot suddenly lost interest in me and sped over to the doorway.

Blue Alpha was enormous—by far the largest robot we had encountered—but even with only one of the doors open, she still could have slipped into the tunnel with room to spare. Instead, she stopped just short of the doorway. An appendage—the one that was equipped with what looked like a giant pair of tweezers —reached up to the band of lenses and plucked one from its fitting. Then, it snaked into the tunnel and shifted back and forth for a few seconds as though it was examining both the tunnel and the stuck door, then withdrew and replaced the lens back in its fixture. Blue Alpha drifted back to us.

"You were not followed," she said.

I wasn't sure whether that was a question or a statement, so I just said, "No, we weren't." I wondered whether I should tell her about the main doors that had jammed open after we entered the tunnel. I decided against it, at least until we knew whether or not we could trust her.

"Why did you not enter the tunnel?" Chou said bluntly.

"I have not left this facility for... a very long time."

"Why not?" Chou pressed. "An entity of your intelligence and size should be able to find a way out of here."

Blue Alpha swayed gently from side to side as though blown by a breeze. "Then who would take care of the Arboretum? Who would there be to await your arrival?"

"But there must be more of you? This place is too enormous for just you to look after," I said.

"I am the last. Follow me." Blue Alpha began to float toward the same building it had originally appeared from behind.

"Hey! Wait a second," I yelled after her. "What about Silas? We're not going anywhere without him."

I felt Albert's hand take mine and squeeze. I looked down to see him smiling up at me, which went a long way to making me feel a little less guilty about my earlier momentary abandonment of Silas.

Alpha Blue hesitated, then an appendage reached backward and with its claw-like attachment, plucked Silas from where he lay. She continued on her way, carrying our deactivated friend as though he were nothing.

I looked at Chou and Freuchen. "Should we follow?"

"Do ve have much of a choice?" Freuchen said.

TWENTY

BLUE ALPHA STOPPED at the top of a set of six sandstone steps. "Your accommodation is ready. Follow me."

The robot said the only way into the building was called the Arboretum. It was through a large wooden door embossed with an elaborate geometrical design. The doorway, tiny by comparison to the ones in the tunnel, was still large enough for Chou to have stood on Freuchen's shoulders and passed through without hitting her head. But there was no way Blue Alpha could fit without quite literally demolishing half of the building.

"How is she going to—" Albert began then stopped as the bulbous protrusion at the center of Blue Alpha's body popped free of her main chassis and floated where she'd left it. This 'mini' version of Blue Alpha was still the size of a compact car. It had just four lenses around its middle, front, back, and one on each side. A smaller set of the main chassis' appendages dangled beneath it. Blue Alpha swung the door open, and we followed her into a lobby lined with white tile. Two sets of stone stairs, one on either side of the lobby, curved up to a second story. At the opposite end of the lobby, windows looked out onto a lawn with benches, a small lake, and lots of trees.

Blue Alpha floated up to the next floor. We all took the stairs and followed her down a passageway to a large dormitory with five beds on either side. The beds were made, each with crisp gray sheets and pillows and a yellow comforter. Albert leaped on to a bed. He let out a long *Oooooh* of contentment. "It's *so* soft," he said and spread himself out. "I've never felt anything so nice."

Did they have beds like this back in the when Albert came from? Probably not judging by his reaction.

"There are showers and bathrooms through there," Blue Alpha said, indicating with a wave of an appendage a doorway at the opposite end of the dormitory. "I'm afraid I cannot offer you any food. What supplies we had expired long ago."

I caught the sudden narrowing of Chou's eyes. If the supplies Blue Alpha mentioned had expired long ago, then that meant the chances of there being any humans here were zero.

"You said 'we.' There are more of you?" I asked.

"There were, a long time ago."

"But now?"

"Now there is only me... It's musty in here." She floated toward a window, released the latch and opened it. "That's better."

Albert sat up, a pillow clutched to his chest like a Teddy bear. "You must be really lonely," the boy said.

"I miss my comrades, yes, but their sacrifice has not been in vain."

"Sacrifice?" Freuchen said. "Vat do you mean by that?"

Blue Alpha glided back to the center of the room. "What do you know of why you are here?"

I looked to Chou and Freuchen and got both of their silent approval. "We know that we were brought here by an entity called the Architect. That it is responsible for bringing others like us from different times and different dimensions. We know that because another entity that we call the Adversary inter-fered, something went very, very wrong with the Architect's plan."

"What we don't know," Chou said, "is *why* we were brought here. Do you know why, Blue Alpha?"

"No, I am just a maintenance intelligence. I was not a primary part of the Architect's plan. I was designed to maintain the collector I was never supposed to interact with humans on any meaningful level."

"And yet," said Freuchen, "you are very eloquent."

"I was... upgraded."

"How so?" said Chou.

"Shortly before the great translocation was scheduled to begin, I, along with all of the other intelligences in this facility, received new code from the Architect... and a warning. We were told that something had gone terribly wrong; that the Architect was at war with another entity—I assume that must be this Adversary that you mentioned. We were given self-aware-ness and told to prepare for an attack on the collector—an attack that we must stop at *any* cost."

"Why attack this place?" Chou said.

"The collectors are the key to the Architect's plan. Without them, it cannot succeed."

""Vell, it makes sense that the Adversary vould try to destroy the collectors," Freuchen said, sitting on the edge of the bed next to Albert, "The Adversary seems intent on making sure the Architect's plan never comes to fruition. This place..."

"I get that," I said, "but *why*? What are these things supposed to do? How do they figure into the Architect's plan?"

"That information was not shared with any of us." Blue Alpha's tentacles gave a little shake, as if she was frustrated. "We were instructed to defend it with our lives. And so we did."

"What about Silas?" Albert asked. "When will you bring him back?"

"I cannot allow his reactivation until I am certain of his loyalty."

"Loyalty?" I said. "Silas is the one who passed the message from the Architect to me. Without him, we would never have made it here. How could you question his loyalty?"

Blue Alpha hovered directly in front of us at head height. "Because two days after we became sentient, this collector was attacked just as the Architect had predicted."

"So?" I said, my frustration growing by the second.

"We were attacked by SILAS units like your friend. Hundreds of them. They had been reprogrammed to stop at nothing in their attempts to destroy the collector. They gained access to the loading tunnel you arrived through and attempted to attack us directly. We managed to hold them off, but it cost almost three-quarters of my brethren; fifty-two units *gone* in a matter of hours. But we were winning, we had the upper hand. Then, we received reports that a secondary group of SILAS units had scaled the mountain and were dismantling the outer shielding of the collector in an attempt to gain access to the core systems."

I don't know whether it was a conscious action on her part or not, but as Blue Alpha narrated her story, she had begun bobbing up and down in what I took to be the equivalent of human gesticulation.

She continued. "That was when we realized that we had been duped. The SILAS units we were fighting were not there to destroy the Arboretum, they were here to ensure *we* did not leave it. They were nothing more than a distraction designed to weaken our numbers.

"It was Green Theta who came up with the idea to overload the collector's capacitors and force them to vent. The gamma radiation that would be released would be more than powerful enough to destroy the SILAS units. Green Theta's plan worked. It eliminated every SILAS unit and saved the collector. But we must have miscalculated some*thing* because the release triggered a simultaneous cascade effect across the network—every collector activated at once. The effect was devastating... destroying everything for several miles around us."

"The gray dust," Albert said.

"Yes," Blue Alpha said. "And worse still, we could not stop it. The capacitors, instead of allowing the release of energy at a constant, steady rate, were now triggering every twenty-four hours instead."

"What stopped you from just repairing it?" I said.

"Only a few of us remained at that point. All of the technical units were destroyed, and none of us survivors had any knowledge of how to fix the problem. All we knew how to do was to keep the collector working. And so that is what we did. As the years passed, the remaining twelve repair units began to fail. We repaired each other as best as we could, and when one of us became inactive, we used their components to repair ourselves. But there were finite resources, and entropy will not be denied. One by one, units failed. Now there is only me."

"But Silas wasn't responsible for that? He isn't one of *them*," I said.

"I will ascertain that soon enough," Blue Alpha said, gliding toward the door.

"How?" Chou said.

"I will run a diagnostic scan of his systems."

I said, "Blue Alpha, when we first arrived, I asked you two questions, but you only answered one of them: Candidate 1—are they here?"

The robot paused for what felt like an eternity then said, "Yes, Candidate 1 is here."

Freuchen jumped to his feet and grabbed hold of my hand. "You ver right all along, Meredith."

I felt a wave of excitement crash over me. "Are they *here*?" I pointed at the ground beneath my feet.

"No, Candidate 1 is in the citadel."

Citadel?

"The green towers?" I asked, remembering the stunning set of towers we'd seen when we first arrived.

"Yes."

"Can you take us there?"

"Yes."

"Now?"

"If you wish, yes. Come with me." Blue Alpha exited into the corridor and led us back to the lobby, down the stairs, along another corridor and then down a second set of stairs that took us well below ground level. We followed her beneath an arch and found ourselves on a platform where a sleek-looking train with two carriages waited. "The buildings are connected by underground and overground maglevs, but the overground tracks were too badly damaged during the attack, so I have concentrated on ensuring that the underground routes remain in working order. Even so, the connection between two of our outermost buildings has been severed due to tunnel collapses." She seemed genuinely saddened by the loss.

At our approach, the doors to the first carriage slid silently apart, and we all stepped inside. Rows of comfortable-looking seats sat on either side of a central aisle. We took the one nearest to the engine. The doors slid shut again, and a second later, the maglev eased away from the station. It accelerated rapidly, the only sense of movement the occasional light on the tunnel wall that flashed by so fast it left an afterimage like a shooting star on my eyes.

Minutes passed, and the train began to slow, finally coming

to a stop in a station that looked identical to the one we'd just left. The only thing to discern they were actually different was a couple of abandoned metal luggage carts. The doors opened, and Blue Alpha led us out. We followed her down a set of spiral stairs that seemed to go on forever and were barely wide enough to fit Freuchen's broad shoulders.

"I'm cold," Albert said as we dropped deeper into the ground. The kid was right. The temperature had grown increasingly cooler.

"I was forced to salvage the heating ducts, long ago," Blue Alpha said.

I was becoming more and more dubious about this strange machine. If it was telling the truth about Candidate 1, then how could any human survive down here without any kind of heat? It just didn't make any sense to me. I was about to voice my concern when we finally reached the bottom and stepped out into a tunnel made of redbrick and mortar. Three pipes fixed to the wall by brackets ran close to the arched ceiling, while lights, strung like Christmas strands, flickered randomly. It was like we'd descended into the Victorian sewers of New York or London.

"Oh, great," I said, "this is just tremendous."

Fifty paces ahead of us, the tunnel's ceiling had collapsed, totally blocking the corridor with dirt, broken bricks, lumps of concrete, and the occasional enormous boulder.

"What the hell is this?" I snapped, turning on Blue Alpha. "You told us Candidate 1 was here. You lied."

The lens closest to me lit up, the intelligence behind it seemed suddenly as cold as the air in the corridor.

"I do not lie," Blue Alpha said. "Beyond the rubble is what you're looking for. When the attack came, and before we realized that the true target was actually the collector, we were faced with the high probability that we would be overrun. It was then that we made the decision to seal this section. We collapsed the ceiling in the hope that, should we lose, it would hide the custodians long enough that help would arrive. As it turned out, there was no help left, but the attack was repelled."

"Custodians?" I said.

"Yes. We thought that they were the target, but now we believe that the Adversary had no idea that they were here."

"So vy the hell did you not clear it avay?" Freuchen said.

"We had lost so many units during the battle, we no longer had the resources. As you may have already gathered, my main chassis is incapable of making it to this location. And we did not know whether there might be another attack. It was decided that the best course of action was to simply leave it."

"But what about these custodians?" Chou said. "How were they supposed to survive? Do you even know if they are still alive?"

"The custodians were safe and in no imminent danger."

God! This machine was really starting to annoy me.

I jerked a thumb at the rubble. "But if they've been behind that crap for three-hundred years, then how are they supposed to have survived? No food, no water, no nothing. You're lying." The anger in my voice was laced with disappointment, and I realized how very tired I was.

"I do *not* lie," Blue Alpha repeated, with vehemence this time.

Chou touched my shoulder. "Meredith, there are alternatives. It's possible they may be in some kind of suspended animation or cryogenically frozen."

"So, there's only vun thing for it," Freuchen said, interlacing the fingers of his hands and cracking out his knuckles. "Ve are going to have to clear this ourselves."

Chou and I turned to stare at him. "Are you crazy?" I said. "Some of those boulders are bigger than the ones that were trapping Silas when we found him. And at least we had gravity and room on our side then. There's barely room to fit *you*."

Freuchen was offended... "Vell, it is not going to magically clear itself, is it? So, unless you have a better idea, it is our only option."

Albert tugged at my sleeve. "What about—"

"Not now," I said, perhaps a little too harshly. I turned my attention back to Freuchen. "It's going to take us weeks to clear all of that away. And what if the ceiling collapses while we're moving it? We'll all be crushed to death or... or trapped down here until we suffocate."

"Meredith," Albert said, tugging at my sleeve. "What about Silas?"

"What about him?" I snapped. "Blue Alpha has already made it clear she's not going to reactivate him until he's passed whatever stupid test she has planned." My voice was shrill, my frustration finally reaching a boiling point. I was sweating despite the cold of the dusty corridor. "This is all just a nightmare. Just a—"

I flinched as Chou took a step toward me, grabbed my arm, and yelled, "Stop! You are panicking, and panic will do us no good under these circumstances."

I was not going to cry. I was *not*. But right then, I felt like this new life was beginning to echo the old life that had brought me here: success always just out of reach. I sniffed back my tears and clenched my teeth together.

"Freuchen leaned back against the wall, his arms folded across his chest. "Vell, Albert is correct. If ve had Silas' help, ve could clear this corridor in a matter of a few days or less, depending how far it goes on for, of course. I have some experience vurking the gold mines in Alaska." He extended his hand to point at the broken ceiling. "If ve brace the ceiling as ve go, it should be safe."

Now, he turned to face Blue Alpha. "But ve vould need our friend brought back to the land of the living. Vat do you say?"

Blue Alpha remained silent for a few moments, then said, "I will administer the test. We shall proceed from there. We must go to my laboratory." And with that, she floated back up the spiral staircase.

————

Blue Alpha's laboratory was a separate gray warehouse building just beyond the towers. Her main chassis was already waiting for us in front of two aircraft-hanger-sized doors. Silas still hung limply from one of its tentacles like Faye Ray captured by King Kong. The doors slid open as we approached, and we followed Blue Alpha inside.

"Vat in heaven's name?" Freuchen exclaimed.

Within the warehouse were row upon row of heavy-duty shelving. Pieces of machinery had been neatly stacked and ordered on the shelves. Some were as large as cars, others as small as a cellphone, but I had absolutely no clue as to what any of them were.

We followed Blue Alpha down a center aisle big enough to accommodate her chassis... just. There could only have been a few feet of leeway on either side of her. The racks reached all the way to the ceiling, several hundred feet overhead.

Chou said, "You have quite a collection."

"I waste nothing," Blue Alpha replied.

Albert let out a gasp of surprise. "Look! There are more robots like Silas." He pointed to a rack of shelves just off the main corridor.

I broke away from the party and walked over to the rack. The kid was right. Each shelf was piled high with the unmistakable bodies of Silas' brethren. All dismantled. Heads, limbs, torsos, odd tube-like protuberances, multi-faceted silver octagons, eye-bars—all neatly stacked and ordered in row upon row, shelf upon shelf, and box upon box. I felt a sudden wave of nausea. It was horrendous. It wasn't so long ago that I wouldn't have considered that I could have felt such disgust at this... this *butchery*.

"The remains of the SILAS units that attacked the facility," Chou said quietly. I hadn't even heard her approach.

"I... I know they're just machines. They're not human, but I've spent so much time with Silas now, seen how kind he is. This seems nothing short of barbaric."

When Chou did not answer, I turned to look at her and was met with a furrowed brow. "I forget," she said, "that in the *when* you come from, these intelligences would be seen as nothing more than machines." She ran her hand over a dusty torso, leaving a trail of brighter gold behind. "But in my time, that kind of attitude would be met with disgust much as I believe you might feel if you met someone who considered slaves as sub-humans or as property."

"Oh, my God!" I spluttered. "Your husband. He's an AI. I'm so sorry, Chou, I didn't mean to offend you."

She nodded and smiled understandingly at me. "I take no offense. In this world, where so many cultures and beliefs are colliding head-on, we must all allow for a period of societal and personal assimilation. It will take time, but I believe we will have all the time that we need."

"Please, keep up with us," Blue Alpha said, then continued on her way.

A little while later, we reached an area that reminded me of a mechanic's shop. Tools that looked vaguely familiar to me and others sat on benches. I saw compressors, and what I guessed was some kind of welding machine mixed in with high-tech equipment and banks of monitors and displays that I had no idea about. In the center of it all was a raised metal table that reminded me of something you'd find in an operating room but about four times larger. It had outlets and connectors set into its side.

"Please, wait over there," Blue Alpha said, gesticulating with a tentacle toward a set of plastic chairs stacked up against a wall. Her chassis extended the tentacle that held Silas and placed him unceremoniously on the table, then proceeded to rearrange his limbs until his legs were straight and his arms lay at his side. She glided over to a rack of tools, pulled out several, including one that looked like a thin version of a crowbar, then moved to Silas's side. With a speed that left me speechless, she applied the crowbar to what must have been an invisible seam running around Silas' chest, levered it up, so the front half separated from the back, and pried it off with a metallic *ping*. Another of her tentacles took it from her while the four others began to probe around inside Silas' chest cavity.

It was like watching an octopus perform open-heart surgery.

Blue Alpha floated up until she was directly above Silas' open chest. She extended a thin tubular metal instrument attached by wires to a gray box on the floor into his chest cavity. There was an electrical buzz, then we all jumped as Silas' eye-bar popped from its recess. His eyes glowed an intense red. Several lines of numbers suddenly appeared in the air a few inches in front of his eyes. They scrolled up at a blistering speed for over a minute then, just as suddenly as they'd appeared, they vanished.

"*Primary quantum diagnostic check: Successful,*" Silas said, his voice sounding, well, robotic. "*No anomalies found.*"

"Good. Very good," Blue Alpha mumbled to herself. She quickly replaced the top half of Silas' chest then repositioned herself above the bump that passed for his head. One of her tentacles plucked his eye-bar out of the air and placed it on the table while two more proceeded to lever his head open by inserting the same thin crow-bar-like tool into the eye-bar socket. From where we sat, we had a perfect view of what I took to be Silas' brain. I guess I had expected some kind of science-fiction-esque array of flashing lights and whirring cogs. Instead, all I saw was a lump of silver metal with three distinct raised bands running from the back of his head to the front that reminded me of a cyclists' helmet.

Blue Alpha picked up a long black cord with a pin-like connector at one end and inserted the connector into a receiver at the base of Silas' brain. She connected the other to one of the banks of equipment behind her, pressed a few buttons on the control panel, and watched as a tsunami of data washed over the screen. A second screen displayed what looked like a duplicate of the data on the first.

"Do you know what she's doing?" Albert said. He sounded worried.

"I have no idea," I admitted, looking at Chou.

"I believe," Chou said, "that she is comparing Silas' core code to a copy she has which she knows has not been corrupted."

Albert stared blankly at Chou.

"She is checking that the Architect has not altered Silas' personality so that he might cause him to want to harm any of us," Chou elaborated.

Albert pouted. "Silas wouldn't hurt us. Not ever."

I put my arm around his shoulder and squeezed. "Well, *we* all know that, of course, but we just need Blue Alpha to make sure that—"

The data on the screens suddenly stopped and a repetitive, alarm-like, beeping sounded. A large block of code on the left screen was highlighted in a flashing green box. On the right screen, the one Silas was plugged directly into, a row of red **X**'s flashed. The numbers and characters above the row of red Xs looked the same as those on the left screen, but everything after it didn't even come close.

I looked at Chou and she at me.

"That can't be good," Freuchen said, stepping between us.

Blue Alpha stopped probing Silas' brain, her attention drawn to the screens.

"What's happening?" I asked her, stepping up to the table.

Her lens closest to me turned red and focussed on my face. "There is a discrepancy between the original backup code I have for the SILAS units and your friend."

"What do you mean 'discrepancy?'" I asked. I sensed my companions move closer to me.

"This SILAS unit is missing a large portion of code."

"Well, he suffered some kind of memory loss when he was hit by a pile of rocks. Maybe that's what did it?"

"No," said Blue Alpha. "This code is not related to his memory systems. We are talking about his core personality and drives." She floated closer to the two screens. "The difference is quite marked. There is a *significant* amount missing." She turned back to Silas and removed the wiring from his head. Moving in closer, she picked up a new tool that looked like a large pen and began prodding Silas' brain. Where it touched, small puffs of smoke rose momentarily into the air.

"Wait," I said. "I don't care that there's a difference between your damn code and Silas'. There is no way he would do anything to hurt us. No way." I was becoming desperate, desperate enough that I was wondering what the odds were that the three of us could overpower Blue Alpha and force her to reactivate our robotic friend.

"That is apparent," Blue Alpha said. She replaced the pen-like tool in its slot on a nearby shelf and began to replace the outer cover of Silas' head.

"I *don't* care," I said, fear working its way into my voice despite my best attempt to stop it, "we're not going to..." I paused. "Wait a second, what?"

With his head back in place, Blue Alpha placed Silas' eyebar back in its slot. "I said that it is apparent that this SILAS unit would not attempt to hurt you," Blue Alpha said. She gesticulated toward the two screens. "I extracted the code on the left from the brains of the SILAS units that attacked this facility. The *corrupted* SILAS units. The code which Silas is missing is the malicious code that was placed in the other units by the Architect. Your friend is *not* corrupted." There was a flash of light from Blue Alpha's main chassis, and a few moments later, Silas whirred into life, sat upright, swung his legs over the edge of the table, and dropped to his feet.

Albert sprinted to Silas' side, threw his arms around the robot's legs, and hugged him hard enough that the metal man wobbled just a little.

"I missed you, Silas," Albert said, his chin tilted up to the robot's eye-bar.

Silas reached out a hand and gently stroked the boy's hair. *"And I have missed you, too, Albert. Although I must admit, I am unaware of what has transpired since our arrival here."* He looked around. *"Wherever here is."*

I was about to answer him when a thought struck me like a lightning bolt. "Hey! Wait a second. You've been deactivated all this time, and I left your slate in my backpack... but you recognize us all?"

Silas's eye-bar moved to take in all of us. "Meredith. Chou. Peter. Albert. Yes, I recognize you all."

I turned to Blue Alpha. "You fixed something. His memory. You fixed it." I felt a smile broadening across my face.

"Yes. It was a simple repair—just a few synaptic nodes that needed to be reconnected. His power core is another matter, however. I will have to pull one from containment, but it will be a simple transference that should take less than half an hour."

"You mean, Silas vill have his memory back, and von't have to shut down every night?" Freuchen said.

"That is correct."

I resisted the urge to reach out and hug Blue Alpha. Instead, I placed a hand against her metal casing and said, "Thank you. Thank you, so much."

"You are welcome," Blue Alpha replied. "Now, perhaps it would be a good idea for you to explain to your friend that we have need of him."

TWENTY-ONE

"*I THINK it would be better if you and Albert waited in the stairwell. The chance of further collapse is high,*" Silas said.

"Yeah, not going to happen," I said.

We were back at the tunnel Blue Alpha said she and her compatriots had sabotaged to ensure the safety of whoever or *whatever* lay beyond the mound of rubble. Blue Alpha had fabricated ten large metal supports in her workshop, and eight of them lay neatly stacked against the left side of the corridor. Freuchen was working with Chou to put two of them into place to support the ceiling at the face of the rubble. Freuchen had already come up with a plan for how to attack the problem of getting the rubble out of the corridor: we mere humans would stack the smaller pieces of debris along the corridor while Silas would carry the larger items up to the next floor, where they wouldn't be a danger to us.

Freuchen stood back, placed his hands on his hips, and regarded the wall of concrete, rock, and dirt, illuminated by two large portable lights Blue Alpha had brought with her. "The more pressing problem is how ve are going to get the biggest pieces out of here," he said, tapping one of the larger boulders with his boot. "If ve pull out the vong one, the whole thing could come down on us." He mimicked the ceiling collapsing.

"Perhaps we should only remove the ones we have to and leave those that we do not need, so they act as support?" Chou offered.

Freuchen stroked his beard. "An untidy solution and potentially dangerous, but under the circumstances, it might vurk," he said. "Let's get to it then."

Albert wanted to help too, so Blue Alpha scrounged up a small wicker basket, and we filled it with smaller pieces of concrete and broken red bricks which Albert dutifully followed behind Silas each time he took the stairs. It kept the kid occupied and out of the corridor, which had quickly filled with a thin cloud of cloying gray dust.

Every ten feet of progress, Freuchen and Chou placed two of the metal supports. I trusted Freuchen knew what he was doing, but I still found myself flinching every time the ceiling creaked or groaned as we moved deeper into the rockfall.

Not long after they had placed the fourth set of supports, Freuchen called out, "I... *yes*, ve're through to the other side." Twenty more minutes of work, and we had a hole big enough for Freuchen and Silas to fit through if they twisted their bodies just so. We grabbed our flashlights and followed one after the other.

Beyond the barrier, we found ourselves in the same redbrick lined corridor as we had just come through, but at the end of it was a heavy, dust-encrusted, oak door.

"This way," said Blue Alpha, and pushed the door open for us.

———

We stepped into a chamber hewn straight out of the rough

quartzite of the mountain. The room was roundish, about twenty feet across, its walls roughly excavated, with not a smooth surface in sight. A rivulet of water dripped slowly down the wall to form a small pool near where we stood, a trail of green algae marking its random trajectory. The place had obviously been hollowed out in a hurry, with none of the usual attention to detail I associated with the Architect's work.

Ahead of us, a wall of reinforced steel stretched from ceiling to floor and wall to wall, blocking us from going any further. In its center was a large door with a lever handle. There was a numerical keypad next to it, glowing brightly.

Blue Alpha floated to the keypad, tapped in a code while reciting the numbers aloud. "Nine. One. Five. One. Nine. Five. Three. Remember it." She reached out, pulled the lever up, and swung the door open.

We stepped through into a semi-circular, metal-walled vault.

Across from us, near the ceiling, a large computer screen followed the wall's curved contour, displaying data and several histograms that updated in realtime. Below the screen, five identical metal doors had been built into the wall. Each one was uniform in size—eight feet by four and made of solid steel. Each was secured to the metal wall by three large, sturdy hinges and equally intimidating bolts. At each door's center was a large metal wheel. Above that, a square of glass was located at approximately head-height. Over the lintel of each door, a small light glowed brightly. Two of the lights were red, but the lights above the last three doors to our right glowed green. Between us and the doors, set back a little way from the center of the room, was a console with a screen and keyboard fixed to it. A single office chair sat by it.

"What *is* this place?" Chou asked, her voice echoing.

"A repository of sorts," Blue Alpha said. "When the attack came, we brought the custodians here for their safety."

"How many custodians are there?" Albert asked.

"There are three who were responsible for building this facility."

"Three?" I said, turning to face Blue Alpha. "We weren't really expecting three." It was a ridiculous thing to say, I suppose. I mean, we'd been told to find Candidate 1. That didn't mean there wouldn't be others, too. I walked past Blue Alpha to the nearest door with a green light and peered through the window.

I let out a gasp of surprise and took a step back.

"Vat is vong?" Freuchen said, immediately at my side.

I had no idea what I'd expected would be beyond the door—a cell or maybe some kind of cryogenic deepfreeze, maybe. But not this... not *this*.

On the other side of the steel door was a park. Cherry Blossom trees lined a path that encircled a pond, a layer of pink petals covering the ground like snow. Beyond the park, visible through the branches of the trees, the towers of a city I thought might be Tokyo rose skyward. Beyond the city, stark against the blue sky, a snow-capped mountain held sway over everything. Sitting on a park bench next to the pond, caught in the act of tossing a sprinkling of seed from a brown paper bag clutched in one hand, was a woman in her mid-thirties. The seed peppered the air in an arc in front of her, while ducks splashed across the pond's surface toward it.

All were frozen in time, as though I was looking at some incredible three-dimensional photograph.

"Is it some kind of hologram?" I asked, unable to drag my eyes away.

"No, it is all very real," Blue Alpha said.

I felt Freuchen's breath on my cheek and turned to see him standing beside me. "Impossible," he said half-heartedly.

"No, not impossible," Chou said, and I turned to see her standing behind the two of us, Albert held in her arms so he could see through the window too. "We have already experienced something very similar, remember?"

"The Titanic," Albert said.

"That's right, Albert," said Chou. She turned back to look at Blue Alpha. "The technology you are using here is the same technology the Architect used to bring us here, the same technology that caused the unstable multi-dimensional chaos we witnessed onboard the ship. But this is controlled. The Architect has managed to establish a permanent connection between this world and these other dimensions. Am I correct?"

"You are," said Blue Alpha. "Before the attack, we received technical data from the Architect and instructions that we should begin construction immediately on this facility. The custodians would be placed in each of these locations. While it appears that time has stopped for us, it is actually moving at a greatly reduced rate. Watch the ducks."

I concentrated on a duck that was in the process of taking off from the pond's surface. Its body was almost completely out of the water, its wingtips just touching the surface, creating a ring of water. As I continued to stare, the ring expanded ever so slightly outward, as though I was watching in super slow motion.

"For the custodians," Blue Alpha continued, "time is passing at a normal rate."

"How *much* time?" Freuchen said.

"Mere hours since they entered," was the robot's reply.

"Weeks have passed here," I said, shaking my head. "Astonishing." I moved to the next door and pressed my face to the glass, my breath condensing against its cold surface.

A man, his back to me, stood on a deserted beach looking out at a cold gray ocean. Huge foam-tipped breakers poised to crash toward the sand and pebble-strewn beach. The sun was either setting or rising, I couldn't tell, but it was barely visible behind a bank of fluffy white clouds. The man was dressed casually in a jacket and jeans, his hands thrust deep into his pockets. I couldn't tell his age, but he had the beginnings of a bald spot visible on the crown of his head, his brown hair tussled by the sea breeze. He was as frozen as the woman beyond the other door.

"How is any of this possible?" Freuchen asked.

"I do not understand the intricacies of the physics, but I believe that it is a similar concept to how gears work. Our universe is the small gear of a vast trans-dimensional machine. These doorways are teeth on that gear and lead to other dimensions that are the equivalent of far larger gears, relatively speaking, of course. For us, time continues as normal, but on the other side of each of these doors, time to us appears to move incredibly slowly. The doorway is kept slightly out of phase with their reality, so it cannot be seen on that side until we want it to be."

Chou and Albert were already at the third door. Freuchen and I crowded in next to them. Inside, we looked in on what I took to be a workshop. An old man stood at a metal workbench. He had to be in his seventies, maybe even older. He wore flannel pants and a woolen sweater. His hair was silver-gray and slicked back over his head, his age-spotted pate visible here and there. He had a narrow face, studious eyes highlighted by a pair of wire-rimmed spectacles that rested halfway down a narrow nose. Full but pale lips were surrounded by a neatly-trimmed beard and mustache that was either red like my hair or stained by nicotine, I couldn't tell.

"He looks worried," Albert said.

He did look worried. His brow was furrowed in either

concentration or worry. It was hard to tell which. The bench was littered with circuit boards, computer equipment, and tools, as were the four other nearby benches. But the old man wasn't concerned with any of these. His attention was completely focused on a framed photograph he held in his hand. It was a strange feeling, to be getting a glimpse into a time way ahead of the one I had left behind me. It was so personal, voyeuristic, yet it was so... mundane. So every day. So—

"Meredith!" Chou said sharply.

I jumped as though I'd been stuck with a pin. "What?"

"The photograph. Look at the photograph." She stepped aside so I could get closer to the glass window.

The photo was in a plain ten-by-eight silver frame. A woman in her forties stood behind a podium. She had red curly hair that was shorter than mine, a more business-like style. Eight men and women stood around her, captured in that split second of jubilation cheering and smiling, some with an arm raised in an obvious gesture of celebration, others caught mid-applause. A young boy of maybe eight stood to her left, gazing up at her. Red, white, and blue balloons cascaded down from the ceiling where they had just been released.

"Oh my God," I whispered. "It's the photograph Weidinger said the Adversary had implanted in his mind."

"Or one very similar," Freuchen said, turning to stare at me, then the photograph. "She is older, to be sure, but there is no doubt in my mind that *she* is *you*, Meredith."

I spun around to face Blue Alpha and blurted out, "Who is he? Is he Candidate 1? Why does he have a photograph of me? You have to tell us."

Blue Alpha repositioned herself behind the control panel. "I think those questions will be better answered in person." She began to manipulate the switches on the console.

I stepped forward and placed both hands on the console. "No, you need to tell—"

Blue Alpha raised a single tentacle in an obvious "shut-the-hell-up" dismissal. I listened.

"I will need you all to step over to the right of the doorway, please," she said.

We did as we were told.

"Thank you."

Chou said, "You're bringing him back, yes?"

"Yes," Blue Alpha said, focused on the console and the computer screen above the doors.

"How?" Chou insisted, obviously fascinated by the whole experience.

"As I have said already, I do not understand the physics of how this works, but the analogy I used earlier—"

"Of the gears," Albert said.

"Yes, of the gears; imagine we are simply meshing more intricately with the universe behind that door. Changing the size of the target universe to match our own so that they meld together and allow us to connect at the same speed of time." She threw several switches at once. The ground reverberated with a low hum, which grew steadily louder. There was a hiss as loud as a sack full of cobras.

Then there was only silence.

The wheel on the door began to rotate. A creek of the hinges, the door opened, and the old man stepped through the doorway to our side, as if he'd simply been standing there all along.

His attention was fixed entirely on Blue Alpha. If he saw any of us standing off to the side, he gave no indication of it. In his right hand, he still carried the photograph of that other me he had been staring at so intently.

"Blue Alpha, you made it. Are you okay?" His voice was

mellow, American west-coast, but he delivered his words with the professorial precision of someone who was used to being listened to.

"I did."

He raised his right hand and looked at a wristwatch. "Twenty minutes over there. How long here?"

"A little more than a month," Blue Alpha said.

The old man staggered momentarily, reached his empty hand out to steady himself on the control deck.

"The others?" he said after regaining his composure.

"I brought you back first."

"We should begin transporting them back as quickly as possible." He still had his back turned and hadn't noticed us.

"Of course, Michael, but first, there are some people I'd you to meet." Blue Alpha gesticulated with one appendage in our direction.

The man turned, jumped in surprise, and took several steps backward when he saw the five of us standing near the wall. "You let a SILAS unit in here? Are you insane?"

"It's all right," Blue Alpha said reassuringly, "I have checked his core system, and his programming is uncorrupted."

The old man relaxed a little. "Who are you?" he demanded. His gaze moved over all of us, and for a moment, I imagined how we must look to him. A giant, a robot, a child, a woman dressed all in white, and me. We must look pretty damn odd. His eyes met mine, moved to Chou, then snapped back to my face. He inhaled an enormous gulp of air then exhaled it as a gasp of astonishment before taking two teetering steps toward me, adjusting his spectacles.

"My God," the old man said, his voice hushed. "It... it can't be. But it is, isn't it?"

I looked at my companions, but they were all staring at me. I took a couple of steps closer to him. "I understand you probably think you know me," I said, nodding at the photograph he held, "but I'm not—"

He covered the space between us in a couple of quick, long steps and snatched both my hands up with his own. His skin was calloused and warm, and he held my hands with a tenderness I had not felt in a very long time. He seemed unable to speak, words trying to escape his lips pulled back by the gravity of his emotion. Tears welled in his eyes and began to follow the curve of his age-spotted cheeks.

"Mother," he said.

TWENTY-TWO

I LAUGHED NERVOUSLY and let go of the old and obviously crazy man's hand. "Look, sir, I am absolutely not your mother. I know this all must be very confusing but—"

He thrust the photograph in front of my face, tapping the picture of the other me with a wrinkled index finger. "This is you, yes?"

"No. I suppose so. Kind of," I stuttered.

"And this..." he tapped the picture of the little boy, "is me. This is the day you... *my* version of you, won the election for President of the United States." He tapped the image of a tall, good looking man standing next to Photo-Me's immediate left, his right hand pressed against my lower back.

"That's my father." He lowered the photo and wiped the tears from his eyes with a knuckle, composed himself, and continued. "I'd wondered whether I might meet someone that I knew—an alternate version of some old friend—but it was just a daydream. I never imagined *this*, never thought that I might find someone who meant so very much to me. It is a little overwhelming."

"But I'm not *really* her," I insisted. *"My* life took a very different route."

"Of course. Of course," he repeated, not unkindly. "The very fact that you are here means your life-paths diverged early on. My eyes see you, and I know you're not her, but my heart... well, that is an entirely different matter altogether. But I know this: if whatever accident brought you here hadn't denied you of a future, then you *would* have become her, a version of her, with all her strengths and tenacity and fire."

"Perhaps you should sit down?" I suggested, cupping his elbow and nodding to the office chair next to the control panel.

"A good idea, yes." He eased himself down. "Now, why don't you introduce me to your companions?"

I did so, starting with Albert, Chou, Silas, and finally, Freuchen.

"Peter Freuchen... I believe I read a book of yours when I was a young man," Michael said. "You were quite the adventurer."

"Another time and another me," said Freuchen, with his trademark grin.

"Michael," I said, using the name I'd heard Blue Alpha use, "we are searching for a very specific person, and we think, *hope*, that you might be him."

Chou interrupted, "We were all brought here at the brink of certain death, contacted by something we have come to call the *Voice*. The *Voice* referred to us in a very specific manner. Tell us, how did you come to be here?"

Michael paused, seeming to deflate. His shoulders slumped, and he placed his head into his hands as all the energy left his body at once. He took a few moments to himself, then sat upright again and said, "The end of the world brought me here. And yes, I was contacted by this same *Voice* that you refer to. I was offered a choice, remain and perish alongside everyone else on the planet, or be saved. I, of course, chose the latter." He trailed off, his eyes dropping to stare at his feet."

"And ven the *Voice* spoke, how did it refer to you?" Freuchen said.

"Ah!" Michael said, a sad smile creasing his lips. "Well, I can tell you that it knew intimate details of my life, from the nickname I was called in high school to where I met my wife."

"Anything else?" I asked.

He thought for a moment. "Why yes, it referred to me as a Candidate. Candidate 1, to be exact. Is that the answer you were looking for?"

I smiled, exhaling a sigh of relief. A huge weight lifted from my shoulders as a light throbbing pain began to pulse behind my eyes. Finally!

Freuchen said, "Ve have already met one other person who came from a version of Earth ver all human life appeared to be destroyed. Earlier, you mentioned that the 'end of the vurld' brought you here. Did you mean that literally or figuratively?"

"Oh, I meant it quite literally, I can assure you."

"What caused it?" Albert asked.

"Well that, young man, is one question that I can most certainly answer. It was me. I am the man responsible for the end of the world."

"You're joking, aren't you?" I said half-heartedly.

"Oh, I wish that I was, but no. I am the man responsible for—"

Chou interrupted us. "Perhaps it would be better to discuss this later. We have more pressing matters, after all."

The message. Of course. I nodded. Nodding at my robot friend, I said, "When we first discovered Silas, he had been trapped by a rockfall. When we freed him, he gave me a message and told me to look for Candidate 1—you—and tell you something that we think is of great importance."

Michael's eyes glowed with an intense curiosity. "A message? From whom? And why me?"

"The message is from the entity we believe is also the *Voice* —Silas calls him the Architect."

Michael said, "And the message...?"

"'Candidate 13,' that's me," I said, "'humanity is in peril. The plan has been compromised by an external entity. This interference has introduced multiple patterns of disorder; the effects on the outcome have moved beyond predictability. Agents of chaos will be unleashed in an attempt to stop what I require of you. You must travel to the collector immediately and locate candidate 1; they must know that the field is collapsing, and the void follows behind.'"

"Hmmm," said Michael but offered no more.

I watched him for a few long moments. "We've pretty much figured out what the first part of the message means, which is how we found you. And while we don't know who or what the 'external entity' is, we've had a couple of run-ins with its 'agents of chaos.'"

"We call it the Adversary," Albert said chirpily.

Michael smiled back at him. "An appropriate name, if ever I heard one."

Chou said, "The last line of the message, 'the field is collapsing, and the void follows behind;' does it mean anything to you?"

Michael leaned back in his chair and slowly shook his head. "I have no idea," he said slowly. "Not a clue."

I felt the air leave the room.

"Damn it all to hell," Freuchen hissed.

Michael held up a hand. "While I am obviously not the person that line was meant for, I think I know who was."

"What? Who?" I gasped.

Michael got to his feet, his knees popping loudly.

"Blue Alpha, I think it's time we brought back Miko and Vihaan."

———

Miko Tanaka was an astrophysicist. A keen mountaineer, she had been descending from the summit of Everest in 2037 when an enormous avalanche plucked her from the side of the mountain. As she was swept away, sure that she was a dead woman, the *Voice* contacted her and asked if she wanted to be saved. Miko was a slight woman in her early forties, delicate looking but with clearly defined muscles beneath the material of her blouse, and a grip that was vice-strong when we shook hands. Freuchen took to her instantly, sensing a kindred adventurer, and now, the two sat across from each other at the end of the table we were all gathered around in some kind of mess hall or cafeteria, sharing stories of each other's adventures.

Vihaan Deshpande would have been one of several million victims of a nuclear exchange between India and Pakistan in 2028. He was in his early fifties, a tenured professor at the National Centre for Nanosciences and Nanotechnology, University of Mumbai. He seemed to be the most affected by his translocation to this version of Earth. Permanently sad eyes watched us from beneath heavy eyelids, and he rarely spoke unless questioned. Understandable, I realized as the destruction of his beloved city was still so fresh in his mind, having had nowhere near the time to acclimate being pulled here. The rest of us had all become candidates by sheer bad luck, or at our own hand, the kinds of events and endings that you could put down to the vague statistical maybe's that whatever hidden dice roll had been assigned to us by the universe, commonly known as bad luck. But for Vihaan, he had been a victim to mankind's utter stupidity—the kind of stupidity that always seems to have to be paid by the blood of innocents.

"I hope this is to your liking," Blue Alpha said as she reentered the room, carrying seven plastic plates in her tentacles. The plates were heaped with lettuce and spinach and cucumber and a few vegetables I didn't recognize. "I'm afraid I had to cannibalize the cultured meat machine for parts several decades ago."

"You have quite the green thumb... tentacle," I said awkwardly, then tried to save my own embarrassment by asking, "Where did the vegetables come from?"

"I have maintained a greenhouse facility on level four on the off chance that the Architect's plan would eventually come to fruition." She paused, then added with her own hint of embarrassment, "But I must admit that I do find the art of growing and nurturing life, even life as simple as the plants you see before you, very satisfying."

I smiled at her, took the knife and fork from the plate, and began to eat. The salad was delicious, and I told Blue Alpha so. She dipped in midair and rustled her tentacles in appreciation before disappearing into the kitchen only to reappear with glasses and two jugs of the most refreshing water I'd ever tasted to wash the food down. When we were done, she cleared the dishes away.

We took our chairs and formed a circle with them. Michael stood, his legs quivering a little as he rose and said, "Meredith, would you please tell Miko and Vihaan the story you told me?"

I repeated the whole story of how I'd gotten here along with how we'd found Silas and the strange message Silas had given to me and me alone. I mentioned nothing of Photo-me's relationship to Michael. He could tell them that part if he wanted. Otherwise, it was none of their business.

"They've figured out the first part of the message, that's what got them this far, but that last line 'they must know that the field is collapsing, and the void follows behind' means nothing to me. Nothing at all. It seemed sensible to ask you two, as all three of us must have been placed here for a reason." He eyed his companions. "Vihaan, anything?"

Vihaan was concentrating, but shook his head, "No, nothing springs immediately to mind."

All faces turned to look at Miko.

"Miko?" said Michael.

She, too, took a long pause before answering, and I was sure that she was also going to say she had no idea what it meant, but instead, she whispered, "Perhaps, but I hope that I am wrong."

All of us except Albert instinctively edged a little closer to her.

"My main field of research," Miko said, "was the study of the Higgs field and a particle called the Higg's Boson."

"I've heard of it," I said, "but I have no idea what it does."

Miko smiled, "It is complicated, but to put it as simply as I can, it is the particle responsible for giving every other particle in the universe its mass."

"Okay," I said. "Still don't understand, but how does that relate to the last line of the Architect's message?"

"Rather than explain, if you will indulge me, it would be better if I showed you."

"Go right ahead," said Freuchen, his eyes not leaving Miko. I had to smile; it was pretty obvious that the arrival of this brilliant woman had reduced Freuchen to puppy dog status. He would be tripping over his own tongue if he wasn't careful.

Miko pointed at the glass marbles Albert held in his hand. "Albert, may I have one?"

Albert nodded enthusiastically, glad to be invited into the adult conversation.

Miko took a marble and placed it carefully on the table, just a few inches from the edge.

"Imagine the marble is our universe, nestled comfortably within the Higgs field," she said, lowering herself down until her eyes were level with the table. She tapped the tabletop with a knuckle. "To us, the universe appears just fine, everything working as it was intended, with the Higgs field in a stable low-energy state, a state that is known as a true vacuum." She paused for a second, letting her words sink in, then continued. "But it could all be a lie, we could actually be in what physicists call a meta-stable state, one where our universe *appears* to be stable but actually exists in a false vacuum. Theoretically, the universe could stay in that state forever, and we would be none the wiser. But... if a high-energy event occurs anywhere within our universe, it could disrupt the Higgs field sufficiently enough to force a portion of the universe out of its false vacuum and into a true vacuum." Miko gave the marble a gentle nudge with her finger sending it rolling off the edge and into Albert's lap."

"And that would be bad?" I said.

"It would be very, very bad," said Miko.

Chou nodded, adding, "The end of... everything."

Miko said, "The true vacuum would expand outward at the speed of light in an ever-increasing bubble, changing the state of everything within it from false vacuum to true. It would mean the destruction of *everything* that holds our reality together. The very fundamental laws of physics would change; nothing would remain the same. It would mean not only the end of life in this universe but also the end of the *potential* for life."

"I think it might be even worse than that," Chou said. For the next couple of minutes, she explained how she and her husband, the AI of the science vessel *The Shining Way* had been assigned to investigate what she had called Vagrant particles, strange particles that simply should not exist in our universe, that had leaked through from alternate dimensions. "I believe that the Architect may have developed technology to access the alternate universes through these rifts, which allowed it to bring all of us here."

"Okay," I said, looking at Freuchen, "I think we're following." He nodded that he was. "So, what does that mean?"

"It means," Chou continued, grim-faced, not only the end of the universe where the false vacuum event occurred but also the destruction of any other alternate universe connected to it. It could destroy not just everything that is, but everything that has been, too. There would be nothing left. Not only would humanity cease to exist, it might cease to have *ever* existed."

Michael blinked several times. Vihaan seemed to melt into his chair. I'd thought that delivering my message to Candidate 1 would be the end of my role, but it was becoming obvious that, instead, it was just the beginning.

Vihaan cleared his throat. "But surely, if what Miko says is true, then the Architect must have found a way to counteract that disaster, or why else would it have brought all of us here? And why task Meredith with bringing us the message? It would not make any sense unless the Architect had already deduced a way to either stop it or save us."

Chou nodded in agreement.

"Well," Miko said, "let us assume I am correct, there is no way for us to prove it and certainly no way to stop it."

"Vy not?" Freuchen said.

"The bubble generated by the event that shifting from false vacuum to true vacuum is expanding at the speed of light. There is no way for us to detect it."

"Then how would the Architect have known it was even happening?" Michael asked.

"A good question," Miko said. "And one I regret I do not have an answer for."

"I think I do," I said. "If the technology the Architect used to bring us here allowed it to effectively move back and forth through time within any other universe outside of our own, then wouldn't it be possible to have maybe seen this false vacuum bubble destroying other universes?"

Chou nodded solemnly. "I think you may be right. And if that is what the Architect saw, then it would have been logical to draw the conclusion that it was also happening here in this universe."

"There's another possibility," Vihaan said, suddenly animated.

"Go on," Michael said.

"We are forgetting a simple fact: if there are infinite universes out there, then it stands to reason that there are other Architects, too. Perhaps one of them communicated with our Architect and confirmed that the event was indeed occurring and that this universe was in imminent jeopardy."

"Wow!" I said. I hadn't really given the idea that there were other versions of me and my companions out there in alternate universes much thought since we had landed at the bay after leaving Avalon. It was mind-blowing."

"Whichever is true," Michael said, "I think Vihaan is right—it doesn't make sense for the Architect to have brought us here only to tell us it's the end of the universe. They must have thought it through, and there *must* be a way out of it. There has to be more to the Architect's plan than we first thought."

"Now, if only we knew where the Architect was located so we could ask them," I said with a deep sigh.

Michael stood up and began pacing back and forth.

"Are you feeling alright?" Freuchen said.

Michael nodded but continued to pace quickly back and

forth, then suddenly stopped, placed both hands on the table, and leaned toward us. "I think I may know where to find the Architect," he said.

I leaped to my feet. "What? Why didn't you say earlier?"

"I wasn't entirely sure," he said, "but the more I think about it, the more I am convinced that I am right. It all makes sense to me. Why I would be here and why I would be designated as Candidate 1."

"Where?" Chou demanded. "Tell us."

"What's wrong with Blue Alpha?" Albert said suddenly.

"What?" I said, annoyed that the boy had distracted us at such a critical point in our discussion.

"Look at Blue Alpha," Albert insisted, pointing to where the robot hung in midair, unmoving. Her lenses all glowed red, and her tentacles were locked rigidly in place at every joint, so they all pointed straight down like she was a soldier standing at attention.

"Blue Alpha? Are you okay?" I asked, but she said nothing.

Silas began to make his way toward her, "*Perhaps, there is something I can—*"

With a sudden explosion of movement that sent me and everyone except for Chou leaping from our seats, Blue Alpha sped across the room and crashed into the wall, sending bits of plaster and wood into the air. She pulled back six feet and did it again, then again, and again. Silas strode across the room in a couple of huge leaps and threw his arms around her, pulling her to his chest like she was some kind of rogue basketball. But even his immense strength could barely contain her, and she struggled to continue her seemingly insane act of self-harm.

"What is *that*?" Vihaan said, taking a step backward and knocking his chair over.

"Look out!" I hissed when I saw the unmistakable glowing eyes of one of the same robo-bugs that had spied on us when we'd first arrived on Avalon and assassinated the Nazi commander, staring back at me from just over the threshold of the doorway. Before any of us could react, a second robo-bug came through the doorway, climbing across the ceiling, then a third and a fourth appeared.

Chou picked up a chair and threw it at the doorway, scattering the bugs. Two of them vanished back into the corridor. The other two spread out across the walls, one on either side of us.

"Don't let them near you," I screamed. "They're deadly." I grabbed Michael and pulled him backward while Albert, Miko, and Vihaan rushed to join us.

"Get behind this," Freuchen said, flipping the table over onto its side. It wasn't much of a barrier, but it would have to do.

Meanwhile, Chou leaped to her feet, grabbed her chair by its legs, and advanced on the nearest robo-bug. The tiny assassin seemed focused on stalking my little group and didn't see her coming until it was too late. It leaped from the wall toward the ceiling, but Chou's lightning-fast reflexes were too quick for it, she swung the chair and caught it in midair, knocking it back into the wall. It bounced and tumbled to the floor. There was a crunch as Chou brought her foot down hard on it, sending pieces spinning.

Chou whipped around and ran at the last bug. She swung the chair again, but this one was more alert. It dropped from the wall to the floor and leaped for Chou, who was now using the chair like she was a lion tamer. It leaped again, and Chou managed to catch it mid-flight, not hard enough to do any damage, but with enough force to send it skidding across the floor on its back. Chou ran after it to deliver the coup de grâce, but before she reached it, it righted itself and scuttled out the door into the corridor, Chou in hot pursuit.

As soon as the bug had vanished into the corridor, Blue

Alpha relaxed in Silas' arms. Her tentacles returned to their normal graceful ebb and flow. Silas released her, and she floated away from him.

"You have to leave, now," Blue Alpha said urgently, her voice resonating with panic. "Quickly, follow me."

"Why?" I yelled, falling in with the others around our new metal friend.

"The collector has been breached," she said matter-of-factly. "Something is here."

TWENTY-THREE

WE GRABBED our packs and equipment from the dormitory.

"Albert," I said, "I want you to stay back with Michael and our new friends. I'm relying on you to keep them safe, okay?"

Albert nodded enthusiastically. Michael caught my eye and gave his own subtle nod acknowledging that he would watch over the boy. When we reached the foyer, Chou and I crept forward and peaked out through the open doors. Blue Alpha's main chassis was where she'd left it. The open ground between us and the tunnel back through the mountain looked clear.

"Let's go," I said and started to edge through the door only to be tugged back inside by Chou.

"Look!" she hissed, pointing a finger toward the doors of the tunnel we'd entered through.

A tall black shape stepped into the threshold. It looked more like a human-shaped black hole than a man, sucking in all light around it, which was why I hadn't seen it standing in the shadow of the tunnel's entranceway.

"Abernathy," I croaked, my throat suddenly dry.

Abernathy walked a few paces into the open, his black cloak swirling around him as though it was a living, thinking thing.

His head moved from side to side as he surveyed the land and buildings. I instinctively ducked further behind the door as his gaze moved over our hiding place. He stopped, staring, it seemed to me, directly at us.

"Do you think he saw me?" I whispered to Chou.

She shook her head. "I don't think so. It's more likely he's looking at Blue Alpha's chassis." Blue Alpha's main chassis still hovered silently above the ground, where she'd detached herself from it, just a few feet away from the steps leading down from the doorway.

With long, purposeful steps, Abernathy began to walk toward us. Behind him, a steady stream of people began to step out of the tunnel. At least, some of them were still people, most were changed; their skin covered in thin, ropey black coils that covered each of them to varying degrees as though there was some kind of a process of assimilation going on. I stifled a gasp of horror as I saw a creature that was made of conjoined humans, fixed together by the ropey material to create a new, fast-moving, almost crab-like new being. More came into view, scuttling toward their master like a pack of hellhounds.

"Back inside," Chou urged, and we retreated into the foyer where a worried-looking Michael and the rest of the group waited.

"There's no way we're going to get to the exit without being seen," I said. "There's just too many of them."

Chou said, "It's not going to take them long before they reach here. Then it'll just be a matter of time before they find us."

"I have an idea," Blue Alpha said. "There are maintenance tunnels that crisscross the entire property. About thirty feet to the east of this building is an access panel. There's another shaft that comes up close to the entrance tunnel."

"There's no way we will make it across any open ground

without Abernathy or one of those... things seeing us," Chou said.

"I know," Blue Alpha said, "which is why I will need to cause a distraction."

"No," I said, "you have to come with us. You don't know what Abernathy is capable of."

"I swore to protect this facility and everyone in it," Blue Alpha said. "I *will* do that."

"There has to be another way," Miko said.

"*This* is the only way," Blue Alpha replied adamantly. "Now, you must leave. Quickly, come with me."

We followed her down several corridors until she stopped at another, smaller door. "Stay close to the wall of the building until I have time to distract the intruders. I will lead them away. Take the passage and follow it north until you reach the third access shaft. That one will get you closest to the tunnel."

"But—" I began to say in a final attempt to stop her, but I knew it was no use. Instead, I simply said, "Thank you."

Blue Alpha rustled her tentacles, turned, and sped back toward the foyer.

———

One after another, we filed out of the door, pressing ourselves against the smooth, cool tower wall until we reached the building's corner.

"There's the panel," Chou said, pointing to a square metal box protruding out of the ground about thirty feet to our right. From our position, the building effectively blocked us from the sight of Abernathy and his minions, but that also meant we couldn't see what he was doing. Chou was the only one who had a clear view, crouched at the corner, her head angled just enough around it to be able to see what was going on.

"Get ready to run when I tell you," Chou said.

Everyone but Chou jumped as, without warning, Blue Alpha's voice boomed across the fields and open ground. "You are not authorized to be here. You will leave immediately or suffer the consequences."

"Ready..." Chou said.

The sound of metal crashing against metal rang out.

"Now!" Chou yelled, loud enough to be heard over the cacophony.

One after the other, we sprinted toward the access panel—Freuchen, Albert and Michael first, followed by Vihaan and Miko, then Silas and me. Chou was the last to leave. Freuchen was already lifting the heavy metal manhole when Chou and I reached it. Only when everyone but Chou and I were safely in did I dare to look back toward the tunnel's opening.

Halfway between the tunnel and the tower, Blue Alpha had engaged Abernathy's minions. She picked them up in her tentacles and smashed them into the ground or tossed them back away as though they were nothing, cut others in half with her saws, or crushed them with her hammer.

Abernathy stood with his back to us, oblivious to our presence, silently directing the attack. A phalanx of his minions broke free of the main horde and maneuvered around behind Blue Alpha. They dove at her. She managed to fend off most of them, but not all of them. I saw three black shapes clambering up her chassis like mountaineers climbing a rock face.

"Meredith! Move!" Chou urged, pushing me.

I snapped out of my stupor, and continued down the ladder, unwilling to look back at the carnage spilling out across the land.

———

The maintenance tunnel was large enough for Freuchen and Chou to stand shoulder-to-shoulder as they splashed through a couple of inches of stagnant water that had collected on the concrete floor. Silas and I brought up the rear behind Michael, Miko, Vihaan, and Albert. Michael was old, but he was still sprightly and didn't slow our pace.

"Here," Freuchen said when we reached the next access shaft leading back up on the other side of the complex. "I'll go up first." He climbed the ladder and pushed the cover up an inch so he could see out. "My God!" he whispered, his voice echoing down to us. "They are everyvare."

He replaced the lid and climbed back down.

"There are several hundred of those things. The tunnel is about ten yards from us, if ve are quick, I think that ve can make it without being seen. I vill go up first. If ve are spotted, I vill draw them off." That last sentence wasn't a request, and nobody argued with Freuchen. He climbed back up, checked that the coast was clear then pushed the manhole cover out of the way before slipping up and over the lip, using the wall surrounding the shaft as cover.

"Come on, now," he called down to us.

We sent Michael, Albert, Miko, and Vihaan up after him. Then it was my turn, and I quickly followed behind them. In the distance, I heard screams and the screeching of metal, but it was cramped behind the wall, and I dared not move in case we were seen. Silas and, finally, Chou joined us, and we waited for the signal from Freuchen before we raced across the space between our hiding place and the huge tunnel doors.

"Meredith, you first," Freuchen said, then tapped me on the back and said, "Go, now!"

I sprinted for the two huge doors, sure that at any second, I would be spotted, and the creatures would come for me, but I reached them without being seen and stood there, my hands on my knees, panting with fear as the panic washed over me. I turned back to face my friends and beckoned for Michael and Albert (who now seemed inseparable) to come and join me.

"Give me... a... moment..." Michael said, between gasps for air.

I took that moment to peek around the doors back toward the tower complex. "Oh no," I gasped, which got everyone's attention. Chou and Freuchen crowded in next to me.

"Ve need to go. Now!" Freuchen insisted, stepping away from the door.

Chou joined him, taking Michael by the arm and ushering him and the others further into the tunnel.

"Meredith," Freuchen said urgently, beckoning to me to join him. But I couldn't move. I was transfixed by what I saw in the pristine fields. There were hundreds of them, maybe close to a thousand, all under Abernathy's sway. They swarmed across the fields, crashing toward Blue Alpha, who floated in front of the tower. She'd lost most of her tentacles, and of the remaining three, only one was still functioning, the other two hung useless below her, but at great cost to Abernathy's army judging by the pile of bodies around her. As I watched, her final functioning tentacle was overwhelmed by a horde of men, women, and children that climbed up the useless limb, heading for Blue Alpha's control unit.

The last thing I saw before Freuchen dragged me after him was Abernathy's minions swarming over Blue Alpha like ants attacking a beetle, tearing her chassis apart as though it was nothing, as she careened into the ground in an explosion of dirt and sparks.

The collector belonged to the Adversary.

———

"Quickly!" Chou said, urging us forward while throwing a nervous look back over her shoulder toward the doors.

When we finally caught sight of the entrance, I was surprised to see that night had fallen, covering everything beyond the jammed doors with a black veil. Chou and I ushered everyone through the doors, then stopped momentarily while we all caught our breath.

The light from the tunnel spilled out beyond the doors illuminating the carpet of gray ash or dust. When we'd arrived, only our footprints had been visible, but now, I saw hundreds of tracks extending away into the darkness toward the forest. I pulled my flashlight from my backpack and shined it into the darkness beyond where we'd stopped, casting the beam around.

"My God," Michael said quietly when he saw the devastated landscape.

"You've not been outside the collector before?" Freuchen asked, looking to Michael, Vihaan, and Miko in turn.

All three shook their heads.

"There simply wasn't enough time," Michael continued.

"Oh, you're in for a treat then," Freuchen said with a chuckle.

"So, where are we supposed to go from here?" Vihaan asked.

His question stopped me in my tracks. I hadn't even given it a thought. Our quest had been to get *here*, to the collector, but now that the collector had fallen to the Adversary, what were we supposed to do? If we called for help from the *Brimstone,* it would take them too long to reach us. If we stayed in the tunnel, then there was no guarantee the army of those monsters led by that tainted psychopath wouldn't catch us.

"We need to make a run for it," I said. "We can't call for the *Brimstone*, it'll take too long.

"*Brimstone?*" Vihaan exclaimed. "What do you mean 'Brimstone?'"

"Long story," I told him. "We'll explain once we get there." Then a thought hit me like a slap across the face. "What time do you think it is?" I said, turning to Chou and Freuchen.

"It must be somevare close to... oh!" Freuchen's eyes grew wide.

Chou finished the sentence for him. "Close to the aurora."

"We need to get away from here. Right now," I said, ushering Silas and everyone else ahead of us.

"What? Why?" Michael said, slowing. I urged him on with a hand to his back.

"Because, when the aurora comes everything within the direct influence of the collector is going to be turned to this." I scooped up a handful of gray ash from the ground and let it trickle through my fingers. I turned back toward the open doors, the beam of my flashlight sweeping over the ground and up the craggy rock of the mountain on either side of them... and froze. Something was moving across the rock above the doors.

"Chou. Freuchen," I whispered, "there's something moving up there."

Chou swept her flashlight up the left side of the mountain, Freuchen did the same on the right.

"Vat on earth..."

Three shapes moved so quickly across the rough surface of the rock that it was hard for us to keep our flashlight beams on them. It took me a moment to realize what they were—two women and a man, climbing adeptly down the rock.

"Run!" I shouted, but at the sound of my voice, they leaped from the rock to the ground ten feet from us, sending huge puffs of the ash into the air that momentarily hid them from us.

Freuchen grabbed Albert and pushed the boy behind him.

The three figures were human. The two men obviously came from the twentieth century, judging from their clothing and the sneakers both wore. One stood a foot taller than the other and was almost as big as Freuchen, his short-cropped hair and thick-muscled forearms suggested he might be military or police, maybe. The kid looked like any teenager who'd hand you a cafe-latte at Starbucks. The woman was from an earlier time, her simple cotton dress torn in places and soiled with dirt. She'd lost her right moccasin at some point, and her exposed foot was badly cut, bloody and dirty, yet she seemed utterly oblivious to a wound that must surely be extremely painful. All three panted heavily, their shoulders lifting and dropping, and saliva dripped from their mouths like dogs that had been run hard. Their skin was covered in the ropes of black, and this close, I could see that the space between them was spattered with raised nodules, each one about a half an inch in width and spaced six inches from the next nearest. The nodules expanded and contracted every couple of seconds like lungs.

Perhaps it was a trick of the light, but behind each of their widely dilated eyes, I thought I sensed panic, fear even, as though the real person was trapped somewhere within—a passenger in their own body, unable to regain control.

"What's wrong with the people?" Albert whimpered from behind Freuchen.

"I don't know, Albert, but you don't need to vurry, ve vill protect you."

The two groups regarded each other silently across the short distance separating us until the nodules covering the three strangers' skin suddenly vibrated in unison, and the three attacked.

The big man went straight for Michael, Vihaan, and Miko, his eyes focused on Candidate 1 and his comrades. Freuchen and Chou both ran to intercept him. The teenage boy darted around them and made a beeline straight for Silas, leaping on him and wrapping his arms under the robot's arms and his legs around Silas' waist. The woman slipped by Freuchen and Chou as they wrestled with the huge man and ran toward Michael. I drew my sword, something I'd hoped I wouldn't have to do, and dove to intercept her, swinging the pommel at her head, not willing to use the blade unless I had to. These poor people were obviously under Abernathy's control, and if I could spare their lives, I would.

The woman ducked under my sword, but I still caught her a glancing blow across the top of her head, and I shivered inside as I felt the pommel scrape away skin and a clump of brown hair from her scalp. She screeched, dropped down onto all fours like some feral cat, and turned her attention to me, ignoring the blood streaming down her face. She leaped at me, and I instinctively threw a punch at her with my sword hand. A jarring bolt of pain traveled up my hand, wrist, elbow, then shoulder as I caught her square on the chin. She dropped to the ground at my side, face-first in the dust. I tried to roll her over to make sure she was still alive, but my arm hurt like you wouldn't believe, so I left her and turned my attention back to the group.

"Protect Albert," I yelled at Michael, just as Miko grabbed Albert's hand and pulled him to her, wrapping her arms around him.

Out of the corner of my eye, I saw Freuchen wrestling with the big man, who seemed more intent on wrenching himself free of Freuchen's clutches, his eyes never leaving Michael and his group. The man's face was a bloody pulp, his nose broken, teeth shattered from where Chou delivered blow after blow. But he simply wouldn't stop. Unbelievably, he was dragging Freuchen with him, taking one slow step after the other toward Michael.

He wanted Michael, that was obvious.

Vihaan shouted, "Meredith!" and I turned, expecting to see the woman I'd knocked unconscious, getting to her feet ready to attack again, but she still lay face-down in the dust. "Silas," Vihaan added. "Your robot."

I looked for Silas in the confusion of flailing bodies only half-visible through the fog of dust that now hung in the air from our struggles. Silas stood completely still, the teenage boy still wrapped around him, locked in an unwanted embrace. I had to blink a couple of times to make sure what I thought I saw was actually what I was looking at.

The nodules on the teenager's skin had grown, lengthening in an arc from every part of the boy's body and fixing onto Silas' golden skin, like long black fingers. The boy's mouth hung open, his eyes looked vacant, saliva dripped from the corner of his mouth. His chest rose and dropped in fast dog-like pants, his body vibrating as though he was shivering from the cold or excitement.

I shot a look back at the big man, straight into Freuchen's eyes. He was struggling for the pistol he'd stuffed in his belt. He got it free, brought it up to his opponent's midriff, then grunted as the man's flailing arm caught Freuchen's hand with a glancing blow and sent the gun flying away, only to be lost in the layer of ash.

I felt a tremor roll up through my legs. The aurora. It was coming, and it was coming soon.

I stumbled my way to Silas.

"Silas! Silas?" He did not respond. This close, I could smell the boy's rotten, fetid, stench. It was... nauseating. I tried to pry his fingers free from Silas's body, but they were like clamps. "Help me," I yelled, turning back to Michael and Vihaan, who were little more than ghostly outlines in the dust and shadows of the night. They emerged from the darkness and tried to pull the boy from Silas, who remained absolutely still and unresponsive. I caught a glimpse of Freuchen and Chou, silhouettes in the gloom, twisting to try and change their position as the big man reoriented himself to Michael's new position.

"It's... no... good," Michael said between hard breaths, stepping back from the boy. "He won't budge."

"Oh God," I whimpered, as the reality of what I would have to do to save my friend finally hit me. I had tried every day to be the kind of person that I'd silently pledged to Silas I would be back on Avalon, but I would not let my friend die. I simply could not.

"I'm sorry. I'm sorry," I said, barely able to see through the misty haze of hot tears that suddenly blurred my vision. I placed the tip of my sword against the side of the boy's ribcage, roughly where I thought his heart would be, took a shivering, deep breath of the cloying air to try and steady my shaking hands... and ran the tip of my sword into the boy's side.

The blade clipped a rib and then slid effortlessly through the rest of his body.

The teenager shuddered as though I'd hit him with a million volts. His grip slackened, then slipped off Silas, and he fell to the ground, pulling himself from my sword and sending me staggering backward. The black tentacles snapped, sending pieces flying through the air. The parts still attached to Silas shivered and wriggled like leeches that had been sliced in half, then one after the other, they fell into the gray dust and vanished.

Silas was suddenly awake again. *Meredith? What happ—"* He saw the boy, writhing in agony on the ground, kicking up even more ash. *"I must help him,"* Silas said and started to take a step forward.

"No!" I yelled at him. "The aurora is coming. If we don't get out of the zone in the next few minutes, we are *all* going to die. *All* of us, Silas. Do you understand?"

The robot paused for a moment, then said, *"Yes. What do you want me to do?"*

I nodded at Vihaan and looked around for Miko and Albert. Their forms were still visible, but only just. "I want you to get them all to safety. Right now. It's imperative that you keep them all safe. Can you do that for me?"

"Yes," Silas said. "*Follow me, lady and gentlemen.*"

Michael took my hand in his. "What about you?"

It was a surreal moment. This man, my son from another dimension, so much older than me and yet, his concern... his love for me, a facsimile of his own mother, obviously. I could only imagine how utterly confusing and painful my existence must be for him.

"I'll be right there. Now go. There's no time." I ignored the incongruence of the last part of that sentence, because up until this moment, there had been nothing but time, it seemed.

Michael nodded and allowed Silas to lead him and Vihaan into the darkness in the general direction of where I had last seen Miko and Albert.

I spun around just in time to see Freuchen and Chou appear out of the particle-filled blackness not five feet from me, the big man lumbering ever forward in the direction Michael had taken. I took an involuntary step backward, stumbled and fell, my hands flat against the dust and dead ground just beneath it. The earth thrummed beneath my hands... and it was growing stronger by the second. The aurora was coming and, like a freight train barreling toward a precipice, there was nothing any of us could do but get out of its way.

As if to illustrate the comparison, the big man managed to slip one arm from Chou's grip. He delivered a blindingly fast right hook to Chou's head, who, half-blinded by the dust and almost at the point of exhaustion, simply didn't see it coming.

It sent Chou sprawling into the dust. Freuchen immediately threw an arm under the attacker's armpit and pulled him back, but it was obvious that even Freuchen, with his almost superhuman strength, was tiring, and it would not be long before he was unable to hold the big man. And then this tainted monster would barrel through me and Chou, and there would be nothing between him and Michael.

Freuchen knew it too. "I'll join you, but you have to run. Now!" he yelled.

I grabbed Chou and pulled her to her feet, switched my flashlight to my left hand, and slipped a supporting arm around Chou's back. She was dazed, a large welt rising below her eye.

"What?" she mumbled. "What's happening?"

"We've got to go. The aurora."

That seemed to get through to her, and she began to stumble forward with me into the blackness. I wasn't sure I'd be able to spot which direction Silas had taken everyone else, but it wasn't hard to spot the huge indentations he left in the dust, even as the wind from the building energy ate away at them.

The ground was trembling now, dust dancing on the surface layer like iron filings attracted to a magnet.

"We're going to make it," I whispered, repeating it over and over, as the two of us stumbled forward through the growing dust.

A deep reverberating foghorn-like bass note began to fill the air, growing louder by the second and only adding to my disorientation as I stumbled onward through the night, sure that at any second, I would become nothing as the energy released by the collector turned me to nothingness. Now, I couldn't even hear my own breathing, let alone the soundless words that Chou mouthed at me.

"Can't... hear... you," I mouthed back.

Chou broke free of my arm, staggered for a second, then pointed down at our feet... and the layer of pine needles and dead leaves beneath them. I turned my flashlight's beam back in the direction we had come. Ten paces behind us, the edge of the dust-zone whirled.

We had made it. We were out.

I heard Vihaan yell, "Meredith, over here." I followed his voice, and then used the glow of Silas' eye-bar to guide me the thirty steps or so beyond the dust-zone to where Michael, Miko, and Vihaan sat, still covered in the gray dust. I let go of Chou, and she sagged against a tree and slowly slipped down its trunk, obviously still not in control of her senses. I dropped to my knees, huffing in breath after breath until my head began to clear. I looked up and saw Miko standing right in front of me with a horrified expression on her face. It took me a second to realize she was alone.

"Albert?" I wheezed through lips chapped and dry. "Miko, *where's* Albert?"

"I... I don't know. Just before Silas took us, he let go of my hand, and I couldn't find him in the dust."

"The dust interfered with my senses, too," Silas said. *"I could not track Albert through it, and you made it clear that our new companions were the priority."*

Miko helped me to my feet. I turned back toward the collector; it was beginning to glow with that same ethereal light we had seen when we arrived the night before. There wasn't much time. Every second was going to count now, so I unbuckled my sword and handed it to Miko. "Stay with them," I told Silas, "I'll find Albert."

"I'll go with—" Chou started using the trunk of the tree to support herself as she struggled to her feet, then dropped to her butt again, turned, and threw up. She was badly concussed; I was sure of it.

"Stay here!" I ordered, then staggered back in the direction I'd just come from before she could get back to her feet and come after me.

Fear gripped me as I stepped back into the dust-zone. I swung my flashlight left and right, looking for any tracks that might indicate that Albert was nearby, while periodically yelling his name. But there was nothing.

The collector glowed brighter and brighter.

"Albert!" I croaked again, all but ready to give up.

From the wall of dust surrounding me, a vague shape materialized

"Peter!" I yelled. Bleeding and bruised, the man looked exhausted but in his arms, he carried Albert. I grabbed Freuchen by his meaty forearm and started to drag him toward the perimeter of the dust-zone. "Quickly," I urged, glancing back at him...

...and a second shape, bigger than Freuchen and unbowed detached itself from the darkness and resolved into the figure of the giant, tainted monster just a few paces behind us. I reached for my sword, determined to finish him, then realized I'd left it with Miko.

I pulled Freuchen onward, screaming expletives at him to move faster. Then, my flashlight illuminated the trees ahead of us, and we were out of the dust-zone again.

Freuchen slowed to a stop, his chest heaving like bellows, and lowered Albert to the forest floor.

"No," I said, shining the light back over his shoulder, illuminating the monster who was once a man. "Keep moving. We're not safe."

Freuchen turned and saw the man, saw the glowing outline of the collector as it primed to ignite and came to the same conclusion I had. The monster-man was going to make it out of the dust-zone moments before the air would ignite.

I knew he'd made up his mind even before he pressed his hands against my cheek, then ruffled Albert's hair. "Good luck, Meredith Gale. It has been an honor." Then my friend turned and ran at the giant of a man, screaming a banshee war cry as he tackled him and the two fell into the swirling darkness and dust.

I pulled Albert to me and turned away from the collector just as the world ignited into white-hot fire, but not before I saw Freuchen and the monster vanish forever into the blinding light of the aurora.

TWENTY-FOUR

"PETER!" I yelled into the darkness when the aurora had passed. I waved the beam of my flashlight through the cloud of ash like a sword. There was no answer. I knew he was gone, but every cell in my body rejected that conclusion, screaming in protest at the absurdity of the idea that that mountain of a man could be snuffed out of existence so quickly. That there would be no more of his deep belly-laughs. Or the way he sounded more like he was sawing wood than snoring. Or his seemingly endless supply of optimism. The thought simply could not find a place to fit in my brain. It was an agony that even the afterglow of the aurora could not sooth.

So, I kept yelling into the chaos for him... right up until I tripped over something lying on the perimeter of the dust-zone and the forest. It was the monster-man's severed arm, perfectly cauterized just above the elbow. I must have stared at it for at least a minute. It had been *that* close. And again, I understood the difference that a single second can make to the trajectory of a life. If Freuchen had not delayed that monster as he had, it would have hunted us all down mercilessly. It was only then that I accepted my friend's sacrifice, and the razor-sharp pain of that sacrifice found its way into my heart and cut a permanent home deep within it. I sank to my knees, my head facing into my hands, and I wept.

That was where Chou, as good as new after the aurora, found me, Albert at her side.

Oh my, God! Albert! I had abandoned the kid. Simply walked off in my shock at Freuchen's death. Either Albert had found Chou, or she had found him. Either way, they had both found me.

"Where's Peter?" Albert said.

I looked down at the boy's moonlike face staring up at me. Instead of an answer, I pulled him close to me and held him as close as I could. He resisted for a moment, then sank into me, and I felt his shoulders begin to heave as he too began to weep.

From the forest, Michael and the others made their way toward us, led by Silas, his electronic eyes floating through the darkness like two wandering stars.

"We must leave now," he said. "The chances that Abernathy has people searching for us is too high." I heard the others whisper their agreement. I have no recollection of the walk back to the Brimstone, but someone must have used the walkie-talkies to call because Amelia and Bartholomew were waiting for us in the light of the airship's doorway and ushered us all inside, locking the door behind them.

"I am so very sorry for the loss of your... our friend. He will be greatly missed," Bartholomew said, as he led me back to my cot. I dropped onto it and laid there staring, at the ceiling. I said nothing. What was there to say, after all?

"We need to get airborne as quickly as possible," Chou said, from somewhere off to my right. She and my compatriots' voices sounded distant, almost like I was listening to them from the other end of a tunnel.

"Can you at least tell us what the hell is going on?" Amelia said, her voice taking on a worried tone.

"In the morning," Chou replied. "Right now, we need to get to a safe altitude."

"Okay," Amelia said, and I heard her walking off in the direction of the cockpit. Minutes later, the airship gave a shudder, and then we were in the air again. We ascended quickly, then slowed to a hover.

I was alone now, except for Silas. He stood in the corner, out of the way, but never out of sight of me. As everyone filtered from the room, he walked to my side and knelt in front of me, his eye-bar level with my eyes.

"*How are you?*" he asked quietly.

"It just doesn't seem real? How can he be gone?"

"*He made an incredible sacrifice for us, noble beyond words.*"

There was no arguing with that, but it did nada to alleviate the pain that flowed through my body. And intertwined with that pain, wrapped ever so tightly around it, was an absolute hatred. And it wasn't exclusively reserved just for Abernathy, either. There was plenty to share with the intelligence that was really behind all of this—the entity that had ruined everything, not just for my band of friends and survivors, but for all of humanity: The Adversary.

"I'm going to kill them," I said suddenly, surprising myself with the hot venom that dripped from my words.

"*I know,*" Silas said quietly. He paused, then laid a metal hand on my shoulder and said, "and *I understand,*" before turning away and going to join the others.

Outside, the first light of dawn seeped into the world, turning the room a muted orange. I stood and walked to a window and watched for a while as the sun slowly woke the world.

And I began to plan.

A NATIVE OF CARDIFF, Wales, Paul Antony Jones now resides near Las Vegas, Nevada with his wife. He has worked as a newspaper reporter and commercial copywriter, but his passion is penning fiction. A self-described science geek, he's a voracious reader of scientific periodicals, as well as a fan of things mysterious, unknown, and on the fringe. That fascination inspired his five-book *Extinction Point* series, following heroine Emily Baxter's journey of survival after a very unconventional alien invasion.

The Paths Between Worlds, the first book in Paul's new *This Alien Earth* trilogy is now available.

You can learn more about Paul and his upcoming releases via his blog at DisturbedUniverse.com or facebook.com/AuthorPaulAntonyJones

FROM THE PUBLISHER

Thank you for reading *A Memory of Mankind*, book two in This Alien Earth.

WE HOPE you enjoyed it as much as we enjoyed bringing it to you. We just wanted to take a moment to encourage you to review the book on Amazon and Goodreads. Every review helps further the author's reach and, ultimately, helps them continue writing fantastic books for us all to enjoy.

If you liked this book, check out the rest of our catalogue at www.aethonbooks.com. To sign up to receive a FREE collection from some of our best authors as well as updates regarding all new releases, visit www.aethonbooks.com/sign-up.

JOIN THE STREET TEAM! Get advanced copies of all our books, plus other free stuff and help us put out hit after hit.

SEARCH ON FACEBOOK:
AETHON STREET TEAM

Made in the USA
Coppell, TX
01 February 2020